A Selection of Recent Titles by Chris Nickson
from Severn House

The Inspector Tom Harper Mysteries

GODS OF GOLD
TWO BRONZE PENNIES
SKIN LIKE SILVER
THE IRON WATER
ON COPPER STREET
THE TIN GOD
THE LEADEN HEART

The Richard Nottingham Mysteries

COLD CRUEL WINTER
THE CONSTANT LOVERS
COME THE FEAR
AT THE DYING OF THE YEAR
FAIR AND TENDER LADIES
FREE FROM ALL DANGER

The Simon Westow Mysteries

THE HANGING PSALM

THE LEADEN HEART

THE LEADEN HEART

Chris Nickson

This first world edition published 2019
in Great Britain and the USA by
SEVERN HOUSE PUBLISHERS LTD of
Eardley House, 4 Uxbridge Street, London W8 7SY.
Trade paperback edition first published
in Great Britain and the USA 2019 by
SEVERN HOUSE PUBLISHERS LTD.

British Library Cataloguing in Publication Data
A CIP catalogue record for this title is available from the British Library.

ISBN-13: 978-0-7278-8879-2 (cased)
ISBN-13: 978-1-78029-597-8 (trade paper)
ISBN-13: 978-1-4483-0216-1 (e-book)

All Severn House titles are printed on acid-free paper.

Severn House Publishers support the Forest Stewardship Council™ [FSC™],
the leading international forest certification organisation.
All our titles that are printed on FSC certified paper carry the FSC logo.

Typeset by Palimpsest Book Production Ltd.,
Falkirk, Stirlingshire, Scotland.
Printed and bound in Great Britain by
TJ International, Padstow, Cornwall.

ONE

Leeds, July 1899

T he train pulled into Pontefract station with a thick hiss of steam and two short blasts on the whistle. Tom Harper opened the carriage door and watched Mary jump to the platform with an eager look. Annabelle took his hand as he helped her down the step.

She was wearing her new summer dress, a sky-blue colour that swirled around her ankles as she walked, carrying a parasol, a straw boater tilted at an angle on her head. It was another perfect summer day, not a cloud to be seen when he glanced up, the sun hot on his back as they walked along the road.

A solid week of glorious weather. They'd had nothing like it in years. The temperatures had left people across England sweating in their heavy clothes. Hardly any crime, as if the criminals had all chosen to go on holiday. Maybe they had; as superintendent of 'A' Division with Leeds City Police, Tom Harper was simply glad to see the figures plummet. If they stayed low for the rest of the summer, he'd be a happy man. Aye, and if wishes were horses, beggars would ride. Their luck couldn't hold.

Harper held his daughter's hand as Annabelle led the way up the hill and into Pontefract Castle. A romantic ruin, they called it. Well, the second half of that was right, he thought as he gazed around. Mounds of ancient stones hinted at the building that had once stood here.

But it was a fine Sunday to go somewhere, to be away from the stifling closeness of Leeds, to breathe some different air. And his wife deserved it. She'd spent the week running the Victoria while Dan the barman was away. Her pub, her responsibility, she told him. That was on top of her work as a Poor Law Guardian, talking to families around Sheepscar that needed help with their relief money, followed by a board meeting on Friday morning.

'I'm jiggered,' she'd said that evening as she collapsed on the settee with a cup of tea. 'Do you know what the silly beggars wanted today?'

'Go on,' Harper said, 'what was it this time?' It seemed that every session of the Guardians brought fresh complaints.

'Someone brought in a pile of different ulster coats for the workhouse girls and they wanted me to try them all on so they could see which was best.' She shook her head in disbelief. 'At first I thought they were joking.'

That wasn't the end of things, he was certain.

'What did you do?'

'I told them they could stuff it.' She smiled, then sighed. 'Honestly, they don't have a clue. I know some of them mean well, but . . .' There might be elected women Guardians now, but equality wasn't even on the horizon yet. Annabelle looked at him. 'They say it's still going to be nice on Sunday. We should go out for the day.'

The castle was her idea; she'd seen an article in the newspaper. And it was pleasant enough to stroll around, he had to admit that. But after a few minutes they'd seen what little remained, and went to the cafe for sandwiches and lemonade.

Mary was full of questions – what the castle had looked like, and all the battles that had been fought here. Seven years old and inquisitive about everything. He didn't have any answers for her: history had never interested him. Instead, he bought a pamphlet of information to tell her what she wanted to know.

As they walked around the town, she read them information about the king who'd been starved to death in one of the towers. Gruesome, but how many had gone for want of food over the centuries? It still happened, just to ordinary folk now, not royalty. When he was on the beat he used to see it week in, week out. Malnutrition, *starved to death* scrawled on the death certificates. The reality continued, as grim as ever.

Annabelle slipped into a shop, coming out with a brown paper bag.

'Try one,' she said to Mary.

'What is it?' she asked suspiciously, holding up a thick black lozenge.

'You'll never know if you don't eat it, will you, clever clogs? Pop it in your mouth and see.'

Warily, the girl did as she was told, eyes widening as she bit down. 'It tastes like Spanish!'

'It is Spanish. Liquorice. They call them Pontefract cakes and they make them here. See, there's even a picture of the castle stamped on them.'

By the time the train brought them back to Leeds, the bag was empty, Mary's tongue was black, and she was absorbed in the pamphlet again. Harper looked at his wife and smiled. The girl was a sponge for words and facts, her head always in a book, tucking every scrap of knowledge away in her brain. With each year, he could see more of Annabelle in her – the same high, proud cheekbones and bow mouth, the flashes of red in her dark hair when the light caught it. Less of himself, luckily for her. But similar eyes, deep-set, always watching.

He felt content as they walked past the guard checking tickets and out into the sweltering station. A porter hurried by, face glistening as he pushed a trolley loaded with cases and chests. The change of scene had been a good idea. If it was still like this next week, maybe he'd suggest a trip up to the Dales. Grass and clear air; a proper tonic.

He spotted a copper in uniform ambling around, eyes alert for pickpockets. The bobby noticed him and saluted.

Outside, he glanced at the newspaper seller's headlines: tensions rising towards war in South Africa, a burglary at a house in Leeds. Nothing that needed his attention.

Salad for tea. A couple of slices of cooked tongue, a few wilted leaves of lettuce, tomato, cucumber, and some buttered bread. A fine, light meal for a day like this. No factories open on the Sabbath, but still the smell of grime and machines came through the open window, bringing the thin layer of dust and dirt that defied cleaning and settled on everything.

'Da?' Mary raised her head from the Pontefract pamphlet. 'Did you know that in the Civil War' – she took pains to pronounce it slowly and correctly – 'they tried to knock the castle walls down with cannons?'

'From what we saw, they must have succeeded.' He winked at Annabelle.

'Oh no,' Mary told him seriously. 'That was later, when they tore it all down.' She held up the thin book. 'It says here.'

TWO

A warm night, just the sheet to cover them, windows in the bedrooms open wide. Harper left the Victoria early, before heat could blanket the day. Not a whisper of a breeze in the air, the open top of the tram crammed with men.

The factories had started up again and the air shimmered above the chimneys, tiny smuts of soot raining down across the city. He pitied the men at the engine works on a day like this; with the furnaces and white-hot steel, they'd feel as if their skin was on fire.

In Millgarth police station the air was stale and muggy. By the time he reached his office he was already damp with sweat. Harper raised the window sash, pushing hard on the warped wood. But outside was no cooler.

'I saw the headline about burglary,' he said, once the detectives had assembled in his office. 'Have you arrested anyone yet?'

'We're still looking into it, sir,' Inspector Ash replied. 'A big house off Woodhouse Lane, that's why it ended up in the papers. There were six gentlemen playing cards in the study. Three servants downstairs and not one of them heard a thing.'

Nine people in the house and a burglar had crept in and out unnoticed? He was daring. And very good.

'Gentlemen?' He'd noticed the inspector's careful choice of words.

'George Hope and some of his friends,' Sergeant Fowler replied. With his thin face and receding hairline, he looked more like a young professor than a copper.

Harper winced. Hope had owned the foundry on Mabgate. Retired now and on the boards of half a dozen institutions around Leeds. Plenty of friends on the council. Soon enough he'd be receiving a summons from the chief constable on this one.

'How did the burglar get in?'

'Open window in the bedroom, sir.' Walsh's turn. He was the youngest, the newest in the squad, here for two years, still a detective constable and eager to prove himself. 'Looks like he shinned up a drainpipe and managed to edge across. Once he was inside, he made himself at home. Wandered all over the place. Took things from almost every room upstairs.'

'Nobody heard anything?' It seemed hard to believe.

'Not a dickie bird. Went out the same way, only this time he must have been carrying a fair bit.'

'That window's a good fifteen feet off the ground, too,' Fowler added.

Harper thought quickly. 'Pawnbrokers and fences,' he said.

'We talked to the fences last night, sir,' Ash told him. 'There's a list of the stolen items going out to the pawnbrokers this morning.'

'How much did he take?'

'Some money and jewellery, probably worth the best part of fifty pounds.'

The superintendent gave a low whistle. That was a very grand haul. He ran through names in his head.

'The only two I can think of for something like that are Dicky Dennison and Rab Taylor.'

'Taylor died back in January, sir,' Ash said, 'and Dennison's serving two years down in London.'

Someone new, then. Unknown. Damnation.

'Working alone, do you think, or an accomplice?'

'Alone is what we think, sir,' Walsh replied. 'One of the servants nipped out for a smoke and didn't spot anybody else.'

'We'll crack it, sir.' Ash grinned. 'Don't you worry.'

Harper wasn't worried. He had the best team of detectives in Leeds, maybe the country. Better than Scotland Yard with their swollen heads.

But finding an unknown man, that would be a grind. And what advice could they offer people? Don't leave your windows open? In this heatwave, no one would pay a blind bit of notice. They'd prefer some air and take the risk.

At least he didn't have to do the legwork. Very occasionally, rank seemed like a blessing.

Harper had just finished putting together the duty roster for August when the telephone rang, the line crackling harshly enough to hurt his bad ear.

'Tom? It's Billy. Billy Reed.'

Reed had been a good friend once, sergeant to Harper's inspector, until they fell out. Then he'd transferred to the fire brigade and been promoted. Two years ago he'd taken a job in Whitby, in charge of police there.

Annabelle and Elizabeth, Reed's wife, were still close, exchanging regular letters. She ran a tea shop now, close to Whitby Market. Harper and his family had visited the Christmas before last. It had been a pleasant few days, but not the way it had once been. That would never return.

'How are you?'

'I'm fine,' Reed answered quickly. 'I hate to ask, but I could use a favour.'

'What's happened?'

'My brother died, so I have to come back to Leeds for the funeral. I think you met him once.'

Long ago. Charlie? He thought he vaguely remembered the name. Thin and pale, with mousy hair and a waxed moustache.

'I'm sorry, Billy.'

'We were never that close, but . . .'

Of course. It was family. Harper understood.

'Do you need somewhere to stay? Is Elizabeth coming with you?'

'If you don't mind. He lived in Harehills and the Victoria's close. It'll only be for a few days, if that's all right. Elizabeth is run off her feet at the tea room. Whitby's full of holidaymakers and the place is packed every day. Besides, she never really knew him.'

They had an empty attic room at the pub. It wasn't much, but the bed was comfortable.

'Of course. You know you'll be welcome, as long as you need,' Harper said. 'When are you arriving?'

'This afternoon. The telegram only came an hour ago.'

'We'll expect you.'

He lowered the receiver, picked it up again and asked the operator for the Victoria. They'd had a telephone installed at the beginning of the year. Between his rank and Annabelle's post as Guardian, he hadn't been able to fight the idea any longer.

She picked up on the third ring, listening as he explained.

'I'll air it out for him.'

*   *   *

'Billy's already been and gone up to Harehills,' Annabelle said as she kissed him. 'Mary's over having her tea with Maisie Taylor. I said you'd pick her up at seven.'

She'd changed from her usual working clothes into a dress of pale yellow silk with leg-of-mutton sleeves and a high neck. Very prim and proper.

'Meeting tonight?' Harper guessed.

'We're discussing the relief budget for next year. I know they want to cut it. I'm going to try and make sure they don't.' She raised an eyebrow. 'We ought to sell tickets. It's going to be a knock-down, drag-out fight.'

'Do you think you can win?'

'Probably not, but I'm going to try.' A sad smile. 'If I lose, at least I'll go down swinging. Sit at the table, tea's ready.'

Salad again.

'What's this?' He prodded the mound at the side of the plate. Not meat, not quite fish.

'Crab. Billy brought it. Quite the delicacy in Whitby, he says. Mind you, I had the devil's own job getting it out of the shell. Ended up taking a hammer to it.'

Not bad, he thought. They looked at each other as they took tentative bites, then started to laugh.

At six she was gone. Harper settled down in his shirtsleeves, tie off, collar stud loosened, and read the newspaper. Councillor Howe was buying more land. A big noise in the building trade, making money hand over fist as houses kept going up. Never a problem with planning permission, of course.

Noise filtered up from the pub downstairs. Men thirsty for a drink after a long, hot shift.

He slipped out with a wave to Dan, then strolled up Manor Street. Evening heat pressed against the ground. Front doors stood open, inviting a draught that never came, women standing outside waving fans as they tried to cool off.

At the Taylors' he stewed in the kitchen, sipping a glass of lemonade with Arthur and hearing about the brickworks where he was foreman. Then Mary was ready, satchel looped over her shoulder, chattering ceaselessly as they started the short trot home.

* * *

Billy Reed walked down Roundhay Road. People moved all around him, but he barely saw them. His feet moved automatically, one in front of the other as he tried to make sense of what he'd been told.

Sense? How was that possible? How could you make sense of someone dying before their time?

Somehow, he reached Sheepscar. He had no memory of the streets he'd passed, for a moment he wasn't even sure where he was. He looked up, and suddenly the noises of the city crashed into his head, the press of buses and trams and carts. It felt like too much, more than he could take.

'Billy?' Harper turned his head as the door opened. 'I—'

He stopped.

Reed knew what he must look like. A man who was lost, a ghost in his own life.

'Come on, sit down.' Harper moved towards the stairs. 'I'll bring you a drop of brandy from the bar.'

'No,' he answered quickly. 'Honestly. I don't want anything.'

'Are you sure? What is it? You look in a bad way.'

'I just . . .' He tried to grasp the words, but they stayed beyond his reach. Instead, he brought out a packet of cigarettes, hands shaking as he tried to light one with a match. There was only one way to say it. 'Charlie committed suicide.'

'Oh Christ, Billy. I'm so sorry. What can I do?'

'Nothing. There's nothing any of us can do, is there?' he replied. His voice was empty, all the expression bleached away. 'It's too late. I didn't really know him, not for years, but still . . . I couldn't believe it when Hester told me. His wife.'

He paced around the room. Too many thoughts were shoving up against each other until he believed his head would overflow. Images of his brother when they were both young. Charlie had always been the one with charm. The women on their street had loved him, slipping him sweets and little treats.

Reed drew the smoke down deep, keeping it in his lungs before pushing it out.

'He was two years older than me, but we did everything together when we were nippers. A right pair of shavers. We were best mates until I joined the army. I came home on leave, full of myself because I had a uniform. You know how it goes.'

Harper nodded. Billy didn't wait for a reply. He needed to talk, to let it all out.

'There was this lass Charlie fancied. I thought I was cock o'the walk, a proper soldier boy, a big man. I thought I'd show him, so I made a play for her. We ended up arguing, said a lot of things we didn't mean. Then we started with fists.' His shrug held a whole world of regret. 'We didn't speak for ten years after that. Once we did, it was only Christmas cards and a few words at weddings and funerals.'

Young men full of piss and vinegar, he thought. How many other families had stories like that? It was only death made you realize what you'd squandered along the way.

'What made him do it?' Harper asked. 'Does his wife know?'

'They have a shop. Just a little corner place. It's never made a fortune, but it's a fair location. They get by. Hester said that about six months ago, someone came in. Asked if they were interested in selling the business.'

'Your brother said no?'

'What else was he going to say? It's all they have. They've been there for years, they live upstairs. Then last week, they got a letter. A new landlord had bought the building. He was putting up their rent.' He paused for a moment, studying the ash on the tip of his cigarette. 'Doubling it.'

'Double? God, Billy, that's awful.'

'Charlie was at his wits' end. They can't afford to pay that kind of money. Seems like he went to the chemist yesterday morning and bought some rat poison. Never said a word to Hester. Made himself a cup of tea while she was out, put the stuff in and drank it down. Left her a note saying he couldn't cope any more.'

What a brutal way to go. To choose poison . . . Harper couldn't even start to imagine what must have gone through the man's mind.

Reed looked up. No tears, even for his own brother. He'd been a copper too long for anything like that, a soldier for years before. He'd seen too much death, mourned too many men.

'What are you going to do?'

'I don't know,' he said finally. 'The funeral's the day after tomorrow.' He stubbed out the cigarette in an ashtray. 'I just want to be on my own for a while, if you don't mind.'

'Of course. You go ahead.'

'Maybe things will seem a little brighter in the morning.'

But Harper doubted that.

'His poor wife,' Annabelle said as they lay in bed. 'What's going to happen to her?'

'I've no idea,' Harper sighed. 'How was the meeting?'

'I did everything I could, but they're cutting the money for the workhouse.' In the faint light through the window he saw anger and defeat flicker across her face. A battle lost. 'There's something I've been asked to do. I might need your help.'

'What is it?' He turned towards her, seeing the sorrow in her eyes, the fine lines of worry in her skin, a few more with each year.

'Do you remember back in April, when a man drowned his daughters over in Holbeck?'

Of course he did. It had been in the papers for days. Everyone in Leeds had been outraged, then appalled; the girls were only four and six. They lived with their father and a woman. He worked, but spent all his money on drink and gambling. The type of thing Harper heard so regularly that it didn't even startle him.

Finally, the woman had had her fill. A Saturday night. The man refused to hand over his wages to feed his own family or pay for a room where they could all live. At the end of her tether, she'd thrown them out, hoping it would force him to do something. It did. In the small hours, he pushed the girls into the canal and walked away. They couldn't swim.

He was arrested the next morning and taken to Hunslet Road police station. Now he was in prison, waiting to be tried for murder at the Assizes.

'I can't remember his name.'

'James Redshaw,' Annabelle said. She sounded bleak. 'The little ones were called Ada and Annie. He claims he went to the Holbeck Workhouse and asked them to take the lasses in, but they turned him away.'

'Ah.' Now he understood. If the workhouse had accepted the girls, they'd still be alive. 'That's why the Guardians are involved.'

'The master over there says Redshaw had enough money to afford lodging for them all. The Holbeck Union's asked us to investigate, to make sure they did everything properly.' She gave a feeble smile. 'I drew the short straw.'

The female Guardians worked with women and girls. Put on the committees where the men thought they could cause little trouble and have no influence. 'How many on the panel?'

'Three of us. I'm the only woman, of course.' Her hands fidgeted on top of the sheet. 'I've read the statements. It's horrible, Tom. Those poor little things.'

'What do you want me to do?' he asked.

'Take a look at everything and see if it's all legal.' She hesitated for a moment. 'And someone to talk to about it, really. I've come across some awful things since I was elected, but this is the worst.'

She'd been a Poor Law Guardian for two years, voted in with a large majority. Since then he'd seen how hard she worked for the poor in Sheepscar, fighting for a fairer system. Every week it seemed as if there was a new skirmish.

He took her hand and stroked her fingers, feeling the solid gold of their wedding ring. 'Of course. You don't even need to ask.'

'I know, but . . .' The words seemed to fail her. 'Do you know what struck me when I read all the reports? Not a single person ever wondered what Ada and Annie were feeling. How terrified they must have been before they died.' She quickly brushed her eyes with the back of her hand. 'It makes me so angry, that's all.'

In the spare room, Billy Reed lay under the covers, turning restlessly. It was the heat, he told himself. Any excuse. But he knew the truth.

THREE

With a slither and a grunt, an old steam tram passed, filled with people. Harper strolled up Briggate, hands in the pockets of his trousers. He studied people, faces. It was habit, ingrained during the days he walked a beat around here. It was still good to get out, to meander and watch. It kept him in touch with his city.

On the other side of the street, the arcades had torn the guts out of the old courts and yards behind the buildings. Still plenty left, but year on year they were disappearing.

He stopped and peered between some boards, already plastered with advertisements. White Hart Yard had gone, knocked down by the hammers. Soon enough there'd be something new in its place. County Arcade, with more shops, and a way through from Vicar Lane. There was plenty of money in Leeds and people wanted places to spend it. The city was growing prosperous, changing so quickly he could barely keep pace.

But Harper kept wondering what had happened to those people in Fidelity Court and the other tiny streets that didn't exist any longer. Where had they all gone?

Leeds was filled with noise. Voices shouting, carts on the cobbles, machines thudding and pumping. Relentless, battering the senses every day.

On the far side of the Headrow, he sat in a small cafe across from the Grand Theatre, hearing the ghost of Sam the Newsman hawking his programmes. One more character who was history now, like the rest of old Leeds. Harper leaned back in his chair. No familiar faces in here, no one to pester him. A ham sandwich, a mug of tea, and chance to think in peace.

Billy hadn't come down to breakfast. Harper wondered how long it had taken him to fall asleep. The weight of everything he'd learned the day before must be crushing his heart. And he couldn't have done a thing to stop it. Billy was a copper, he understood things like that were a part of life. Always different when it was family, though, and you realized how powerless you really were.

He stirred a spoonful of sugar into his tea. No call from the chief constable yet, but no progress on the burglary. His men had questioned Hope's servants: they were all clean. Well over a quarter of a million people in Leeds, more coming and going every day, and they had to find one. The needle in the proverbial haystack.

Answers. That was what he needed, Reed thought. He heard the Harpers moving around downstairs, smelled the bacon cooking. He didn't want company, no questions or sympathy, the ordinariness of family life. His brother was dead and he had to know *why*. Hester had given him the facts, but when were they ever enough? Who was behind it all? Why raise the rent like that? What made

the location of Charlie's shop so important? Discovering things
was his job. And it seemed like the very least he could do. The
final thing.

He'd written a pair of letters during the evening. One to Elizabeth,
telling her what had happened and saying he might need to stay
on for a few days. She'd understand; anyway, at the height of a hot
summer, she'd be too busy with the tea room to miss him.

The other was to his chief constable, requesting some extra leave.
He had the time coming, and even in high season, crime in Whitby
had been quiet.

As soon as the doors closed downstairs, everybody gone, he
slipped out, coughing as he walked up the street. Two years of clean
air on the coast had spoiled him. Leeds was hot and filthy; it caked
his nostrils and tasted burned and bitter in his mouth as he walked
towards Harehills.

The bell tinkled as he entered the shop and he saw Hester glance
up from the other side of the counter. She was a small woman, a
long apron wrapped around her body, dark hair going grey, cheeks
sunk where most of her teeth had been pulled. A woman like so
many of the others around here, pummelled by life and grief.

'I didn't know if you'd open up today,' Reed said.

'Got to make some money.' She lifted her head, as if his comment
had been a criticism. 'I still have to eat and pay the bills. And find
the brass for his funeral.'

'I told you yesterday: I'll pay for that.'

She folded her arms and stared at him.

'And *I* told *you*: I won't take charity from anyone. Charlie never
would, and I'm the same.'

He was never going to win against stubborn pride. Instead, Reed
said, 'Would you mind if I took a look through all his papers? I'd
like to have a sense of what was going on.'

Hester shrugged. 'Help yourself. They're in his desk. For whatever
it's worth. We both know how it's going to end.'

He sat on his bed at the Victoria, poring over the papers he'd brought
back from the shop. He'd glanced through them there, but it was
impossible to concentrate with Hester bustling around. Serving,
talking to neighbours and the undertakers to arrange tomorrow's
funeral.

For a short moment he wondered about Whitby, missing the place, the plain routine of work and the company of the men he commanded. More than anything, he missed Elizabeth. But he had to be here, he needed to stay until he'd taken care of this. After all these years he owed his brother that much.

Reed ran a hand through his hair and returned to the documents. He'd taken a walk around the area by Charlie's shop before coming back to the Victoria. New houses were starting to go up, street after street of them, back-to-backs, one long row of terraces with tiny front yards. Foundations laid, brick walls beginning to rise. Another three months and they'd be finished. Trade at the corner shop would increase. Easy enough to see why someone had wanted to buy the business; soon enough there'd be very good money to be made here. Must have had advance information, if the offer was that long ago. He could even understand a landlord raising the rent. But doubling it? That was pure gouging. No wonder Charlie had felt so desperate.

He'd found something in the papers that made him suspicious. Payments to a man named Davies. Every month. They'd begun two years before, small at first, then a little more and a little more. Never enough to cripple, but still a constant, niggling amount. He knew what it sounded like. He'd discover the truth. Then he'd go hunting. Start paying back a very old debt.

'You were quiet during supper,' Harper said. They'd gone down to the bar, two glasses of lemonade in front of them. All the windows and doors open wide, begging for a wisp of breeze.

'Just thinking,' Reed replied. He lit a cigarette and blew out a stream of smoke. 'I discovered that Charlie had been paying money to someone for a couple of years. A little every week. Michael Davies. The name is in his accounts. Do you know him?'

'Oh yes. Mickey bloody Davies.' His voice was filled with disgust. 'Protection racket. You know how it works, Billy. How much was your brother forking out?'

'Five bob a week.'

'He was getting off lightly, then. What about this new landlord? Have you discovered who it is?'

'There's nothing in Charlie's papers. I'll find out tomorrow, after the funeral. I'd like to stay on for a few days, if you don't mind. Sort everything out.'

'Of course. As long as you need. Once you come up with some names, let me know. We'll work it together. I'll take care of Mickey. Don't worry about that.'

'What about your burglar? I saw the papers.'

Harper shook his head. 'Ash and the men are looking after that. There's not much else going on. Either all the criminals have vanished on their holidays or the heat's making them sleepy.'

Reed had always been an excellent detective, ferreting and nibbling away at things until he found the truth. They'd made a good team in the old days. Before the falling-out. But they were older now, both of them higher in rank. Maybe even a little wiser, Harper thought wryly. Perhaps it was time to make sure those old wounds healed properly. Well past time, really. The whole thing had been his fault in the first place.

'Let's make sure we do right by your brother, shall we?'

'Billy seemed a little brighter after you came back up.' They lay in bed, barely touching; the night was too warm to snuggle. Harper could feel the dampness on the back of his neck where it touched the pillow.

'He needed to get a few things off his chest. You didn't have much to say for yourself earlier.'

'I was thinking,' Annabelle replied. 'I went over to Holbeck Workhouse today and talked to the master.'

'The one who turned the family away? What did he have to say for himself?'

'He showed me the records. It's all there. He made Redshaw turn out his pockets. Seventeen and threepence. The master counted it himself. That's more than enough to afford lodgings for him and the girls. The master was in the right. Those are the rules, Tom. He did everything by the book.'

'Could he have altered the entry later?' Things like that happened all the time; any trick to make themselves look better.

'No. There are others right below it. He was being straight. He did recall that Redshaw didn't seem to quite know what he was doing. Begged the workhouse to take the girls.' She let the words hang in the air.

'Did he threaten to kill them?'

'Not there. Turns out he had earlier, when he was in the pub. I took myself there, too, and had a word with the landlord. He claims he kicked Redshaw out when the man was too drunk to make sense. After that I went and looked at where they'd been living. It was an old stable. The door wouldn't close properly and half the roof was gone. Can you imagine trying to raise two kiddies in a place like that?'

He could. He'd seen people living in worse. But he didn't need to mention that now.

'If he had the money, why didn't he rent somewhere?' Harper asked. 'Redshaw was in work, wasn't he? He could afford it.'

'He liked to keep his brass for drink and betting. That's what everyone said.'

Harper didn't speak for a long time. What could he really add?

'From all you've told me, it sounds as if Redshaw was the only one to blame.'

'In the end, he was,' she agreed. 'But it's awful, Tom. The system worked the way it's supposed to, and we still have two little girls dead.'

'What can you do, though? *Really* do, I mean.'

'I haven't stopped digging yet. I want to know it all. I can't bring Ada and Annie back, but maybe I can change things so it won't happen to someone else.'

'How?'

Her silence lasted a long time. 'I'm still trying to sort that out. But if I don't try, I don't think I'll be able to live with myself.'

Sometimes he wondered if she cared too much. But she wasn't about to stop now. Deep in the night, his mind drifted into the silence.

FOUR

Billy Reed glanced around the church. It was filled with Charlie's neighbours and customers who'd come to pay their final respects. Women offered hurried words of condolence to Hester before taking their seats in the pews, faces set and grim.

They'd held the inquest first thing that morning. A quick verdict of accidental death to give a gracious lie that spared everyone and allowed a proper burial. The service itself was short, a pair of hymns and a few prayers, then a eulogy from a vicar who sounded as if he'd never met Charlie in his life, before the hearse made its way to Beckett Street Cemetery. Familiar streets; Reed and Elizabeth had lived a stone's throw away until they moved to Whitby. But it seemed as if a lifetime had passed since then.

He'd received a letter from her that morning. Full of seaside gossip, but he could sense the exhaustion beneath her words. Business was good at the tea shop. She was making money, but working from first thing until long after dark, six days a week. Next summer she'd hire more staff.

Elizabeth understood his need to stay, to know what had happened, why his brother had killed himself.

Find out what you can. But don't be too long, Billy. I miss you. Love you.

He smiled for a brief moment, hearing her voice in his mind. The parson began the service at the graveside as the coffin was lowered into the ground. Beside him, Hester's head was bowed, face hidden behind a black veil as her shoulders moved with silent tears.

Reed waited his turn, then picked up a handful of dirt and sprinkled it into the grave. Another few minutes and they'd be filling in the hole. After that, the funeral tea and life would push on in its daily procession. All this would become a memory.

The rooms above the shop seemed to burst with people. He stayed a few minutes, made his excuses and left. He didn't know any of them, and there were things to do. A tram into the centre and meet Tom Harper at the Town Hall.

The burglar had struck again during the night. Another big house, this one on Clarendon Road. The owners out for the evening, servants playing gin rummy for matchsticks in the kitchen. They hadn't heard a thing.

'We still don't have a clue, sir,' Ash said. He exhaled and ran a hand through his hair. 'Not one.'

'What did he get away with this time?' Harper asked.

'Some money, a few bits of jewellery the wife wasn't wearing. Silver-plated hairbrushes. He was probably inside for five minutes at the most.'

'Whose house is it?'

'Mr and Mrs Collins. He's the vice-chancellor at Yorkshire College.'

Another important person. But with an expensive address like that, it was a given.

'No word from the snouts? Nobody trying to sell the goods to the fences?'

'Nothing yet,' Fowler told him. 'Barring a piece of luck, this one's going to be a long slog.'

He was right, Harper thought as he dismissed the detectives, a drawn-out case when they needed a quick arrest.

'Ash, I need a word.' The inspector settled back on his chair.

'Of course, sir.'

'You've probably heard that Mr Reed is in Leeds.'

Ash's mouth twitched under his heavy moustache. 'One of the beat men saw him and told me. It's very sad news about his brother.'

'Mickey Davies is involved.'

'Is that right?' He raised his eyebrows. 'Putting the squeeze on the brother, was he?'

'Yes. Seems there were something else going on, too, but I don't know if he's involved in that.' He hesitated. 'Can Fowler and Walsh track down this burglar on their own?'

'They'll manage that, sir.' Not a trace of doubt in his voice.

'I want you to find out about our friend Mickey. Gather as much as you can.'

Ash grinned. 'Leave it with me, sir. I'll be happy as Larry to bring a ton of bricks down on his head. I should still have a little time to work on the burglar. Did you say there was more?'

'Mr Reed and I are going to handle that.'

'Of course, sir. But if you need a hand . . .'

'I'll let you know.' He glanced at the clock. Twenty minutes to one. Where did the time go? He needed to meet Billy at the Town Hall, then dash over to Hunslet.

Reed was waiting, leaning against one of the stone lions on the steps. He looked uncomfortable in his black suit of thick, scratchy wool.

'How was the funeral?'

'Same way they always bloody are.' He sounded bitter. 'I'm sorry, it's just . . . how can it ever be worthwhile when a man's killed himself?'

'I told you, we'll take care of the people who drove him to it.'

Reed took a final draw on his cigarette and ground it under his heel.

'Too late for Charlie, though, isn't it?' He shook his head, as if he was trying to clear away the sorrow. 'You know, I just saw the strangest thing while I've been standing here. One of those motor cars I've read about.'

Harper laughed. 'That'll be Roland Winn. He sells them, has a garage on Woodhouse Lane. We had him up before the magistrate last year for driving twelve miles an hour. Progress, Billy. That's what they call it. Telephones, electric light, moving pictures, motor cars. A new century in a few months.'

'Just another year. It doesn't mean anything. Sometimes I wonder if any of it's worth a damn,' Reed replied as they entered the building. Inside was marble and wide staircases, all the expense of civic grandeur. And at the rear of the second floor, the planning office, where a clerk with stooped shoulders and wild, grey hair seemed surprised that anyone would visit.

But he was efficient, bringing out a large map to locate the shop, then ledgers to discover who owned it.

'This is very unusual,' he muttered slowly. 'It was sold six months ago.'

'What's so strange about that?' Harper asked. People bought and sold places all the time.

'Two things, sir,' the clerk answered. 'First of all, it was bought by a company, not a person.'

'What's the name of the company?'

'The Harehills Development Company.' He read the words from the page.

'Who owns that?'

'It doesn't say. I'm sorry, sir.' The clerk bit his lip. 'I'm not familiar with them at all.'

'You said there were two unusual things.' Reed's voice cut over him.

'Yes. According to this, the buyer paid the same for the property as the original owner.'

'Maybe it hasn't risen in value.'

'No, sir.' He shook his head, absolutely certain. 'It should definitely have gone up. Definitely.'

'Why?'

The man was silent, staring down as he framed the words.

'By the time it was sold, it was common knowledge round here that planning permission would be given for more houses in the area.' He stared at them, making sure they understood. 'Everyone in the trade would have been aware, too. Word travels quickly in this business. That meant any commercial property would have gone up in value. Even a small one like this.'

'Where can we find out about this Harehills Development Company?' Harper asked.

'You can try the office three doors along,' the clerk said doubtfully. 'A lot depends on what type of company it is, and there's nothing here to indicate that. I'm sorry, sir.'

At the door, Harper turned. 'Who's building these houses?'

'Mr Regis, sir.'

Regis, Regis. He knew that name.

'Isn't he—'

'Yes, sir.' The clerk looked shamefaced. 'Councillor Howe's son-in-law.'

Nothing like keeping it in the family.

Out in the corridor, away from the musty smell of old paper, Harper pulled out his pocket watch. They'd spent an hour in there.

'I'm sorry, Billy, I'm going to have to leave the rest to you. I have an appointment.'

'Don't worry. Thank you for the help. At least we've made a start.'

We. He liked the sound of that. 'I'll see you later. You can tell me what you've found.'

Harper hurried along the pavement to Hunslet Road police station. Annabelle was pacing as she waited. A rose-coloured dress with white lace on the collar today, standing out brightly against the drabness of the buildings.

'I'm sorry I'm late.'

She raised an eyebrow. 'I'll be getting myself a reputation if anyone spots me loitering outside a place like this.'

'Not if you're seen with a handsome detective.'

Annabelle glanced around. 'You'd better hurry up and find me one, then. All I can see is my husband.'

He took her arm and they went in. A familiar smell, exactly the same as Millgarth, that mix of sweat, hopelessness, and fear.

Superintendent Patterson was waiting; he showed them through to his office and sent a constable to bring tea.

'I appreciate you taking the time for this, Brian,' Harper said. 'Especially as it's a bit non-regulation.'

'I'm happy to help any way I can. I don't think there was a man here who wasn't shocked when we pulled those two lasses from the canal.' He was a big, bluff man who'd started out plodding a beat in Wortley. 'Most of us have kiddies of our own.'

'My wife's a Poor Law Guardian. She's been asked to look into it, to make sure everything possible was done.'

Patterson dipped his head. 'Whatever you want to know, Mrs Harper.'

She was about to speak when a bobby entered, carefully balancing three full mugs.

'I'm afraid we don't run to the bone china here,' Patterson said.

'It wouldn't last a minute in our house, either.' Annabelle gave a fleeting grin, then her expression turned serious. 'The first the police knew about this business was when someone reported Ada and Annie in the canal. Is that right?'

'Yes.' Patterson turned the cup in his hands, staring into the liquid. 'The constable who pulled them out tried to revive them, but it was too late. It didn't take long to discover their names. From there, my men did their job. Asking questions, looking for the father. We found him the next morning. Have you seen the reports?'

'I have,' Annabelle told him. 'I can't say they're pleasant reading.'

'What I wondered,' Harper began, 'is whether there's anything that wasn't put on paper. You know, the little bits that don't fit and don't help the case. Not to blame anyone, nothing like that' – he glanced at his wife for confirmation, waiting until she nodded in agreement – 'but just to find out everything we can.'

'I talked to the constables involved this morning after you telephoned me. They all remember it clear as day. I doubt they'll ever forget. Everything is in the reports. Only—' A high, metallic screech rose over his voice.

'What on earth was that?' Annabelle asked, eyes wide, hands over her ears. 'It sounds like something's tearing itself apart.'

Patterson laughed. 'Just the engine works testing the brakes on a new locomotive. Spend any time down here and you get used to it. No, the only thing not in the report is that when Redshaw was arrested, he didn't mention the girls at all.'

'Not a word?' Annabelle asked in disbelief.

'No. He seemed dazed, that's what the constable told me. Like he'd just woken up and didn't remember a thing.'

'What do you mean? Lost his mind?'

'For a little while, perhaps,' Patterson replied cautiously and leaned forward. 'Are you sure this is just between us?'

'Absolutely confidential,' she promised.

'Right then. Everyone here wants this to be a murder case. *Everyone.* Those daughters of his never had a chance. We want him to hang and we're not about to give a lawyer any ammunition that could bring a different verdict.'

'The outcome isn't my concern,' Annabelle told him. 'I need to make sure the workhouse acted properly. That's all.' A small hesitation. 'And I don't want anything like this to happen again.'

'Mrs Harper . . .'

'You'd best call me Annabelle,' she said. 'If you're on Christian name terms with my husband, you should be with me, too.'

'Annabelle it is, then. As far as I can discover, the workhouse master did everything he was supposed to do,' Patterson said.

'That's how I'm beginning to feel.' She sighed. 'The question is always going to be how we ended up with two dead girls, isn't it?' She sighed and stood, extending her hand. 'Thank you for your time. And your honesty.'

'I can't say I gave you much. But if there's anything else, just ask.'

'Was it worth the visit?' Harper asked as they stood on the pavement.

'I think so,' she answered hesitantly. 'Everything I can learn helps.'

'They've sent for a hackney; it should be here soon. I need to go back to Millgarth.'

'I'll see you at home.' She ducked forward and kissed him. 'Thank you for arranging this.'

'I told you I'd give you a hand.'

'You did. That's one thing about you, Tom Harper, you always do what you promise. With most men, it's just talk.'

*   *   *

'Right,' he said. 'The burglar. Have you turned up anything at all?'

Late afternoon, the sun hazy and hot above the thick layer of smoke that covered the city.

'Nothing, sir,' Fowler said. He took off his glasses and rubbed his eyes, voice weary. 'It's not for want of trying. The snouts don't have a scent. I've written to other forces to see if they've had anything similar.'

'Good idea,' Harper said. 'Whoever he is, it looks like he's just started here. Maybe things became too hot for him somewhere else.'

'Well, he's definitely not trying to move anything through the local pawn shops or the fences,' Walsh added. 'I tried them all again today.'

'Keep worrying at it. Something's going to give sooner or later.'

He just hoped it was sooner. The men left, but Ash didn't move from his seat.

'You wanted to know all about Mickey Davies, sir,' he said.

FIVE

Reed sat back with his tea and cigarette, listening as Mary sang the song she'd learned that afternoon at school. *Begone Dull Care*, wavering around the notes in a high, piping tone. Two verses, every word correct. Like her parents, he applauded as she finished and curtseyed, before dashing off to her bedroom to play.

'Her voice might never be her fortune,' Annabelle said, 'but at least she's got plenty of front. You could never pay me to sing for anyone.' She gathered the last of the plates. 'You two look like you need to talk. I'll leave you to it.'

'What did the companies' office have to say?' Harper asked as he poured another cup of tea from the pot.

'Not enough,' Reed replied. 'Nowhere near enough.'

'What do you mean?' He stared. 'Who owns this Harehills Development Company?'

'Another company.' He could hear the tight frustration in his voice. 'And the office doesn't know who owns that. The only contact named is a lawyer.'

'A lawyer?' Harper asked. He didn't understand.

Reed sighed. 'The clerk said he's come across this before. According to him, it's a way to hide the real owners.'

'This Harehills Development Company bought the property where your brother had his shop, but it doesn't really own it?'

'That's right. The real owners are this other company, the North Leeds Company,' Reed said.

'North Leeds?' Harper raised an eyebrow. 'Not short of ambition, are they?' He rubbed his chin with the back of his hand. 'And the only name we have there is the lawyer. Who is he?'

'Dryden, in Park Square. Do you know him?'

'Oh yes. Very well.' Charles Dryden, retained by the rich crooks who could afford his services, and worth every penny. He was sly, cunning, a man who knew all the twists in the law. What was he doing in something like this, though? He dealt with criminals, not companies. Something was starting to smell rotten. 'It's not good news.'

'Why?' Reed asked.

'Charlie Dryden knows the law inside and out, and he gives up information like it's money from his own pocket. It's going to be a battle.'

'We need to know, Tom.' He could hear the metal in Billy's voice, the need.

'In the morning,' he said. 'We'll go down together.'

Reed nodded. That was enough. He sat back on the chair. 'I looked in on Elizabeth's oldest two this afternoon.'

'I'd forgotten they'd stayed here.'

He shrugged. 'All grown up now. In lodgings, caught up in their own lives and their sweethearts.'

'You blink and they've grown up.' Harper shook his head. 'Every time I look at Mary I wonder where the last seven years went.' A small cough. 'We're moving along with Mickey Davies. How often is his name in your brother's account books?'

'Every week,' Reed told him. 'I can bring them downstairs, if you like.'

Harper shook his head. 'No need. As long as it's there when I need it. Do you think your sister-in-law would testify?'

'I can ask her.'

'Ash is looking into it. The problem is, we've never had much real evidence against him, and no one's been willing to stand up in court and speak. And there have always been more important things,' he admitted.

'What now?' Reed asked.

'Ash has found a couple of people willing to give evidence. Once we have enough, we'll drag Mickey down to the station.'

'Ever had dealings with him before?'

'Once,' Harper said. 'Years ago now. You know the type – reckons he can get away with anything he wants.'

'I only have the rest of this week,' Reed said hesitantly. He wanted to go home with something. Some small sense of justice. 'My leave's up after that.'

'Can you take more?'

He shook his head. 'My sergeant goes on holiday from Monday. He's been looking forward to it all year.'

'You can't go upsetting sergeants. We'll keep on with the investigation. That's a promise, Billy.'

Reed stretched in the chair and yawned. 'I'm going up to bed. It's been a rough day.'

'Poor Billy. He looked like he was carrying the weight of the world on his shoulders,' Annabelle said as they lay in bed. The heat seemed to cling to their skin. Even a single thin sheet on top of them felt too heavy.

'Hardly surprising, is it?' He said nothing for a long time. 'How about you? How do you feel with this Redshaw case?'

'Hopeless,' she answered. 'I still want to find the woman Redshaw lived with and hear her side of things. But the workhouse master isn't at fault.'

'Then your job's done, isn't it?'

'That part is.'

'I was wondering . . . do you think they chose you for this to stop you harassing the board about cuts?' The idea had been niggling him since she first mentioned the panel.

'Distract the troublemaker, you mean?' She snorted. 'Probably. But they won't be happy when I tell them that we all failed, Tom. *We* let those little girls down. We're the ones who let them die.'

'No,' Harper told her. He couldn't let her believe she bore any of the guilt. 'That was their father. It's not your fault.'

'We need a better system. One that allows people to use their judgement. So no more end up dying like that.'

She began to cry, tiny sobs, and he held her close until it passed. It wasn't just Billy Reed who was carrying his sorrow.

'We might have something on our burglar, sir,' Fowler said as he glanced at the letter on his desk.

'A name?' Harper asked hopefully.

'We should be so lucky. I heard from Newcastle. They had one just like this. Plagued them for three months, two or three incidents a week.' He lifted his head and pushed the spectacles up his nose. 'Stopped a month ago.'

Not long before they began in Leeds.

'Plenty of time for him to come here and start over,' Ash said.

'Did they manage to uncover anything at all?' Harper asked.

'No. They think he must have worked alone, never a word to anyone else.'

'Same as our man, then,' Harper said. 'What about selling the loot?'

Fowler shook his head. 'Nothing ever turned up, sir. They were glad to see the back of him.'

'The fences and the pawnbrokers are still reporting nothing,' Walsh said.

The superintendent rubbed his chin and counted the points off on his fingers.

'One: we have a very daring burglar who *may* have arrived from Newcastle. Could be a Geordie. That's the good news: if he is, someone's bound to notice the accent. I want you to ask about that, about anyone who's come here in the last few weeks. Two: he's not doing this for the fun of it. He's selling what he steals *somewhere*. If he didn't get rid of his loot in Newcastle, then he probably has a buyer he trusts between here and there. A place he can reach easily.'

'Sunderland?' Ash suggested. 'Durham? Middlesbrough? They're all easy enough on the train.'

'I'll write to them,' Walsh said.

'Telegraph them,' Harper told them. 'It's quicker.' They had a sniff of the man now. Things were starting to move.

He was reading through reports and making notes in the margins when he became aware of someone in the office. He looked up with a start to see Chief Constable Crossley.

The man smiled. 'I knocked, but you must have been engrossed.'
A polite way of ignoring his bad hearing.

'I'm sorry, sir. Have a seat. Would you like some tea?'
He waved the offer away. 'I was passing and thought I'd pop in for a chat.'

Millgarth wasn't a place anyone simply passed. More of Crossley's politeness. But he'd been expecting to hear from the chief since the first burglary at George Hope's house. After another, it was inevitable.

'I wanted to talk to you about South Africa.'

'Sir?' Harper said. The statement took him by surprise.

'Come on, Tom, you must have seen the papers. There's going to be war there very soon. They're already beating the drums for England.'

He'd read the stories. Small pieces growing day by day into headlines. But he didn't understand how it would affect them.

'Some of our men are bound to enlist,' Crossley said. 'Might be quite a few. We need to be prepared, ready to plug the gaps. We're going to need trained men.'

'Special constables?'

The chief nodded. 'That's what I've been thinking. I'm planning a recruitment drive. I wanted to let you know.'

'Thank you, sir.' But it wasn't the reason for his visit; he could have put that in a note.

'While I'm here, what's going on with these burglaries?'

Here was the meat of the matter. Harper had a little progress to offer. Crossley listened and nodded, jotting a few lines in a small notebook.

'It sounds as if you're doing all the right things.' He coughed. 'I've had some grumblings from the council. The usual thing, influential people having a word with their friends. No need to worry. Not yet, anyway. I just wanted you to be aware.'

'Thank you, sir.' *Not yet*. Get the job done and someone behind bars, that was the message. What did the councillors think? That the police wouldn't investigate?

'I'd love to know where this chap is selling what he takes, though,' Crossley said.

'Makes two of us, sir. There's something else we're working on, too. It involves Inspector Reed. You might remember him.'

He'd barely had a chance to start when the man appeared, as if the words had conjured him from the air.

'Inspector.' The chief rose. 'I heard about your brother. I'm sorry for your loss.'

'Thank you, sir.'

Crossley slipped his notebook into his jacket. 'I should go, Tom. More meetings waiting. Keep me informed about the burglar.'

'What was that about?' Billy asked once they were alone.

'His gentle way of giving me a warning. Two important men have their houses broken into. You can guess who's been having a word in his ear. Are you ready to go?'

Leeds was sticky. As they marched along Commercial Street, Harper felt the shirt clinging to his back. Frazzled faces everywhere. This heatwave had lasted too long. The joy of it had become an annoyance, with short tempers and the stink of sweating people.

The houses in Park Square were all immaculately kept. Trees and carefully clipped grass lay behind a fence in the centre, a few people sitting on shaded benches, reading the newspapers. Harper led the way to a door painted in brilliant black gloss. A brass plaque read *C. Dryden* in curling script. Nothing more needed. Anyone coming here knew exactly what the man did.

A plush waiting room, with heavy leather armchairs and a secretary whose fingers moved swiftly over the keys of one of the new typewriting machines. Finally, on some hidden signal, they were ushered into the office.

Dryden was a sleek man, wearing a lounge suit that cost as much as most working men made in a month. Thick legal texts lined the shelves. He settled behind a partner's desk under the window.

'Superintendent,' he acknowledged with a short nod. 'And . . .'

'Inspector Reed. Whitby Police.'

'Whitby?' Dryden's face clouded for a moment. 'Forgive me. I don't have any business there.'

'This is about business here,' Harper told him. 'One business in particular. The North Leeds Company.'

'I see.' If the lawyer was surprised, he hid it well. 'Why do you want to know about it?'

'Some enquiries, sir.' Harper smiled. 'I'm sure we can count on your cooperation. We'd like to know who owns the company.'

Dryden pursed his lips. 'I'll ask again, Superintendent: why?'

'Various dealings with properties, sir. At this stage I'm not free to go into details of the investigation.'

The lawyer shook his head. 'Do you know why my name is listed for the company?'

'You take care of things for them,' Reed said.

'I do,' he acknowledged, 'but it's more than that. The owners don't wish to be known. In English law, that is their right. That's why they nominated me to handle everything, and it's why you found my name.'

'So you won't tell us who owns the North Leeds Company?' Harper's voice was harsher now.

'No, Superintendent, I won't. If you check, you'll find that's completely legal.'

'We're the police. This relates to a crime.'

Dryden stood, bunching his knuckles and pressing them down on the desk.

'I'll put it in words even you can understand, Superintendent. I don't care if you're God Almighty. That information is protected by the law of this land, and I do not have to divulge it.'

'The North Leeds Company owns the Harehills Development Company, is that correct?' Billy Reed's question filled the dangerous silence.

Dryden turned his head. 'It is.'

'And who runs that?'

'It's a matter of public record.' Dryden smiled as he opened a ledger. 'I'm surprised you don't know. John and Jack Smith. Perhaps you'd care for the address, too? I'll write it down for you.'

Harper blazed up the street, his face set. 'I don't like being treated like I'm a bloody fool. Not by someone who defends the worst criminals in town.'

'Where are we going?' Reed asked as they crossed the Headrow towards the Town Hall.

'The police lawyer. We'll find out how we really stand on this. John and Jack Smith. Dryden loved it. He must think we're simple.'

The lawyer was out on business. But his senior clerk was there, a wizened man who probably knew the statutes better than his employer.

'I'm sorry to say it, sir, but for once Mr Dryden is telling the truth.' His voice wheezed and creaked after a lifetime surrounded by books and dusty papers. 'It's a basic legal principle in this country, a matter of privilege between a lawyer and his client. We can't compel him to name the owners of the company, even in court. It's a trick that slum landlords use quite often. Even the church does it, believe it or not.'

'How *can* we find out, then?' Harper asked.

'If one of the properties is condemned and they want to claim the compensation, the real owner has to come forward. That's the only way I know, sir. I wish I had better news.'

The tram stopped by the long parade of shops in Harehills. Barely two years old and the brickwork was already turning black from the soot. Not like Whitby, Reed thought. The sea air kept everything clean and fresh there.

Tom seemed a little calmer now, just sitting and staring out of the window. Still seething, but he was quiet, more in control of himself. A little more, anyway.

'I tell you what,' he said as they walked along, checking the numbers on the buildings. 'The way I feel, I'm likely to drag the information out of these Smith brothers with my bare hands.'

'Let's see what we find,' Reed told him.

'This can't be right,' Harper said as they stopped in front of a grocer's shop. *Cameron, Grocer to the Trade and the Home.* Large, open sacks of dried beans, yellow, green, red, stood on the pavement. Reed took out the note. 'This is what the lawyer gave us.'

'If he was telling the truth.'

The air inside was thick with spices, an overwhelming, heady mix of scents. Pepper, cinnamon, so many more he couldn't identify. They had to step around boxes to reach a polished wooden counter where a man in a brown canvas coat waited, a smile on his face.

'Can I help you, gentlemen?' He was no more than thirty, with a thick, unfashionable beard that hid a weak chin, and curious, beady eyes. 'I'm Douglas Cameron.'

'We're looking for the Harehills Development Company,' Reed said. 'I have this as their address.'

'It's their *postal* address,' the man corrected him with a smile.

'Everything is delivered here, then someone comes to collect it. We have several customers who use the service. The busy ones who are out and about a great deal find it very useful.'

'Where would I find the business? Their office.'

Cameron rubbed his hands together. Long, white fingers, carefully trimmed nails. A man who was vain about his appearance, Reed decided.

'I'm afraid I couldn't tell you.'

'We're police officers, sir. I'm Inspector Reed and this is Detective Superintendent Harper. We'd value your help.' He shaded the words into a threat, but the man didn't seem worried; the bland look remained fixed on his face.

'What I mean is, I don't know where to find them. They pay to use this as their address, and that's as far as it goes. I have no way of contacting them at all.'

'What happens if they don't pay or don't come for their letters?'

'After two months everything goes in the bin,' Cameron said.

'Who collects it?' Reed asked.

'They have a lad who comes. I've always assumed he's the office boy. He's sixteen or seventeen, I suppose. Keeps his hair cropped very short. Always wears an old suit and scuffed boots.'

'What's his name?'

'I've no idea. He just collects the letters and leaves.' His expression soured for a moment. 'Never even buys anything.'

'What happened when they signed up for your service?' Harper asked. 'You must have insisted on some details then.'

'It was the same boy. About a year ago. He paid the money and gave me the name of the business. That's all it takes, Superintendent. The simpler the better, that's what I've found.'

'Do they receive much post?' Reed asked.

'There was very little at first,' Cameron pursed his thin lips, remembering. 'Then it became one or two a day. For the last few months it's been five or six letters every morning.'

'How often does the lad come to collect them?'

'Twice a week.' He paused. 'More often, recently, now I think about it.'

'Any set times? Days?'

The shopkeeper shook his head. 'It varies. I'm open from seven in the morning until ten at night.'

Outside, Reed lit a cigarette and started to walk, leading the way through the back streets.

'There's something wrong about this,' he said. 'Every proper business has an office.'

'An accommodation address is legal,' Harper answered slowly. 'Just like hiding the owners' names. But you're right. This feels bad.'

'The Smiths,' Reed began. 'I've never come across them before. But I want a long talk with them now.'

This was Tom's patch, Billy thought. He was supposed to know what was going on. That was his job.

'Let's talk to Hester,' he said. 'She might be able to tell us something.'

But the blind was down on the shop door. No notice to announce a closing. Reed peered through the window and drew in his breath.

'What is it?'

'The place is a mess. Things strewn all over the floor. I'll go in the back way,' Reed said.

Through the ginnel and into the yard. He tapped on the door. No answer, but the knob turned in his hand.

'Hester?' he said quietly. She wasn't in the office; he climbed the stairs. The door to the flat was open. No one in the living room or kitchen. He heard a quiet cry and stiffened, waiting until it came again. The bedroom.

The curtains were closed, the room stifling in the heat. He could make out her shape, lying on the bed.

'Hester, it's Billy. What's happened?'

She turned her head. There was just enough light to make out the bruises on her face.

'What's been going on?' he asked, but she looked at him with empty eyes.

Downstairs, he unlocked the front door.

'You'd better come in, Tom. This has just become real police business.'

SIX

I t took two cups of tea to draw out the story. Harper listened, letting Billy ask the questions. He was the brother-in-law. Even if Hester barely knew him, they were related.

'Two men came in,' she said. Her voice was shaky and frightened. 'It was just after half past nine, I remember the church bell ringing. One of them pulled down the blind on the door and locked it.'

'What did you do?' Reed asked quietly. He sat on the other side of the table, holding her hands.

'I asked what they thought they were up to. They said they owned the place and wanted me out by Saturday. One of them started kicking things over. When I told him to stop, the other one hit me.' She lifted her fingers to her face.

'What else did they say?'

'If anything of mine was still here on Saturday night, they'd put it out on the pavement.' She lifted her head, looking from one of them to the other. 'And if I tried to stop them, it would be worse for me. Then he hit me again and again, and they left. I . . .' The words faded and she sobbed again. 'I came up here. I didn't want anyone to see. Not like this, right after the funeral.'

'I'll make sure the beat constable keeps a close eye on the shop,' Harper promised. 'What did the men look like?'

'Big, the pair of them. They could have been brothers. They both had dark hair, parted in the middle.' She closed her eyes. 'I won't ever be able to forget them.'

Could have been brothers. Billy looked at Harper. A small nod.

'How old do you think they were?' Reed tried to coax out the information gently.

'I don't know. Not very.' Her voice wavered as she pictured them. 'Thirty? Somewhere round there. The one who hit me was smiling when he did it.'

She looked drained. Her husband's death had left her with no reserves. Now this. The men had picked their time well. Threats and a beating when she was at her lowest.

'Is your rent paid? Harper asked.

'Until the end of the month. Charlie took care of it before he
. . .' She couldn't bring herself to say it. Everything was too raw,
just waiting beneath the surface 'It's in the rent book.'

'We'll make sure they can't do anything.'

Billy could see Tom had more questions, dozens of them. He
made a small gesture with his fingers: they could wait.

'I'll stay here,' Reed told him. 'Clean everything up and make
sure she's all right.'

Harper scribbled down the address and handed it to Sergeant
Tollman.

'I want a constable going by this shop every half hour.'

'Yes, sir. That's Barstow's beat. He's a good man, he'll do it.'

'Tell him that if there's any sign of trouble, I want arrests, not
words. Understood?'

'Absolutely, sir.'

'John Smith and Jack Smith. A pair of brothers. Does it ring any
bells?'

Tollman started to laugh. 'We've had more of both over the years
than I've had hot dinners.'

'These two would be somewhere around thirty. Might well be
brothers. One of them has a nasty streak.'

The sergeant's face became serious. 'Doesn't sound familiar, sir.'

'See what you can find, will you?'

The men were all out. No matter; he could do this himself.

A sweltering walk over to the Town Hall. The kind of weather
when anger flared. But it was too hot, too wearying for violence.
Except for a pair of men wanting to take over a corner shop, he
thought.

Why hadn't he heard about them? They'd developed a business
right under his nose, and he didn't know a damned thing about it.
He'd seen the way Billy looked at him. Accusing. And he had every
right. He should have been aware, on top of something like this and
stamping it out.

Hester Reed's beating had been deliberate, calculated. They wanted
to intimidate. The Smith brothers . . .

What about the real owners, hiding themselves behind a
lawyer? What did that mean? Who were they?

The clerk in the planning office glanced up in surprise as he entered.

'The other day you discovered that the Harehills Development Company had bought a place,' Harper said.

'I remember, sir,' the man said. 'I remember it well.'

'I want to know what else they own. Everything. It's police business. Can you find that? And the names and addresses of the sellers, please.'

The clerk nodded. 'I'll have to go back through all the transactions. It might take me a few hours. There's only me here, sir.' He gave a wistful, lonely smile.

'This afternoon?' Harper asked. No harm in pressing; this was important.

'Tomorrow,' the clerk answered. 'By eleven, sir. I'll make sure the list is ready for you.'

'Mickey Davies has been a busy boy,' Ash said.

Harper had sent the others home. Fowler and Walsh had spent another frustrating day hunting the burglar. Plenty of shoe leather and talk, but no results. Tomorrow he'd have them tracking down the Smith brothers. Now, though, he sat with the inspector.

'Go on.'

'The usual story, sir. He picks businesses whose owners are too scared to fight back or come to us.'

The police had failed. They should have arrested him long ago. *He'd* failed. This was his responsibility, his area. He'd never really gone after Mickey. As he'd told Billy, it had never seemed important enough.

'Do you have a list?'

'I'm getting there, sir.'

'How many of them are willing to testify?'

'Three so far. Four if Mr Reed's sister-in-law will join them.'

'She has other problems at the moment.' He explained what had happened.

Ash ran a large hand over his moustache. 'Smith . . . it's always a good alias, isn't it? I don't recall this pair, though. The Harehills Development Company. I'll keep my eyes open. When do you want me to bring Davies in?'

'Find one more willing to testify,' the superintendent told him.

'I want him sewn up so tight that he can't escape. Anyone who works with him, too. And let's get after these Smiths. I want them off the street.'

'Fowler and Walsh on it, sir?'

'Yes.' Short and terse. He'd been too cocky and let things slide with Davies. He wasn't going to make that mistake again.

'What about the burglar?'

'They're going to have to cover both.'

'I can't sleep, Da.'

Mary had kicked off the sheet, lying there in her nightgown, a heat rash on her calves. He'd read her two stories as she squirmed around on the bed.

'Would you like me to tell you a secret?'

Her eyes grew wide. She nodded. He brought his head close enough to feel the warmth coming off her skin and began to whisper.

'An old copper once told me the best way to go to sleep. He said he'd learned it when he was a soldier in India. Do you know where India is?'

'No.' She shook her head from side to side, hair flailing across the pillow.

'It's a long, long way off, on the other side of the world. He told me that you have to lie very still and imagine each part of your body falling asleep. One by one. Start at your feet and move up. It works, too; I've done it myself. Go on, close your eyes and try it.'

He sat and waited. Five minutes later he crept out of the bedroom with a smile on his face. That part was a joy. But the evening turned sober as he sat with Annabelle and Billy.

'Hester's bruised and battered,' Reed said. 'That man has experience. He knew exactly what he was doing.'

'Poor woman,' Annabelle said. 'Give me ten minutes with him and I'd make him wish he'd never been born.'

'Was she able to give you a better description?'

Reed shook his head. 'She's still too shaken. Her cousin is staying tonight. Keep an eye on her. Hester's determined to open up in the morning.'

'Do you want me to pop in and see her?' Annabelle asked.

'She has plenty of family in the area. I'll be there all day tomorrow, too.'

'The man on the beat will go by often,' Harper said. 'We have one advantage. This pair don't know the police are looking for them yet.'

'Saturday's going to be the day,' Reed said. 'When they return.'

'We'll be ready.'

'I go back to Whitby on Sunday.'

'I know. We're going to find them. We'll make them pay.'

With a nod, Reed left, footsteps climbing to the attic.

'At least you two seem to be making some progress,' Annabelle said.

'If that's what you call it.' He sighed. 'Rough day?'

'I've spent most of it trying to track down this woman Redshaw lived with. It's like she's vanished off the face of the earth.'

That was easy to do when you were poor. Disappear into a crowd, change your address, change your name. No one would ever know.

'Ask the man on the beat in Holbeck. They should be able to help.'

'Could you introduce me? It might grease the wheels.' She hesitated. 'There's one other thing, Tom. I'd like to speak to the police surgeon.'

'Dr King?' he asked in surprise. 'Why?'

'He did the post-mortem, didn't he? I want to hear it all.'

'Are you sure?' King's Kingdom, that was what they called the mortuary under Hunslet Road police station. Not a pleasant place for anyone to visit. Especially a civilian.

'I need to know.' She stared at him imploringly. 'For myself.'

He had to visit, anyway. King was retiring at the end of the month. Going out with the century, he said. He was in his eighties now, already long-established in the job when Harper joined the force years before. His leaving would mark the end of a long era.

'All right.' She'd go with or without him. Things might be easier if he was there.

'Looks like we might have a winner, sir.' Walsh's voice was full of excitement as he held up a small sheaf of letters.

'What?' Harper asked as Fowler and Ash crowded round the desk.

'I've heard back from the forces in York, Middlesbrough and Durham,' he said, laying the replies out like playing cards. 'They've all had a man going round the pawnshops selling jewellery. Not the same places or towns each time. None of it was reported stolen locally, that's why the pawnbrokers bought it.'

'And those places are all on the railway line between here and Newcastle,' Fowler pointed out.

'Anything since our burglar started working here?'

Fowler glanced at the letters again.

'No. The last was a month ago. That means he's probably due another visit.'

'Send them a list of everything taken in Leeds and ask them to circulate it. Do they have a name? Any idea what he looks like?'

'He calls himself Brown.' Walsh shrugged. Almost as anonymous as Smith, Harper thought. 'He's in his thirties. Dark hair, plenty of pomade. Clean-shaven. Good suit. That's it, sir.'

He could be any one of ten thousand men in Leeds. Still, they'd snagged a thread. Now they could begin tugging. Meanwhile . . .

'Good job,' he told them. 'Keep on that. But I want you after these Smith brothers too. We know they're clever and they're a vicious pair – you've heard what they did. Let's drag them out from under their rock. I want them absolutely terrified.'

'I have your list, sir,' the planning office clerk said. Two sheets of paper, neatly folded.

'Thank you. How much do they own?'

'Thirty-five properties, sir.' The man's voice was grave. 'All purchased in the last nine months, and none of them for full market value. That's the best part of one a week. I should have noticed. I've listed the addresses, the sellers, purchase price and date.' He gave a small, dry cough. 'I included when planning applications were submitted for the new houses near each one, and when they were passed, plus the names of the builders.'

'That's very thorough. Thank you.'

Thirty-five, Harper thought as he walked back to Millgarth. Thirty bloody five. They'd pulled together an empire right under his nose and he'd known nothing about it. It didn't matter how little they paid for each property, it still spelled money. Real money. And behind all that, this North Leeds Company. What the hell was going on?

'If you're going to spend the day here, you might as well make yourself useful,' Hester said before Reed could settle in the office at the shop. 'There's stock needs to go out on them shelves and two sacks of beans that need shifting.'

The bruises had flowered into brilliant yellows and greens and purples on her face, and she moved stiffly, trying to mask the pain in every step. But she was standing behind the counter with a fresh, clean apron wrapped around her body. There'd be no shortage of customers today; plenty would be curious about her being closed the day before.

'Glad to help.' He did as she directed, took a broom to the floor, sweeping out all the dust to the street, then on to the cobbles of the road, before going up to the flat and making them both a cup of tea.

'How do you feel?' he asked as he put a mug down in front of her. Hester glanced around, making sure the shop was empty before she spoke.

'Scared.' Her voice was subdued as she stared at the liquid. 'I suppose that's what they want, isn't it?'

'It is. We won't let anything happen.'

'I know, but . . . you won't be here after Saturday, will you? I'm not saying as I don't appreciate all you've done, but what happens when you've gone? There's next week and the one after, and the one after that.'

'Tom Harper promised,' Reed said. 'He'll do what he says.' He had to hope the man was as good as his word.

'Like as not,' she said. 'After all the pressure, then Charlie, then the funeral, them two caught me when I was low.'

'You said Charlie paid the rent to the end of the month.'

'That's right, luv.'

'What will you do after that? If they put up the rent again?' He had to ask. He needed to know before he returned to Whitby.

'Pay, I suppose,' she replied in a weary voice. 'We have a little bit put by.' Her mouth twitched into a brief smile. 'I can't just do a flit, now can I? I don't want to, anyway. This is my home. I'm staying.'

'Good,' he told her. 'You can't leave. Not with all your friends round here.'

'That's right.' The bell tinkled as a customer entered, and she straightened her back. 'Morning, Mrs Chappell, luv, how can I help you?'

*   *   *

'I've found five people willing to testify against Mickey Davies,' Ash said. 'When do you want me to drag him in here, sir?'

Harper sat back in his chair and smiled. 'Right now would be perfect.'

'My pleasure, sir.'

'Take a constable with you.'

'Sir?' He raised an eyebrow, as if Harper had insulted his dignity by suggesting he'd need help.

'It's always more impressive when a uniform puts the cuffs on someone and marches them off. People remember it.'

'You're starting to think like a superintendent, sir.'

Harper laughed. 'God forbid. Bring him in and let him stew in the cells for a few hours, then we'll have a talk with him. Any news on the Smiths?'

Ash shook his head. 'Nothing so far.'

Damn.

'I hope Fowler and Walsh can track them down.' He nodded towards the map of Leeds he'd put up on the wall, pins showing every property they'd bought. 'They've managed all that on the quiet. Every place on there is close to where new streets have been built, and we've never even had a whisper.' That was what really angered him. Not knowing, letting a couple of thugs grow rich without anyone realizing. They were bright. They were dangerous. So was the man behind them. 'As soon as Mickey's in his cell, I want you to visit some of those places. Ask how much the rent's gone up, whether they've had visits from the Smiths.'

'Yes, sir. It doesn't make us look good, does it?'

'It makes us look like a bunch of fools.' He could feel the anger rising and took a few breaths. 'I'd like to catch this burglar before the chief drops by for another little visit. I have a job for Saturday, too. For everyone.'

For once, he was there before her. Hunslet Road felt airless, heavy with the stink of metal and oil. Harper ran a finger round his collar, feeling the dirt and grit. The shirt stuck to his back again and there were lines of sweat inside his hatband. Finally a hackney drew up, the driver slipping from his seat to open the door, and Annabelle stepped down.

'I'm sorry I'm late,' she said. 'That's usually your line, isn't it?'

'Are you absolutely certain you want to do this?' Harper asked again. 'It's not pleasant down there.'

She looked into his eyes. 'I told you, Tom. I've got to. I've seen enough bad things in my life.'

But not like this, he thought. It took a strong stomach for the mortuary.

Down the stairs, and he saw her wrinkle her nose and cough at the harsh stench of carbolic soap. Dr King was waiting in the corridor. He was growing rounder by the year, eyes still bright and eager behind his spectacles, the stub of a cigar between his lips.

'Superintendent. And you must be Mrs Harper. A pleasure, although I don't know why you'd want to marry this one.' He gave a small bow.

'I won him in a raffle and they won't take him back.'

King roared with laughter, eyes twinkling with approval. 'You'll do, my dear. You'll do very well. Your husband says you're a Guardian.'

'That's right.' She gave a brief summary of the investigation.

'I see. We'd better go into my office.'

Thank God for that, Harper thought. At least he wasn't taking her into the examination room.

'Do you remember the girls?' Annabelle asked.

'Of course,' King replied, striking a match and lighting the cigar. At least the smoke covered the other smells. 'I remember them all.' He tapped his bald head. 'Everything up here.'

'How long did they survive in the water?'

'That's not an easy question to answer,' he replied slowly. 'I was told they couldn't swim. They were probably panicking, so no more than a few minutes.' He shrugged. 'That's an educated guess. But it would have been a terrible time for them.'

'What if they'd cried out and someone had come along to help . . .?'

'If it happened quickly enough, I expect they'd have survived,' King told her.

'Five minutes?'

He thought, studying the ash on the tip of his cigar, then said: 'Less. Closer to three. It was April, so the water was still very cold and they were both small. Malnourished, but that's nothing unusual.'

'But could they have been saved?'

'Of course.' He snorted. 'Their father could have done it by not throwing them in the canal, for a start. If I remember the notes, he did it and walked away, hoping someone would hear, and save them.'

'That's what he said in his confession,' Annabelle agreed. 'He took it all back later, though.'

'Then he was lying,' King told her. 'They didn't jump in of their own accord.'

'What about bruises?'

'More or less what I'd expect to find. They were petrified, they must have been flailing around and trying to save themselves. To climb out, I expect.'

'I've been down to the canal. There are no ladders or handholds.'

King nodded. 'That makes sense. I've been a police surgeon for fifty years, Mrs Harper.' His eyes looked around the room. 'I've worked down here since they built the place. That's why they call it King's Kingdom. A strange little tribute. I've seen enough to ruin my faith in man. But I'm not sure I've ever seen anything quite as callous as that. Still,' he added, 'if you're asking whether Redshaw beat them regularly, the answer is no. Just the usual childhood bumps and scrapes.'

'Why didn't they call out? Why didn't they scream? That's what I don't understand. There were people not far away. They'd have heard.'

That, Harper thought, was the crux, the question she'd come to ask.

'I can't give you an answer.' He sighed. 'Fear? Panic? They'd have been too exhausted and chilled after a minute. Their strength would have been failing. I wish I knew. I really do.'

She stood, held out her hand to shake his. 'Thank you. I appreciate your time.'

'For whatever good it did.'

'It all helps.'

Harper didn't immediately follow her out of the office.

'The end of the month, eh?' he said.

'It's time,' King told him. He gazed at the cigar stub and tossed it in the ashtray. 'You'll like the new man. Younger and less cantankerous.'

'It's been an education, working with you.'

'And it's been a pleasure to see you rise through the ranks, although I'll deny that remark if you ever repeat it. I suppose there has to be a leaving event?'

'Of course.'

He nodded at the door. 'You have quite a wife.'

Harper chuckled. 'She keeps me on my toes. I'll see you at the do, Doctor.'

'Having a word behind my back?' She was standing on the pavement, out in the heat.

'Saying goodbye,' Harper told her. 'He's retiring. I've known him a long time.'

'His mind's sharp enough.'

'He's good. And he seems taken with you. Did he give you what you needed?'

'Yes.' In the harsh light, the lines on her face seemed deeper than ever. 'I might not have liked it, but he did.'

SEVEN

Saturday morning and the heat still smothered Leeds. Harper left the Victoria at six, hoping for a lick of coolness as he walked to Millgarth. No such luck. By the time he arrived, his clothes were soaked with sweat.

'Morning, sir,' Tollman said from his desk by the front door. 'Worse than Burma, isn't it?'

'Burma? I thought you'd never been further than Wakefield.'

'Well, no,' the sergeant admitted, 'but that's what everyone's saying. Whistle you up a cup of tea, sir?'

'I'd be happy to see one.'

Walsh was there before him, already sitting at his desk in the detectives' room.

'Found the Smiths?'

He knew the answer. If they'd been arrested, someone would have telephoned.

'Nothing, sir. Absolutely nothing at all.' He frowned. 'I do have some news on the burglar, but it's not so good, I'm afraid.'

'Go on.'

'Some of the jewellery taken from Mr Hope's turned up at a pawnbroker in Middlesbrough.'

Harper leaned against a table and folded his arms. Damn it. Nothing was going right.

'How? I thought you sent them the list.'

'I did,' Walsh insisted. 'The police up there were slow in circulating it. Evidently our man had been through the day before.'

Harper closed his eyes and breathed deep. If the force up there had been on the ball, they could have had him in custody.

'I don't suppose we have a better description?'

Walsh shook his head. 'More or less the same as we had before, sir. Still calling himself Brown.' He shrugged.

'Right. I want you to send a list of stolen items everywhere on the line from here to Sheffield.'

'Sir?' Walsh looked at him questioningly.

'Just in case he decides to go south next time. Let's make certain.'

'Mr Ash said you want us on something else later.'

'That's right. With a little luck, we'll take down the Smiths tonight.'

'On remand.' Harper replaced the paper on the pile. 'It's a start.'

'Mickey Davies didn't look like a happy man when the magistrate told him.' Ash grinned.

'Good. Let's hope it's a little while before he has his day in court.'

'Just until Monday, sir. Two days. Still, it'll give him a chance to get used to the routine. He howled when the constable put the cuffs on him. Right in the middle of the Fleece. Gladdened my heart.'

'I told you it was a good idea.'

'Right enough, sir.'

Davies had spent four hours in the cells before Harper brought him to the interview room. Windows closed, the air stuffy and damp. He'd sweat; that was fine. He wanted Mickey to suffer. And he wanted to conduct this interrogation himself.

Davies held up his hands as he sat on the battered chair. He was a heavy, fleshy man, his crooked nose broken several times over the years, and the promise of menace at the back of his eyes.

'You can take the cuffs off now. I'm not going to hurt anyone.'
Harper shook his head. 'Is that what you reckon? Threats are
how you make your living, Mickey. Can't trust a man like that.'
'You what?' His eyes narrowed. 'Who says so?'
'We have testimony from five different people.'
'They're lying.'
'Protection.' Harper clicked his tongue. 'That's a nasty game.
Preying on people. It's my fault. I should have stamped on you
long ago.'
'I told you, they're all lying. You probably told them what
to say.'
The superintendent ignored the words. 'We even have account
entries from one man. Every week, right there in ink. You're going
to jail, Mickey. With any luck, it'll be for quite a few years.'
'Who wrote that he was paying me?' Davies protested. 'I'll sue
him for libel.'
'You'll have a hard job. He's dead. Committed suicide last
weekend.'
'Then you don't know!' Davies sat back, triumphant.
'His wife's still alive. You didn't do your homework properly. His
brother's a police inspector in Whitby. Used to work here, in fact.'
It was a pleasure to see the man's face fall, the way he tried to
recover, all bluster and bravado that meant nothing. Harper let him
talk, then said: 'The inspector's waiting outside. He was telling me
he'd enjoy a word with you. Would you like me to leave the pair
of you alone while I have a cup of tea?' Threaten the man who
liked to issue threats. Turn the tables and bully the bully. He started
to rise.
'No.' Davies was sweating hard, the drops shining on his face.
He wasn't so tough after all. Half an hour and Harper had a
list of the businesses that paid Davies money. Maybe not all, but
enough; he'd been making a comfortable living from it. Now he'd
damned himself.
'What do you know about buying property?' Harper asked.
'Eh?' Davies stared at him, not understanding. 'Property? What
are you on about?'
'Making sure you pay as little as possible for it.'
'That's not my racket.' Harper believed him. It was far too subtle
and complicated for a man like Mickey.

'Ever heard of the Harehills Development Company?'

'Don't mean a thing. Honest, it don't.'

'What about John and Jack Smith?'

'Are you having me on?' he asked. 'Names like that?'

'Do you know them?'

Davies simply shook his head.

'Take him back down to the cells,' Harper told the waiting constable.

Salad for tea once again, with a few slices of ham. If this heat lasted much longer, they'd turn into rabbits. But it was too hot to cook. Noise drifted up from downstairs, men already celebrating payday.

'Don't you like it, Da?' Mary asked. 'You haven't eaten much.'

Her plate was empty, as always. But she knew the rule: no pudding if you don't eat everything in front of you.

'I'm just thinking. I have to go out to work again soon.'

'But it's Saturday night,' she said.

'That's what happens when you're a policeman,' he told her. 'Your mam has a meeting, too, so you'll be with Ellen.'

'And spoiled rotten, probably,' Annabelle said as she came from the kitchen with three small cream cakes. 'These are from that new bakery on Chapeltown Road.' She sniffed. 'I can't say they look that good, but we'll give them a chance.' She'd run her own small string of bakeries in the past; her standards were high. 'Harehills tonight?'

'Yes.' Billy had been there all day. Fowler and Walsh should have reached Hester Reed's shop already. Ash would arrive soon enough. The beat constable would pass every half hour. Between them, they'd keep Hester Reed safe. 'Guardians meeting for you?'

'For what it's worth.' She sighed. 'We've written an interim report of the Redshaw investigation. I still haven't been able to track down that woman he was living with. That's on my list for next week.'

Harper turned to look at Mary. The cake had vanished from her plate, not a crumb left, and she was beaming.

'I'd better go,' he said, kissing her on the forehead. 'You be good for Ellen.'

'I always am, Da. You *know* that.'

A quick peck on the cheek for Annabelle.

'I hope it goes smoothly.'

Then he was away, striding up Roundhay Road.

Saturday night was full of music. Somewhere in the distance a German band was playing. Trombones and tubas bellowing away, something with no real tune to it. At the bottom of the street where Reed's shop stood, an organ grinder cranked out his noise. The children loved it, dancing all around, eyes wide, laughing like they'd never known anything so wonderful. Women stood in the doorways, fanning themselves as they talked, toes tapping, one or two singing along.

It was quieter after he closed the door. As the bell rang, Hester appeared. The bruises were still there, vivid and awful.

'They're all in the back,' she said. 'I suppose you'll want a cup of tea.'

'Have you ever met a copper who refused one?' Harper asked.

'No,' she agreed. 'Nor a biscuit, neither.'

With five men packed inside, the room was cramped.

'Any trouble today, Billy?'

'Nothing at all.' He sat at the desk, smoking a cigarette and rubbing his chin. 'It's been busy. Hester's kept me working.'

The superintendent turned to Ash. 'Right. What have you found?'

'I went to see some of those people in properties the brothers own, sir. Rents have all gone up. Enough to squeeze them hard. They're all shops. They can just make enough to get by if they struggle and scrimp. New houses near all of them, so more trade. Looks like the Smiths picked their places very well.'

'Tell me what you've learned about them, Sergeant.'

Fowler turned towards Walsh, then back again. 'Very little, sir,' he admitted. 'They don't seem to go to the usual places. Some people think they've heard the name.' His mouth turned down. 'But it's Smith, so who knows? Best I can tell, they seemed to pop up out of nowhere a bit under a year ago.'

The same time they began buying property. Who the hell were they? Where did they come from? They hadn't just sprung up from the ground. How had they operated without the police hearing even a whisper? Someone had to know.

'The moment they show up here, we arrest them,' he said. 'Understood?'

And then they'd find out who was behind this mysterious North Leeds Company that ran everything.

They were prepared. Now they simply had to wait. Every time the shop door opened, they tensed, ready, holding their breath as they stared at each other. But nothing more than a stream of customers.

'What time are you going to close?' he asked Hester when she came through with more mugs of tea.

'Ten,' she replied. 'Eleven if we're busy.'

The minutes dragged by. Fowler took a book from his pocket and began to read. Ash produced a pack of cards, laying them out to play solitaire. Walsh brought out a folded magazine.

Harper sat, bored. He'd forgotten what this was like, all the tricks to while away the time. Billy sat with his eyes closed, looking as if he was sleeping. Thinking, most likely. Remembering.

Finally, Hester came through to the back with a broom in her hand.

'I'm calling it a night,' she said. 'It'll go faster if you lot help me.'

Sweeping the floor and the pavement outside, taking the back door key off the hook on the jamb, then putting the rubbish in the bin, making everything neat. And no sign at all of the brothers. Barstow came by on his beat, saluting as he passed. Quarter past eleven and they were done. The street was quiet, most of the windows dark.

'What do you think, sir?' Ash asked. 'They might have had word we were here.'

Not a bad thing if true; at least they'd think twice before returning. He glanced over and saw Hester lowering the blind. Light from the gas mantle caught the bruises on her face.

'Tomorrow you're going hunting.' Harper looked at the men. 'I want them. Do whatever you have to do.'

'I'll stay here tonight,' Reed said. 'Just in case. There's a spare bed in the flat. Sunday tomorrow, the shop won't be open.'

EIGHT

Harper stirred his tea.

'How was the meeting?'

'What you'd expect.' They'd avoided the subject all through breakfast, until Mary had gone off to spend the morning with Maisie. 'As soon as they heard the workhouse master in Holbeck did everything correctly, you could practically hear the relief in the room.' Bitterness seethed under her words.

She'd been asleep when he returned the night before. He'd tumbled into bed, itchy from the heat. But he'd still managed eight solid hours.

'You haven't given up on this, have you?'

'No.' Annabelle said. 'I—'

They heard the footsteps on the stair. Billy returning.

'No problems during the night,' he said before Harper could ask. 'I'm going to pack my grip and get off to the station.' He vanished up to the attic.

'What were you going to say?'

'I'm not done with it by a long chalk.'

Reed didn't like farewells. Never had. They always reminded him of the army, comrades leaving for different postings, men you might never see again.

'You make sure you give Elizabeth my love,' Annabelle said as she hugged him. 'And look after yourselves, the pair of you.'

Harper walked with him into town. The roads were empty, no more than a few trams passing. Quiet, the factories closed for the day. Almost peaceful. Only the haze and the pressing warmth remained.

'They probably got wind we were waiting,' Reed said after a while. 'They'll be back.'

Harper knew he was right. Men like that always returned. It was their nature.

'We'll find them. Mickey Davies goes on trial tomorrow. He's off to prison. I'll make sure they end up the same way.'

'Once you catch up with them.' He worried about Hester. She seemed strong enough, but it was all a front. He could see it in her eyes. Charlie's death, the threats, the beating; she was barely clinging on. 'Look out for her, will you, Tom? I'd stay longer if I could.'

'I will. I'll keep you up to speed.'

It had been a bad few days in Leeds. Still, a tiny sliver of good had come from it; he felt closer to Harper than he had in years. He was starting to trust him again. And he'd be glad to be back in the clean air, feeling the sea breeze. Seeing Elizabeth. The brief separation was a powerful reminder of how much he loved her.

The smell of coal filled the station. People bustled around, porters pushing their carts full of luggage. It was dirty, smoky, shrill with sound, alive.

On the platform, they shook hands.

'Take care of yourself, Billy.'

'Always. You look out for that family of yours.'

As the train pulled out, Reed stared at the miles of houses and streets, red brick and black soot. Something bad was going to happen. It was out there, just waiting for its moment. And all Tom Harper's promises wouldn't be able to hold it back.

On Monday afternoon Harper sat at the back of the courtroom and saw Mickey Davies found guilty of extracting money with menaces and intimidation. The testimony of four shopkeepers and Charlie Reed's account book left him with no defence, no matter how his attorney blustered. The jury only needed ten minutes for the verdict before the judge sentenced him to three years.

But he barely felt any satisfaction as he walked back to Millgarth. One down, that was a start, but two still to go. At least the burglar hadn't struck again.

The Smiths. Buying property ought to mean a trail of paper and forms. Yet those led nowhere: just the stone wall of a lawyer. Their names: John and Jack Smith. As anonymous as bloody air. Where had the money come from to buy so many places? It was business. A new type of crime and a new type of criminal. Clever, elusive, vicious, and they barely left a ripple. Try as he might, he couldn't begin to understand them. It was like trying to grasp mercury.

*　　*　　*

Tuesday morning, a little after six, and he felt the stir of a breeze as he stepped out of the Victoria on to Roundhay Road. He stopped, turning his head to face it. By the time he reached Regent Street, it had grown into a light wind, the first he'd felt in weeks. Harper passed men on their way to work, smiling with the simple pleasure of being outside.

With the window wide, his office was cooler. He settled down to the paperwork that came with running a division. Four years into the job, he'd finally come to accept it, to surrender to the routine.

He was halfway through the pile when Ash tapped on his door. His face was grave, eyes thoughtful.

'We need to go out to Harehills, sir.'

'Why?' He could feel an alarm ringing in his head. 'Did the Smiths come and see Hester?'

The small pause before the man replied set his heart beating faster.

'I don't know, sir. But she didn't open her shop this morning. The constable knocked but there was no reply. He managed to get in, and he found her dead in her bed.'

'What?' Harper pushed the chair back as he started to rise.

'He says it looks like it was in her sleep. But . . .'

The timing.

He was already reaching for his hat.

Hester lay on her back, two pillows under her head, the covers over her body. Nothing disturbed in the room, nothing awry. Harper bent, studying her face. It looked peaceful enough, eyes closed. The bruises had begun to fade; now her skin was waxy. No new cuts, nothing on her hands.

The same layer of fine grit and dust on the furniture as everywhere else in Leeds. But nothing smeared or smudged. Everything looked normal in the kitchen and sitting room. Downstairs, the office and shop were both orderly, yesterday's takings counted, sitting undisturbed in the drawer.

He'd barely met the woman, but he'd liked her. A hard shell, there to ward off the world. Underneath, a widow trying to face everything alone.

'The body goes to Hunslet,' he ordered Ash. 'I want Dr King to do a full post-mortem on her.'

'Yes, sir. Puzzler, isn't it?'

'Very.' It could be natural; in most cases he wouldn't even question it. But under the circumstances . . . this felt wrong. With each pace around, he was more certain. No evidence, but he *knew* it. He moved from room to room, eyes searching. Something was missing. For the life of him, though, Harper couldn't place what it was.

Constable Barstow stood outside the door, keeping away the curious.

'Were all the doors locked when you arrived?'

'Yes, sir.'

'How did you get in?' Nothing had been forced; he'd checked.

'I, um, have a way with locks, sir.' He reddened and stared down at the ground.

'Did anything look unusual to you?'

The man shook his head. 'If it hadn't been for all the fuss about these brothers, I'd have said she just died in her sleep. She was very upset, what with Charlie topping himself like that. The shop was open yesterday, same as ever.'

'Mrs Reed had relatives nearby, didn't she?' This was Barstow's beat; he knew who was who.

'Plenty of them, sir. A cousin two streets away, another at the top of the hill. A pair of aunts and uncles on Harehills Lane.'

'You did the right thing here.'

'Thank you, sir. I don't know, there's just something not quite kosher about it, somehow.'

'I feel exactly the same.' He shook his head. 'By the way, if I were you, I'd just keep that lockpicking skill quiet.'

'I will, sir.'

A thought struck him. 'Where was the back door key? Do you know?'

'No idea, sir.'

Harper strode back inside. Not in the lock. He saw the empty hook on the wall. He'd used the key himself on Saturday night. He opened drawers and cupboards. No sign of it anywhere. Hester was too neat for anything to be awry. *That* was what had been troubling him. Someone had come in, then taken the key after locking the door on his way out.

Murder. Now he was sure.

* * *

Reed stared out at the estuary. The sky was blue, just a few clouds
high in the sky, a hint of wind from the North Sea to stop it feeling
too warm. Perfect weather for the holidaymakers. It seemed like
a mockery.

The conversation played over and over in his mind.

'Billy?' The connection was poor, crackling and buzzing.

'Tom?' He could feel his heart beating faster. 'Have you arrested
them?'

'No. It's Hester.' The line faded to silence, then returned. 'I said,
it's Hester.'

'What about her?'

'I'm sorry, Billy. She's dead. Didn't open the shop this morning.
When the bobby went in, he found her in bed.'

'But—' he said, not sure he'd heard correctly. Dead? She
couldn't be.

'I've been up there. I wish I had better news. I'm as certain
as I can be that it's murder.'

'Tom . . .' He closed his eyes and tried to swallow.

'I'll have more details soon. I just wanted to tell you.'

'Yes,' he said after a moment. 'Thank you. Better than a telegram.' He knew the words sounded empty, mechanical. 'I can't
come. The chief will never agree. There's just me and a constable
here this week.'

'We'll find them.' But Tom had promised him they'd look after
Hester, too.

He took out his cigarettes and lit one. The bad thing had
happened.

God only knew what Charlie had been feeling, the despair that
crushed him and made him take his own life. At least he'd made
his own decision. Hester intended to battle on. Bastards.

He hadn't even asked how she'd died. He'd been too shocked
by the news. *As certain as I can be.* That meant he had nothing.
Found her in bed. She was always careful about locking the doors;
he'd seen that on the night he stayed. He knew who'd done it. So
did Tom. They hadn't needed to kill her. They'd already buried
her alive when they drove her husband to suicide.

Now he had to rely on someone else to bring them some
justice.

A knock on the door. A young constable, barely past his training.

'Sorry to disturb you, sir. But a man's just come in. Says his pocket's been picked.'

'Can you look after it?' Reed asked. 'Take down the details.'

Still early, but the tea room already had a few customers. Elizabeth was out in the yard, checking a delivery and laughing with the driver as he left. She turned as the back door opened, seeing the expression on his face.

'Billy, what is it?'

He told her and watched the colour rush from her cheeks.

'That's . . . that's awful. What did Tom say?'

'Not much. He's going to tell me more later.'

She put her arms around him. 'I'm sorry, Billy, luv. I really am.'

Too late for sorrow, he thought. Hester's death needed more than that.

'Suffocation,' Dr King said. 'No doubt about it.' He looked at the younger man beside him. 'What do you think, Dr Lumb?'

'Definitely.' He was an inch or two smaller than King, in his early fifties. Creased, weathered skin like aged leather, a full head of dark hair, intense eyes, thin lips.

'This is my replacement, Superintendent. And a very fine police surgeon he'll be. Experience in Egypt.'

They shook hands. The man was wearing a pale linen suit, just right for the hot weather.

'My guess would be smothered with a pillow,' Lumb said. 'It fits with the pressure. She was found in her bed?'

'That's right,' Harper agreed. 'But I didn't see any signs of a struggle.'

'It's there – we found some light bruising on her wrists.' Lumb looked at him questioningly. 'Could there have been two people working together who killed her?'

'Yes.' Oh yes.

'Then I'd say one held her while the other forced the pillow over her face.'

King beamed, like a teacher watching his pupil perform well.

'What else can you tell me?' Harper asked.

'We found some cotton fibres in her mouth. That's why we believe it was a pillow,' Lumb continued. 'I could give you all the medical jargon, but suffocation is probably enough.' He gave a nervous smile and glanced at King.

'The superintendent has seen his share of bodies, Doctor. The summary is all he needs.'

'It is.' He smiled at Lumb. 'Thank you. Don't take this wrongly, but I hope we don't see too much of each other.'

The man chuckled. 'That might just be the strangest welcome I've ever received.'

He had his confirmation. Murder. Billy had been right: men like the Smiths always returned.

'We put everything into this,' Harper told them. 'Everything. I want these men found and in custody.'

'What should we do about the burglar, sir?' Walsh asked.

'On the back-burner for now.' With a little luck, he'd remain quiet for a while. 'The inspector's talked to a few people who live in properties the brothers own. Walsh, you have a word with the ones who sold to them. Bring me every detail you can find.' He turned to Fowler. 'They've paid cash for over thirty properties. That must have cost a few thousand. It came from somewhere. Very likely this North Leeds Company. I want to know about them.'

'Why would they set up this Harehills Development Company, then?' Walsh asked.

'It's a good way to keep their distance,' Harper said. 'Whoever runs the North Leeds Company tells the Smiths which properties to buy. They're the front for it all, and they handle all the problems. If there's any comeback, the people at the North Leeds Company can deny any responsibility.'

'And the Smiths do all their dirty work,' Fowler added.

'Exactly,' Harper agreed. 'In return, they get a slice of the money. And the people pulling the strings can stay safely in the background.'

It was clever, he had to admit that. And thanks to the law, impenetrable.

Ash spoke quietly into the silence. 'Once we catch the Smiths, do we have any solid evidence against them, sir?'

No, and he knew it. 'We will.'

'If they're that clever, they'll have a lawyer. He'll get them out inside an hour.'

'Not if he can't find them,' Harper said. 'Bring them in, and we'll play hide and seek with his clients. Let him try and find the buggers while we build a case against them.'

Ash grinned. 'Just like the old days, sir.'

'Find them,' Harper ordered. 'I want this pair put away.'

NINE

Someone had placed a bunch of flowers by the door of the shop. They'd wilted in the heat, the colours already fading. But it was a touching gesture.

Constable Barstow wasn't the only one with lockpicking skills; every copper who'd walked the beat knew a trick or two. A few seconds and he had the back door open. Inside, the building was stuffy and dusty, as warm as a hothouse.

He needed to see it with fresh eyes.

The faint scent of death lingered in the bedroom, the sickly-sweet hint of decay. The bed lay unmade, as if someone might come back at any moment to tidy it. The curtains were closed, but light still streamed in, enough for him to search. Harper crawled on the floor, looked under the bed.

The sense of Hester Reed still filled the place, as if her ghost was hovering, but there was nothing to find, not there or anywhere upstairs. In the office, the bag with the takings was still in the drawer. Leaving it had been a clever touch, another way to make the death seem natural.

Half an hour and he gave up, letting himself out again, then used his tools to make the door secure. As he opened the gate, a man was waiting. Older, in his seventies, a couple of patches of white stubble on his face that the razor had missed, and a pair of intelligent brown eyes. He seemed to stoop more than stand, one hand gripping a heavy walking stick.

'What do you think you're doing?' He raised the cane; there might not be a lot of strength in those arms, but it could still do some damage.

'I'm with the police,' Harper said, and brought out his card.

His expression changed. 'Finally reckon there was something

wrong about her death, do you?' As he spoke, Harper saw the
gaps where the man's front teeth had been pulled.
The superintendent stared. 'Do you know something, sir?'
'I live over there.' He pointed across the ginnel. 'Don't sleep too
well, I get these pains in me legs most nights.'
'Did you see anything the night Mrs Reed died?' Please God,
let him be a witness.
'Heard. Couldn't get up to see, it were too painful. But me hearing's as good as ever. Sounds, like scraping and someone
whispering.'
Dammit. Still, he'd listen to the man.
'What time was it? Do you know?' he asked.
'Ee, I couldn't tell you.' The man shook his head. 'Don't have
a clock. Always had the knocker-up to wake me when I could
work.' He thought for a moment. 'Long since dark, and not near
morning. That's the best I can do.'
Even in the short nights of late July, that still covered a few
hours. 'Could you try and remember everything you heard?'
'It was like they was trying to be quiet, you know? My missus,
she didn't even stir.'
'They? More than one?'
'Oh aye. Definite. I could pick out two voices.' He was quiet for
a moment, eyes narrowing as he tried to remember. 'Not what they
said, mind. They was too quiet for that. Two men.'
'Young? Old?'
The man shrugged. 'Couldn't tell.'
'How long could you hear them?'
'Only a little while. Then, a bit later, there was more and the
sound of footsteps. Going that way.' He gestured down the ginnel.
'Did anyone come around yesterday, asking if you'd seen or heard
anything?' He'd ordered a house-to-house for the entire area.
'Some young bobby. Didn't look old enough to wipe his own arse.'
'Did you tell him all this?' If he had, and it hadn't been
reported . . .
'Course I didn't. Not with me missus there. She'd think I was
going daft. But I know it was real.'
'You're right. You tell your wife that if she asks. And if you
remember anything else, let Constable Barstow know. He'll make
sure it reaches me.'

'Reet enough.'

It wasn't much, he couldn't take it to court. But it was confirmation. Now he just had to find these men.

Reed sat in his office, the receiver tight against his ear.

'I'm sorry, Billy,' Harper said as the line crackled and fizzed. 'She was suffocated with her pillow. They did everything they could to make it seem natural. Didn't even steal the day's takings.'

'I see.' He'd known it since the first news arrived. Known it in his gut. He ought to feel angry. But there was nothing, just emptiness. He was in Whitby, looking out at the water and hearing the gulls, not in Leeds. There was nothing he could do.

'The funeral's tomorrow.'

'I told you, Tom, I can't go,' he said. 'I asked my chief and he refused. We're at the height of the season. I'll have to send a wreath.'

'I've put everyone on the case.'

'Catch them soon.' Words. A little salve on an open wound. For who, though? Tom or himself?

'We will.' A hesitation at the other end of the telephone. 'I really am sorry, Billy.'

'Just find them, will you?'

'The Board of Guardians has voted to provisionally give the workhouse master in Holbeck a clean bill of health. No responsibility for the deaths of Ada and Annie Redshaw.' Annabelle sighed.

'You told me he did everything properly. By the book.'

'I know.' Her voice was tired. They lay in bed. A thin breeze fluttered the curtains. Not a cloying heat, but warm enough for the old cotton sheet to feel like a weight on his body. 'I'm not saying he did anything wrong.' She rolled on to her back. He could just make out the silhouette of her body as she stared at the ceiling. 'It's the rules. They're the problem. If *this* happens, you have to do *that*. The master told me himself that something looked wrong with Redshaw. But since the man had enough money for lodgings, he couldn't take in the girls. His hands were tied. I told the board I'd put my name to it if we debated ideas to make sure something like this never happened again.'

'How did that go down?'

'How do you think? They didn't need my vote to pass the motion.

Very grudgingly, they told me to come up with some proposals and they'd be discussed if we had time.'

'A better system?' Harper asked.

'Like I said before: something that would let him use his own judgement.'

'And do you think they'll make time to listen?'

'Two minutes at the end of a meeting if I'm very lucky,' she snorted. 'They just want something simple, keeping the books in order, everything cut and dried. But how can we look after people if we turn them away?'

He thought about Hester Reed. What more could he have done to keep her alive? Nothing. In his head, he knew that. But it didn't stop the guilt growing inside. He'd failed her. He'd failed Billy.

'How much did it cost them to buy all those houses?' he asked Ash.

'Best part of five thousand pounds by my arithmetic, sir. You won't get that by saving your ha'pennies.'

Harper let out a low whistle. More than most people would see in their entire lives.

'Have you discovered where it came from?'

'Has to be this North Leeds Company, sir.' He rubbed a hand across his moustache. 'After all, they own this company the Smiths run. It's just two and two, isn't it?'

'And it's legal.'

'We've never come across this type of crime before.'

'Find out whatever you can. With what they're bringing in from increased rents, someone's making money.'

Harper attended Hester Reed's funeral. He had to go, a quiet observer at the back of the church, then at Beckett Street cemetery, standing a little distant under the shade of an elm tree. She was buried next to her husband, his grave still so fresh that the mound of earth hadn't even begun to rest.

He bowed his head at the prayers, feeling a weight settle on his shoulders. Billy's wreath lay by the coffin as it was lowered. One by one, relatives came forward to drop their handfuls of earth.

He gazed around the crowd. Nobody who resembled the description of the Smith brothers. Yet he spotted one familiar face, hanging on the fringes. Jeb Pearce. What was he doing here? He'd never even lived in Harehills.

As the service ended and people began to cluster in groups, Harper followed Pearce down the path and out past the railings that guarded the dead. The workhouse stood across the street, the stark warning of poverty. Pearce wasn't strolling. He was hurrying down the street towards the tram stop outside the Fountain Head pub.

Easy enough to catch up with him. Jeb was short and round, the black suit tight around his belly as he waddled away, sweat running down his face from the effort. A bowler hat sat awkwardly on his head.

'Going somewhere?' Harper asked. 'You'll miss the funeral tea.'

'Superintendent Harper,' Pearce said, as if he'd never noticed him in the crowd.

But he knew Jeb all too well. Half the force did; they'd been dealing with him since he was a boy shoplifting sweets in Little London. Spells in and out of jail. Nothing violent, that wasn't his style. Just schemes that promised the world and came to nothing. Jeb Pearce was everyone's fool.

'I saw you at Mrs Reed's burial.'

'My ma asked me to go. Mrs Reed was her second cousin,' he replied. 'She's poorly, back's giving her gyp. Someone from our side had to be there.'

It might have sounded plausible if Pearce's mother hadn't been sentenced for receiving stolen property just the month before.

'Very thoughtful of you,' Harper said. He pulled out his pocket watch. 'I tell you what. The next tram won't be along for a while. Why don't we walk into town? We'll have time for a catch-up.'

'I need to get over to Bramley.'

'You'll be fine. Trams go there every quarter of an hour from the Headrow.' He made sure the words didn't brook any refusal. Pearce's face fell. He put his hands in his pockets and started to shuffle along. 'Now, Jeb, why don't you tell me what you've been up to lately?'

Billy Reed walked along West Cliff, past the Royal Hotel to stare down at the water. The tide was out, leaving a long expanse of beach stretching all the way to Sandsend. Families sat under parasols, enjoying the sun. Children were paddling and playing games. A perfect late July day. He ought to feel happy to be here. Instead, darkness crept around the edges of his mind.

He should have asked to stay in Leeds a few more days. That could have changed everything. With him around, Hester might still be alive. Instead, he'd had to make do with sending flowers for the funeral. It wasn't enough. He'd let her down. Her and Charlie. He lit a cigarette. Part of him knew it was all stupid, pointless. He couldn't have spent the rest of his life guarding her. Tom was good. He'd do his duty; he'd ensure the murderers paid. But that didn't make it any easier. *He* should have done more. He'd be carrying this around for the rest of his life, the thought of *what if* haunting him on nights he couldn't sleep.

He needed something brighter. Something hopeful.

On a bench, an old couple leaned into each other, whispering and laughing, happy. Would that be him and Elizabeth in twenty or thirty years? he wondered. Would they even be alive then? The new century was right around the corner. A world full of something or other, one that was going to leave him behind. A man out of time.

Maybe Whitby was the right place for him. A sleepy little town that lived on fishing and history. Busy for three months every summer, then quiet, hidden away and forgotten for the rest of the year. A place that could happily let the rest of the world pass by.

He turned, walked through the whalebone arch and out of the breeze, down into town. Time to go back to the station and see if there was any crime worth the name today.

TEN

'Have you come across Jeb Pearce?' Harper asked Detective Constable Walsh.

'No, sir,' he answered in surprise. 'Should I have?'

'Good. If you don't know him, he won't know you. Find him, start following him. I want to know who he talks to and where he goes.'

'Yes, sir.' He hesitated. 'Is there a special reason?'

'He was at Hester Reed's funeral, and he lied when I asked him why.'

'Right, sir.' He picked up his notebook, crammed a hat on his head, and left.

'You don't think Jeb's involved with the money, do you, sir?' Ash asked.

The superintendent shook his head. 'He wouldn't know where to begin. But he was there for something, and it's a pound to a penny that someone paid him.'

'I've got more on the burglar, sir,' Fowler said with a frown. 'I did what you said and sent out the list of stolen goods to other places. He's been selling to the pawnbrokers in Doncaster and Barnsley.'

'Same name and description?' Harper asked.

'Yes, sir. Still using the name Brown.'

The superintendent rubbed his chin. He'd made a good guess. That wasn't much consolation.

'The forces up north start asking questions and suddenly he changes tactics. Make me wonder if he has an informant there.'

'Going south to sell the loot is closer from Leeds,' Ash pointed out. 'He's there and back in half a day with the money in his pocket. It's barely even an excursion.'

'Still no word from the snouts?'

'Nothing, sir,' Fowler replied. 'It's like he doesn't exist.'

But the burglar did exist, large as life and twice as troublesome. And he'd be back at work sooner or later.

'Forget him for now,' Harper told them. 'I want you concentrating on the murder. Maybe we won't bang our head on a brick wall with that.'

'I spent the morning in Holbeck,' Annabelle said as she reached around and undid the buttons on her gown. It spilled to the floor around her feet. A few more movements and she let out a sigh of relief as her corset loosened. 'That's better.'

'I thought you had a meeting at the workhouse today.' He was already in bed, watching her; he'd never tire of the sight.

'Postponed until Monday.' She arched an eyebrow. 'Two of the gentlemen Guardians had conflicting luncheon appointments.'

'Have you managed to find the woman Redshaw lived with?'

'Not yet. No one will say if they've seen her. It would help if I could talk to the man on the beat, Tom.'

'Tomorrow?' He'd talk to Brian Patterson and arrange it.

'If you can.'

A few minutes later she cuddled up beside him, fresh with the scent of Pears soap.

'I'm glad you're not giving up,' he said.

'Don't be daft. I need to *know*. I've told you that. Know it for myself.'

He put his arm around her shoulders. Night had brought a little coolness to the air. Maybe this heatwave was slowly beginning to fade. About time, too.

'This woman might be trying to put it all behind her,' he said.

'I've worked that one out for myself. I still want to hear her side of the story, though. Maybe you won't be the only detective in the family.'

'Can we stand more than one?'

She gave a small laugh. 'Better watch out, Superintendent. I might be after your job next.'

'We had another burglary last night, sir,' Fowler said as Harper walked into the office. 'Our man again.'

He sighed. This wasn't news he wanted to hear.

'Who was it this time?'

'A family called Miller. Out for the evening, gave the girl-of-all-work the night off. He had the run of the place.'

'Are we sure it was our man?'

The sergeant gave a weary nod. 'Twenty feet up a drainpipe, then six feet across the roof to an open attic window. It's him. Unless we've got another—'

'Don't you dare think that,' the superintendent warned.

'—then it's him. No clues left behind, of course.'

'Have you circulated the list of stolen goods?'

'Already gone out, sir. Locally, as well as up and down the train line.'

What else could they do? Harper wondered.

'No one nearby saw anything? Where was this?'

'Blenheim Square, sir. I talked to a few of the neighbours last night. I'm going to see the rest this morning.'

'Have a word with the man on the beat, too. He might have noticed a stranger around during the day, sizing the place up.'

This burglar might be new in Leeds, but he was finding his way around quickly enough. There was money in Blenheim Square, plenty of the professors from Yorkshire College lived there.

'That last burglary . . .' Harper began.

'What about it?' Fowler asked.

'Didn't the victim have something to do with the college?'

'Vice-Chancellor, sir.'

'This one, what's his name?'

'Miller.'

'What's his job?'

The sergeant checked in his notebook.

'Professor of Latin at Yorkshire College.' His voice slowed as he spoke. 'I'll look into that connection, sir.'

It might be nothing, Harper thought. Pure coincidence. But he'd never believed in those.

'See what you can turn up.' A thought struck him. 'George Hope was the first victim. Find out if he has anything to do with the place, too. But I want most of your attention on this murder.' That was what was burning inside him. 'The people who sold to the Smiths. What did they have to say?'

'The ones I spoke to were all older, sir. Owned the property for a few years, happy to take the cash. Better to have a lump sum than a little trickling in every week. Sounds like the brothers kept pressing those who were reluctant. Going on for hours until they wore them down. No violence,' he added.

Everything legal, everything above board. Not a shred he could use in court.

'Talk to the rest of them,' Harper ordered, then turned to Walsh.

'What about our friend Jeb?'

'It took me a couple of hours to track him down.' He grinned. 'I must be losing my touch, sir.'

'That's Jeb for you. Elusive as the wind,' Ash said from the corner.

The others all turned to stare at him.

'Elusive as the wind?' Harper asked. 'What does that mean?'

The inspector smiled. 'Saw it in a book my Nancy made me read. It's true, though. Pearce is all over the place, sir. You know that.'

'I finally found him at the White Stag on North Street,' Walsh continued. His eyes widened. 'Do you know they have a monkey there?'

'I've seen it,' Harper said. The pub was only four hundred yards from the Victoria. A sailor had brought the animal home with him and taken it to the pub, hoping for free drinks. It had run off. By the time they found it in the cellar, the sailor had vanished. The landlord had decided to keep the monkey; it brought in trade. God knew, the place needed it. 'What was Jeb doing there?'

'Nothing much. Hardly a soul in the place. I had the impression he was waiting for someone. After half an hour he left. Went up to Harehills. Looked around the shops and went into a grocer's.'

The superintendent sat upright. 'Which one?'

'I don't know, sir,' Walsh answered. 'I wasn't paying much attention to the name. I couldn't follow him inside. Too obvious.'

'Would you remember it?'

'Of course, sir.'

'Get your hat. We're going to take a tram ride.'

'Are you certain it was this one?' Harper asked.

'Positive, sir. I remember the sign.'

Hard to forget. *Cameron, Grocer to the Trade and the Home.* Gold letters on an olive background. It stood out on this parade, where everything else looked so drab.

'How long was Pearce inside?'

'Couldn't have been more than two or three minutes. And he wasn't carrying anything when he came out.'

'No,' Harper said thoughtfully. 'I don't imagine he was. Why don't you go and catch up with him? Let's see what he gets up to today.'

He stared at the shop. Go back in? No, he decided. He wanted more before he talked to Cameron again. An accommodation address was perfectly legal. The man could claim he didn't know Pearce, that he'd never seen him before in his life. At the tram stop back into town, the superintendent considered his choices.

Back at Millgarth he left a note for Ash: *Grocer called Cameron in Harehills. Find out about him.*

Reed sat in the Inglenook Tea Room and read the letter again, the sixth time since it arrived that morning. He knew the words by heart now, but he wanted to see them on the page once more.

This looks as if it will be a slow investigation. We still don't know who these Smith brothers can be. But we will get there, Billy. I promised you that, and I will see that we do right by Charlie and Hester.

He *wanted* to believe it. But what was going on? What if they couldn't find the kind of answers that would see two men standing in the dock?

Reed folded the sheet and put it back in his jacket. All those years when he and Charlie could have been friends again, but both of them had been too stubborn. They'd settled for grudging politeness, when a good talk over a couple of pints might have cleared the air. Too much bloody pride, the determination not to be the first to back down. Look where it had left them: one in the ground, the other feeling as if his heart was splitting apart with the knowledge that they wasted all those years for nothing at all.

Without Elizabeth, he'd have been drowning his sorrows. Marriage to her had changed his life. He'd talked to her about the old days, when he and Charlie had been close, and all the stupid little things that stopped him from mending the breach. She hadn't judged; she'd listened patiently and hugged him, looked after him. Never mind that she was up to her ears with her own work at the tea room. Very quietly, she made the time for him. How had he ever been lucky enough to find someone like her? Every single day, he was grateful that she was there.

He counted out the pennies for his pot of tea and placed it on the tablecloth, leaving with a nod to Mrs Botham. Time to go back to work.

ELEVEN

'What did Jeb do yesterday?' the superintendent asked Walsh.

'Nothing worth mentioning, sir. He lives with his aunt. Spent most of it at home.'

'Stick with him.'

'I intend to, sir.'

'Cameron,' Harper said to Ash. 'Our friendly grocer to the trade and the home. What do we know?'

'I'm still working on it, sir. He's had his shop for two years, but nobody around Harehills Parade seems to know much about him. Doesn't seem to go out of his way to make friends. Has ambitions to cater to the higher end of the market.'

That fitted with the man he'd met, the neat clothes, beard carefully trimmed, the clean fingernails.

'What's his background?'

'I'm still trying to find that out, sir. I should know a bit more by tonight.'

'Good.' He looked at his men. 'Don't forget we're dealing with murder here. Fowler. Anything else with the others who've sold property to the Smiths?'

The sergeant pushed the spectacles up his nose. 'The same as before, sir. Older. Easy to persuade. Or bully,' he added.

Harper nodded; he'd spent the afternoon visiting a few of them himself and seen exactly the same thing. The Smiths were smart. Persuasive. Born salesmen.

'They put the money right there on the table,' a widow had told him. Just her and a maid in a house that was far too big in Hyde Park. She was in her seventies, her clothes shabby, grey hair so sparse that he could see the pale pink of her skull. 'Said that was mine if I sold to them, that it was better like that than a little bit of rent every month.'

'What did you do?' he asked.

She continued as if she'd never heard his question. 'Then they started to put it away. Told me that I'd had my chance and that was it.' The woman looked up at him with sadness in her eyes. 'My Bob didn't leave me much and I've gone through it. I took what they were offering. Did I do the right thing?'

'Maybe you did,' Harper said.

The brothers had been tougher with some of the others he saw, staying and talking for hour after hour, simply hammering away with words, grinding them down until they accepted the offer. Everything a hair on the right side of legal. By the time the day ended, all he felt was an overwhelming sorrow for the people he'd met.

Ash and the others left. They knew what to do. Meanwhile,

Harper thought as he looked at the papers waiting on his desk, he wouldn't be able to escape Millgarth today.

'You look all in,' Annabelle said.

His jacket was hanging by the door and he'd removed his collar and tie before stretching out his legs with a sigh. The end of another hot day.

'I've spent most of the day reading and signing my name on forms.'

Mary looked up, her eyes suddenly curious. 'Did they make you practise writing your name all day, Da?'

He laughed. 'It felt that way,' he told her. 'But some days a superintendent's job is like that. Don't ever become one.'

'Chance would be a fine thing,' Annabelle said. But he wasn't about to start on *that* discussion; he was too weary. 'It's just going to be you two tonight. I need to go and see a couple of families.'

'Work?' he asked, and she nodded.

'They've applied for relief and the officer turned them down after a visit.' Her eyes hardened. 'I know them both, so I want to see for myself. No rest for the wicked.'

'Have you been wicked, Mam?' Mary asked.

'Not yet,' Annabelle told her. 'But I might be after this evening.'

Time with his daughter was the perfect medicine. First she wanted to play shop, bringing out a box filled with tiny pieces of wooden fruit and cheese for him to buy as she totted up the prices on a piece of paper. Correct every time. Then it was the memory game.

How had he ever managed to father such a clever girl, he wondered as she slipped into bed. He'd never been a bright spark at school; joining the force had been the making of him. But Mary was streets ahead of both her parents. Every day it astonished him. Worried him, too. What opportunities would be there for young women when she grew up?

All they could do was hope that the world became a better place. He had his doubts about that: during the afternoon a pair of constables had come to him, saying they intended to enlist if war broke out with the Boers. Men and their urge to fight. The chief constable had been correct; they were going to need plenty of special constables. From the stories in the papers it was probably only weeks before the fighting started.

After Mary was asleep, he read for a while, windows open to the warm evening, voices and laughter drifting up from the pub.

By the time Annabelle returned, he was starting to doze in the chair, eyes jerking open as the door closed. One glance at her face told him all he needed to know.

'That relief officer and I are going to have words,' she told him as she tried to pace away her anger.

'Bad decisions?'

'Oh, I'm sure he'll insist they were completely justified.' Her jaw was set, eyes flashing. 'But I'm going to overrule him. I've met him. He's one of this new breed, reckons everything comes down to pounds, shillings and pence. He cuts relief to families for the smallest thing, or he denies it to them altogether.'

'You've had enough?'

She held a hand to her neck. 'Up to here. I was elected as a Guardian to *help* the poor in Sheepscar. I'm blowed if I'll see them punished for things they don't even understand. I've sent him a note telling him to report to me at the workhouse Tuesday morning.' She exhaled slowly. 'Let's go to bed. If I think about it any longer, I'll have steam coming out of my ears.'

'We're meeting that bobby in Holbeck tomorrow afternoon.'

'I haven't forgotten.' She brightened a little. 'When I was walking home I had a few thoughts that might stop anything like the Redshaw girls happening again.'

Something had happened. He could feel it as soon as he walked into Millgarth. The air seemed to buzz. Men moved around with purpose. Ash, Fowler, and Walsh had their heads together in the detectives' room.

'What is it?' Harper asked.

'We've just had word about a body, sir,' Walsh replied. 'Five minutes ago. At one of those little quarries close to Roundhay Park. Discovered when the men arrived for work this morning.' A small hesitation as he swallowed. 'It's Jeb Pearce.'

'What?' The word exploded from his mouth. 'You were supposed to be following him.'

'I saw him all the way home to Bramley. About nine last night, sir.'

'What happened after that?'

'I don't know, sir. I wish I did.'

Harper believed him; Walsh wasn't one to shirk on his duty. But how . . .?

'You're coming to Roundhay with me. Fowler, I want you in Bramley, see what you can find out. Jeb didn't fly across Leeds to die.'

'Yes, sir.'

'Ash, I want *everything* about Cameron on my desk later.'

It was all connected; he didn't know how yet, but it had to be.

'Very good, sir.'

Out past the Victoria and up Roundhay Road. Beyond the grocer's shop with its gold and green sign on Harehills Parade, already open for business, a striped canvas awning for shade.

'How much detail do we have?'

'Just the name,' Walsh told him. 'He had a letter in his pocket.'

The quarry was set back from the road, no more than a hundred yards from the entrance to the park, out of sight, tucked into the hillside. A uniformed policeman stood by the entrance. Behind him, Harper saw a wooden hut and ton upon ton of stone. Large blocks with rough edges, more half-worked, some ready to be hauled away. Five workmen stood around with doleful expressions, smoking and drinking tea from tin mugs. And there, in the hole, the body. It was definitely Jeb, impossible to mistake that round body and hopeless face.

He wasn't quite at the bottom, though, Harper thought as he scrambled his way down the slope. Pebbles and chippings slid away under his feet as he tried to keep his balance. It looked as though Jeb had tried to climb out. On the other side of the dip, a cliff rose twenty feet in the air, a sheer expanse where blocks of stone had been quarried.

A rippling sound, a shower of pebbles, and suddenly someone was beside him. A man in a dusty suit, bowler hat perched on his head.

'I'm Saul Waters. The foreman here. Found him when I opened up today. Came down to see if he was still alive. I looked in his pockets and found the letter. Put it back after,' he added.

'Is all this locked at night?'

The man shook his head. 'No need. A few kids play here, but that's it. Never had a problem before.'

That seemed like a miracle in itself, Harper thought.

'What do you think happened?' He turned his good ear towards Waters.

'My guess?' He nodded at the cliff. 'He probably went off the top, was hurt and tried to crawl out.' He brought a pipe from his pocket and lit it with a match.

'Why would he be walking around up there in the dark?' Harper asked. 'He lives in Bramley.'

Waters shrugged. 'Couldn't tell you. You're the copper.'

He was, and he had a few guesses of his own.

'Who owns this place?'

'Chap called Nicholson. Had it for a year now.'

It was an unlikely place for a killing. Most people wouldn't know it existed, not even visitors to the park.

'I'm going to need a list of all the people who've worked here over the last five years.'

Waters sucked on his teeth, then nodded. 'Might take a little while.'

'This morning,' Harper told him. 'Or do you think this man decided to jump of his own free will?'

'I'll see you have it.' He moved away, climbing easily over the scree.

The superintendent squatted to examine Pearce's body. Cuts all over his hands and face, blood dried around them. Dr King would be able to tell him more when he examined the corpse. Stone dust covered the clothes, trouser knees torn from crawling. He felt an overwhelming sense of sorrow. Poor bloody Jeb. He'd tried to live, done his best to crawl out of here. But once again, his best hadn't been good enough. Now it never would be.

Harper followed the dirt path to the top of the cliff. Nothing to show a struggle, but it had been dry for so long that the earth was hard and packed; impossible to tell anything.

He looked down. It wasn't that high, but sharp, jagged lumps of rock waited at the bottom. Enough to break a body. He sighed and stared, eyes tracing the path Pearce must have taken on his hands and knees. How long had it taken him? He'd died with the rim of the quarry just three yards away. So close, but it might as well have been the other side of the moon.

'Well?' he asked Walsh. The constable had been talking to the workmen. 'Do any of them know him?'

'No, sir. I asked them about the Smiths, described them, but that didn't ring any bells, either.'

'They brought him here. They threw him down.' And once again, not one shred of proof. But he knew. Had they stood up here and laughed as Jeb tried to save himself?

'Makes you wonder what condition Pearce was in when they arrived, doesn't it, sir?'

'We'll see what the surgeon says.' He heard the anger in his voice, felt it like iron in his body. 'I want you after them.'

Charlie Reed's suicide had opened the lid on something far bigger than he could have imagined. Two murders so far. And if Billy hadn't come for his brother's funeral, the police might never have known.

In the cab back to Millgarth he was silent, lost in his own thoughts. Where did they go from here? And how was he going to find out who owned the North Leeds Company?

'Sir?'

'What?' The superintendent glanced out of the window. The hackney was trotting along Regent Street. 'Sorry, I missed what you said.'

'I can't believe the Smiths are the brains behind this,' Walsh said.

'Why not?'

'It looks like they're muscle. Bright enough and good with words, yes. But all this, it's . . . too convoluted.'

Completely true. Add in the knowledge about planning applications, and the money to buy the houses; five thousand pounds was a fortune. The North Leeds Company was pulling the strings. Someone with connections. Someone who knew what was going on in the city.

Another hour or two and Pearce would be in King's Kingdom. But the post-mortem couldn't give him the answers he really needed. Why murder Jeb? What had he done?

Dr Lumb had performed the post-mortem, with King peering over his shoulder. The body still lay on the slab, chest cut open, all the blood drained away, the organs weighed and bagged somewhere.

'Your victim had been badly beaten before he fell in the quarry,' Lumb said.

'How badly?'

'He definitely wouldn't have been in any condition to walk by himself.'

'He was still alive when he landed,' Harper said.

'Only just, as far as I can judge. How far did he crawl?'

'Ten yards or so.'

'Then he did that with a broken pelvis, four ribs smashed, a hairline fracture on his thigh and three broken fingers. Plus plenty of internal bleeding.'

Sweet God. 'Was there any chance he could have lived?'

'None at all,' King snapped. 'All it did was make him suffer more. That was what you wanted to know, wasn't it?'

'Yes.'

'Then just come out and ask it.' His voice was hard, echoing off the tiled walls. 'The Lord only knows what kind of pain he was in. And he didn't *crawl* that distance. He couldn't. He *dragged* himself along the ground. His hands are in ribbons, all sorts of stone and dust under his skin and fingernails.' He glared and stalked away.

'Most of those injuries happened before he landed on the ground,' Lumb continued after a moment, a raw sorrow in his voice. 'I saw brutal things out in Egypt, Superintendent, but believe me, nothing as . . . deliberate or as thorough as this. The beating must have lasted half an hour.'

'Christ.' Tossing him down into the quarry was the final touch. Throwing him away in a last humiliation.

Jeb had been a crook most of his life, a con-man, a pickpocket, trying anything illegal that brought in a few shillings. Not a good man, but never one of the worst. He didn't deserve a death like that.

'Could one man have moved him?'

'It's possible,' the doctor replied after a little thought. 'Difficult, though, he'd need to be strong. Much easier with two.'

'That's what I thought. Thank you.'

The constable was standing near the Cross Keys pub, rocking back and forth on his heels. He snapped to attention and saluted as soon as he noticed Harper and Annabelle.

'Afternoon, sir. Missus.'

'At ease, Cartwright.'

The bobby was good at his job; that was what Brian Patterson had said. Conscientious, well-liked by the locals, he knew the area like the back of his hand. Seventeen years on the same beat, and not the slightest ambition for anything more.

'This is my wife. She's on the Leeds Board of Guardians. She's been asked to look into the deaths of the Redshaw girls.'

'Ah.' His face clouded. 'They were lovely little lasses, those two. 'Bout broke my heart when it happened, that did.'

'Mine, too,' Annabelle told him, then reached out and put her hand on his arm. 'I'm sorry, you must have known them since they were born.'

That was all it took. A small gesture and a few sympathetic words and she'd won a new friend. He could see it in Cartwright's expression.

'I did, missus. A pair of little bobby dazzlers, them two. Smiles that could charm the birds out of the trees.' He looked away for a moment and quickly wiped a hand across his eyes. 'Sorry, sir. Ma'am.'

'It's all right,' Harper told him. He took out his pocket watch and looked at Annabelle. 'Do you need me here? With . . .'

'I'm sure this gentleman will be able to help me,' she told him. 'You've got enough on your plate.'

He glanced over his shoulder as he strode away. The two of them were already talking as if they'd known each other for years.

Six o'clock in the evening. The sun was hidden somewhere behind the haze that covered Leeds. Noise blared through the windows as people made their way home in the lingering heat. People, trams, carts, carriages. The ugly honk of a horn, then the distant mechanical blur of a motor car.

Harper ignored it, sitting with the others in his office. All Fowler had found in Bramley was a grieving aunt. Someone had come for Jeb a little after nine the night before, she'd said. He'd answered the door himself, then told her he had to go on the water for a while. That was the last she saw of him. Neighbours had reported him going off with two men in a horse and gig.

'Was there a driver as well?'

'No one remembers, sir. They weren't really paying attention.'

'The next we see of Jeb is this morning, dead,' Harper said. 'Is there any connection at all between the Smiths and the quarry? Why would they choose that place? It's out of the way, on the other side of town. There must have been somewhere quiet much closer to Bramley, surely.'

'The foreman sent a list of employees,' Walsh said.

'Check every one of them,' Harper ordered. 'The owner's called Nicholson. I want to know about him. Put the fear of God into all your snouts. For God's sake, these brothers aren't invisible. Let's drag them down here.' He turned to Ash. 'Cameron. I hope it's something good.'

'He started out as a grocer's boy in Harrogate. Then he went to prison for three months.'

Harper raised an eyebrow. 'What did he do?'

'Stealing from his employer.' He rubbed his chin. 'Yet he ends up a grocer himself. Strange world, isn't it, sir?'

'You've got that look in your eye.'

'Our Mr Cameron seems to have had an interesting little life, sir.'

Billy Reed climbed the steps up to Whitby Abbey. One hundred and ninety-nine of them, that's what they claimed; he'd never bothered to count. One thing about living in a place with so many hills; he was fitter than he'd been in years. Not a single pause on the way up and he was hardly winded by the time he reached the top.

A small group was waiting. The bishop, in brilliant white surplice, colourful stole and mitre. The mayor and two councillors. Reed was wearing full fig, the cutaway coat, wing collar, and the top hat he brought out for special occasions. All to re-dedicate an ancient block of stone that a drunk had tried to steal. He'd managed to drag it all of six feet by the time he collapsed and the constable arrested him. Bound over to keep the peace for twelve months. And now this ridiculous ceremony to make it holy again.

He didn't listen to the words, letting his mind drift and his gaze wander out to sea. Calm today. Only a few fishing boats still out; most had long since unloaded their catch for the morning. The tide was coming in, slowly forcing the holidaymakers off the beach.

How many were buried up here? he wondered. Centuries of monks under the ground, piles of old bones, the way Charlie and Hester would be when the worms were done. He sent up a silent prayer for his brother and his wife. His mind turned to Tom's investigation. Not done yet; he'd have sent word.

Then it was over, a few handshakes and he strolled back down the hill while the others stayed to talk. Reed always felt uncomfortable around people like that, out of place among the great and the good. No matter, he was on his way to some better company. Dinner at the Black Horse with Harry Pepper, the man in charge of Whitby's customs office.

A last look towards the water before he turned on to Church Street, and the lingering, hopeless wish he could have done more for Charlie.

TWELVE

No cooler the next morning, the night had held the stifling heat. Now the sun shimmered somewhere off to the east as Harper walked into town, wondering when the weather would finally break. All night, the image of Jeb's body had kept falling through his dreams, jerking him awake.

Why kill him? That was what he couldn't understand. Pearce hadn't given the police any information. He hadn't done anything at all. Yet the killers had relished every moment of beating and murdering him.

He stopped at the post box, dropping in the letter he'd written to Billy. He deserved to know what was happening.

Not that he had much to tell. Just the hope that the brothers would make some mistake, and so far they'd shown no sign of that. Even if they did, the police had little evidence. Nothing that would stand up to a lawyer's questions. No one had seen them with Jeb. Hester Reed wasn't alive to testify against them. Not a thing.

He couldn't let men like that roam free around Leeds. People who'd kill that way deserved to hang. And who was behind it all? Someone was giving the orders and keeping his hands clean. And *he* wasn't even leaving a shadow at the moment.

Fowler and Walsh were in the office, still wearing yesterday's clothes as they sifted through statements.

'Well?' Harper asked.

'We haven't managed to come up with a clue, sir,' the sergeant answered. 'Nobody saw or heard a thing, and there are no houses close to the quarry.'

A very good reason to choose the place.

'We've been going through the list the foreman made,' Walsh said. He looked weary, hair standing on end where he'd run his hands through it. 'So far, they all look straight enough.'

'The Smiths?'

Fowler simply shook his head.

Ash arrived, hanging his old bowler hat on the hook. He sighed, running his hands down his cheeks.

'Nicholson,' he said. 'The quarry owner.'

'Go on,' the superintendent told him.

'I spent a very frustrating few hours yesterday going through records at the Town Hall, sir.'

'Do you have an address for him?'

'I do, sir.'

'Then we'll start by paying him a visit. Walsh, get some uniforms to go through the rest of the quarry employees. I want you out and talking to people. Find out everything Jeb was up to in the week before his death. And keep hammering every informant about the Smiths.'

'What about me, sir?' Fowler asked.

'You're going to Harehills to talk to Cameron the grocer.' Ash had told them all about the grocer's shadowy past the evening before. After that first prison sentence for stealing from his employer, there had been two more, both for forging cheques, all before he turned twenty-three. After that, a long, quiet period until he suddenly appeared with his own grocer's shop on Harehills Parade, with no hint of where he'd found the capital for the business. Was Cameron tied in with all this? Harper's instincts said yes. But how? Fowler was the right choice to go there. He didn't look like a copper, didn't have the manner of one; he was more like a young professor from the college, with his thinning hair and distracted air. 'Tell him you want your post sent there. Make up some company name. Get him talking.'

'Yes, sir. One other thing. About the burglaries. You asked if George Hope had anything to do with Yorkshire College.'

Hope, the first of the burglar's victims. 'I remember.'

'He's on the board there.'

'I see. Leave it with me.'

A quick word with Sergeant Tollman, then a walk to Woodhouse
Lane to catch the tram, and out to Far Headingley, leaving the bustle
of the city for wide streets, cleaner air and big houses. The address
they wanted lay behind a low stone wall, oaks and elms hanging
over the drive to offer cool, beautiful shade.

'Must be good money in stone,' Ash said.

'There's brass in plenty of things,' Harper said. 'Just not policing.
What happened to the previous owner of the quarry?'

'Died of old age.'

Stained glass in the front door, a sunrise shining in reds
and yellows. The superintendent pulled the bell, hearing it ring
inside, and waited for the slap of shoes on the tile. A maid looked
up at them quizzically. Harper removed his hat and produced his
card.

'We're looking for Mr Nicholson.'

'Is this about the death at the quarry?' she asked. 'Only I read
about it in the papers.' She was middle-aged, wide-eyed and nervous,
alarmed at finding two policemen on the doorstep.

'It is, miss,' Ash said. His voice was warm and friendly. 'Don't
you worry, these are only routine enquiries. Is he in?'

'He's not here. He and the missus have gone away.'

'When did they go?' Harper asked sharply.

'A week ago Sunday. They do it every year. Take a house up in
Staithes. They say the sea air does them good.' She rolled her eyes.
'Fat chance I get to see it.'

'Has he been in touch since the . . . incident?' Ash asked gently.

She shook her head. 'Not with me.'

'When are they due back?'

'Another week yet.'

Staithes, Harper thought; that was in Billy's area. The maid gave
them the Nicholsons' address up there. And Reed had a vested
interest in discovering the truth behind all this. Definitely worth a
telephone call once they were back at Millgarth.

'What do you reckon, sir?' Ash interrupted his thoughts.

'Honestly? I don't know.' He kicked at a stone, sending it skittering down the street. 'I keep wondering how the Smiths even knew about the quarry.'

'I read the post-mortem on Jeb Pearce. Not much mercy in his death.'

'None at all. Done for the sheer pleasure of it.'

'Why, though? Any ideas, sir?'

'I wish to God I did.' He shook his head. No answers at all. 'We'll ask them when we catch up with them. I'm sure they'll be happy to tell us.'

'I daresay they'll be quite eager to explain after a while in the cells.' He sighed. 'Do you know what worries me about all this, sir? If crimes like this are the future, all business and money, people like you and me are going to be left behind.'

'I'm sure there'll always be a place for the old school.' But where would it be?

It was a fine afternoon for a trip up to Staithes, Reed thought, as he guided the horse and trap along the road. A gentle breeze off the sea, barely a cloud in the sky. And finally, some proper police work to do.

Staithes seemed an odd place to choose for a holiday. Not even a village, just a tiny fishing hamlet that barely survived. Picturesque, clinging to the hillside, and a good, small harbour. But still . . . he'd never heard of anyone going there just for the fun of it.

His notebook held the words he'd scrawled as he talked to Tom on the telephone. Questions he needed answered.

'If he can tell you, we'll be one step closer to finding the men who killed Hester and Jeb Pearce,' Harper had said. He hadn't needed to add the rest – they'd be nearer to finding the men responsible for Charlie taking his own life.

The house was at the bottom of the hill, not one of the grand buildings perched at the top with their wide views of the North Sea. Nicholson was down among the life of the village. A good enough place, though, built for the gentry a hundred years or more ago. His hand came down on the knocker.

'I'm Inspector Reed, Whitby Police,' he told the flustered maid who answered the door. 'Is Mr Nicholson here?'

'He's not,' she answered, then her eyes narrowed. 'Is this about that death at the quarry?'

'It is.'

'He got the letter this morning. Went white as a ghost. Picked up his easel and painting things and left. Didn't even have breakfast.'

'Do you know where he's gone, miss?'

'Harbour, like as not,' she told him. 'That's where he goes to paint. He's been over on Car Bar Bank a lot this year. The other side of the beck,' she explained.

'What about Mrs Nicholson?' he asked.

'Not been well since we got the news,' she replied, and her eyes flashed a warning: don't disturb the woman. That was fine. It was the man he wanted to see.

Two cobles sat in the low water, ready to head out to sea in the morning. Six or seven more anchored in the harbour behind the breakwater. He picked out a figure sitting in the sun near the lifeboat station, easel and canvas set up in front of him. But the man appeared to be staring, not painting.

That wasn't quite true, he saw as he approached. He'd made a start on things, the colours of a dark, threatening sky, so different from what was in front of him. The man had talent; it looked very real.

'Mr Nicholson,' he said, and the man's head jerked round, snapped out of his daydream. He was in his fifties, a full head of grey hair, wearing a pale summer suit of good linen, a shirt and tie, the straw boater lying on the ground beside his bag. Soft blue eyes and an expression of sadness on his face, a man whose world had been shaken. Reed introduced himself and said: 'It's a terrible thing that happened.'

'That it is, Inspector. That it is.'

'The man who died was called Jeb Pearce.' No mention of murder yet. Start out easy, Tom had suggested. 'Did you know him at all?'

'No. I don't believe I'd ever heard the name until I received a letter from the foreman this morning. I – we were shocked. Nothing like that has ever happened before.'

'How long have you owned the quarry, sir?'

'A year.' His gaze shifted, looking out to the water.

The story was straightforward. Nicholson was an engineer. He'd owned a small works in Hunslet, built up his business and finally sold out to a larger company. But retirement didn't sit well with him, and he'd looked around for something new. He'd always been fascinated by stone, he said: the texture, the shades, the way it was cut and shaped. When he heard that the quarry was for sale, he'd put in a bid. But the price was too high. He tried the bank for a loan. They weren't interested, so he began casting around for money. 'A loan?' Reed asked. He could feel the hairs on the back of his neck begin to rise. 'Who lent you the money in the end?'

'Someone I'd done business with before. He's a sleeping partner. But I'd tried several others first.'

'Do the names Jack and John Smith mean anything to you, sir? Two brothers.'

Nicholson looked startled, and Reed's heart began to pound.

'I talked to them about a loan to buy the quarry. Nothing came of it in the end.' He looked up curiously. 'Why?'

Reed ignored the question. 'Why didn't it happen, sir?'

'Honestly, I'm not sure.' He produced a cigarette case from his jacket, took one out and lit it, watching the smoke curl into the blue sky. 'It was no secret that I was looking. They approached me, but we couldn't agree terms.' He cocked his head. 'Why would they be important?'

'Just asking, sir.' He made sure his voice was bland, giving nothing away. 'Did they ever come out to the quarry?'

'Of course. That's normal. Why do they interest you?'

'Background, sir, that's all.' Reed smiled. 'And you're absolutely sure you've never heard of Jeb Pearce?'

'Positive. I told you. The first time was my foreman's letter.' He reached into his pocket. 'Here. Take a look if you like.'

It was simple, just the facts. Nothing Tom wouldn't already have seen for himself.

'Thank you.' He handed it back. Nicholson's hand trembled slightly as he reached for it. 'Have you had any other dealings with the Smiths, sir?'

'None.' He breathed slowly. 'Do you suspect them in this man's death?'

'I couldn't say, sir.' Reed chose his words carefully. 'All I have is what the people in Leeds wanted me to ask you.'

'I see.' A moment of silence, then a quick nod. 'Anything else?'

'Did you ever go to the Smiths' office?'

'No.' Nicholson's voice was firm. 'They came to me or we communicated by letter.'

'I don't suppose you remember an address for them?'

The man smiled and gave a brief shake of his head. 'As a matter of fact, I do. It was all a little strange, that's why it stuck in my head. Do you know Leeds at all?'

'I do, sir. I worked there before I transferred up here.'

'It's in Harehills.'

'A grocer's shop, perhaps?'

Nicholson looked astonished. 'Yes. I pass it most days on my way to the quarry. How did you know?'

'It's related to some other enquiries, as I said.'

Five more minutes of questions, but he'd already learned everything useful. John and Jack Smith remained as anonymous as they'd been before.

'The Leeds Police are looking into things,' he said. 'They'll get to the bottom of it.'

'I hope so, Inspector.' Nicholson's voice sounded weary. 'I really hope so. And soon.'

Before he left, there was one more question Reed wanted to ask.

'I'm curious, sir. Why Staithes for a holiday? There's nothing here.'

For the first time, Nicholson smiled. 'We've been coming for a few years.' He gestured at the easel. 'I like to paint. I've never seen anything quite like the light here. I like to try and capture it.'

As he walked back to the cart, Reed felt his breathing ease. He had information to pass on. A connection. Tom would be able to use that.

At the top of the hill, he let the horse rest. He turned back, glancing over the sea. The light? It was the same here as everywhere else, wasn't it?

THIRTEEN

Harper stared at the map of Leeds on the wall, pins showing all the properties owned by the Harehills Development Company. But that didn't bring him one inch closer to the Smiths.

He stepped back. Only two common factors: the Smith brothers, and the grocer in Harehills where the company received its post.

Nicholson was innocent. Billy had sounded certain of it when he telephoned the evening before. The quarry owner was genuinely shocked by the death, he said. Still, they'd learned something. At least they knew why the Smiths were familiar with the place. Now they needed to find out why they murdered Jeb Pearce.

Sitting at his desk, he took a pencil and a clean sheet of paper and began to write down questions. Perhaps having everything in stark black and white might make things clearer.

Who was behind all this? With the law blocking the way, he couldn't know. But it had to be someone with access to the planning system, who understood how it worked. Councillors would know, and that brought one or two names to mind. A start. *Why do it?* That was simpler. The increased rents would bring in a good profit over the years. That meant that someone was looking to the long term with this. *Why use the Smiths?* They were a pair of clever, persuasive, brutal thugs; they made an ideal front for the operation. *Had the pair moved out of control with the killings?* He hesitated. Maybe so. In the end, he left that blank. He didn't know enough to give an answer yet. *How to catch them?* Another empty space. None of his ideas so far had worked.

He was still staring at the page when Fowler came in, a broad smile on his face.

'You look happy,' Harper said.

With a magician's flourish, the sergeant produced a thin stack of letters.

'Correspondence for the Harehills Development Company, sir.'

He raised an eyebrow. 'How did you manage that?'

'I went to talk to Cameron like you wanted, sir. Told him I was interested in having my post delivered there. I'm a financial company, by the way.' He winked.

'Then I wish you large profits.'

'From your lips to God's ears. He was only too pleased to show me everything. Where he keeps the letters in pigeonholes behind the counter.'

'How did you manage to grab them?'

Another smile. 'I went not long before he was closing. While he was outside dragging in those sacks of potatoes, I had a chance to be light-fingered. I didn't think you'd mind a little theft, since it's in a good cause.'

'What theft?' Harper asked. 'I don't see a thing, Sergeant. Go through them, then visit whoever wrote them. There might be something juicy.'

Ash arrived with a quick report on Nicholson. It seemed to confirm what Reed had said: the man was clean.

'What about Jeb?' He turned to Walsh. 'What was he up to in his last week?'

'Not a great deal, sir. That's what his friends told me, anyway. They can't believe he's dead. All of them were horrified when I told them how it happened, so I'm sure it was true. He was scuffling for pennies most of the time. Had a few quid a week or so ago, but he ran through it quickly.'

'Where did that come from?'

'He never said. Kept hinting to people there might be more of it soon.'

Easy to guess at the source of the money. But what had he done to earn it, and how had he displeased his masters so quickly?

'What have the snouts given you on the Smiths?' His eyes moved from one face to the next.

'Blank looks,' Walsh replied. 'They don't go in the pubs, don't seem to go anywhere that I can find. They keep their noses clean.'

'Suffocation and beating someone to death is hardly clean.'

'Nobody knows them. I mean, not at all. They don't spend any of their time with criminals.'

'It's exactly like I was saying yesterday, sir: this is a different type of crime,' Ash said quietly.

Harper sighed and rubbed his temples. 'Keep pressing. Something has to give. I want enquiries sent to every force in the country. They came from *somewhere*. They have a past. Meanwhile, Walsh and Fowler have their work for the day. Ash, you're coming with me. I think we'll go and see our grocer friend.'

The inspector laughed. 'Right you are, sir. I'll bring my shopping bag.'

First, though, he needed an hour going through the papers waiting on his desk. The duties of rank. What he wanted was to be out there, doing something worthwhile. But the pile here wouldn't vanish if he ignored it.

He was grateful when Sergeant Tollman tapped on the door.

'I've got Sissons here, sir. Exactly the kind of bobby you wanted.'

'Send him in.'

Harper had asked the desk sergeant to find him an intelligent copper in his early twenties, someone who didn't look like he was on the force. With a grin, he'd said he knew the perfect candidate. And the young man who stood to attention in his stiff uniform seemed the part. Ungainly, still growing into his body. An innocent face with big brown eyes. Tall, with long limbs and scrawny arms. Nothing like a copper at all. Perfect.

'Did the sergeant explain why I wanted to see you?'

'No, sir. I don't think I've done anything wrong,' he blurted out.

Harper laughed. 'You haven't. Take a seat.'

He perched on the edge of the chair, keeping his back perfectly straight.

'How old are you?'

'Twenty-two, sir.'

'And how long have you been with us?'

'I joined when I was eighteen, sir.'

He had experience, he'd have seen a few things. 'Any ambitions? To work in plain clothes, maybe?'

'Yes, sir.' Sissons's face lit up and Harper had to hide his smile. Exactly the way he'd been at that age.

'You might just have your chance.' Time to see how clever the lad was. 'Sergeant Tollman says you're bright. Ever studied anything?'

Sissons blushed. 'I know it'll sound daft, sir . . .'

'Go on,' he said. 'Tell me.'

'I like to read Latin and Greek. My mam thinks I'm cracked.'

Hardly what he'd expected, but it could work well.

'Where did you learn?' Someone like Sissons wouldn't have been in school long enough to be taught any of that.

'From a book, sir.' He blushed again, the colour rising all the way to his forehead. 'And, well, night classes at the Mechanics' Institute. I like it, sir. Don't know why.'

Harper sat back in his chair. 'How would you fancy spending a couple of days at Yorkshire College?'

'Sir?' He sounded confused. 'I'd love it, sir. But why?'

The superintendent explained about the burglar and the connection to the college.

'I need you to go there and be sharp, keep your eyes and ears open. Look like you're part of the place. Poke around, ask a few questions. But do it carefully. Stay especially alert for any Geordies. We've no idea if our man is a student or works there. And for God's sake, don't let anyone know you're a copper. Can you manage that?'

Sissons nodded. His face was serious now, thinking about the possibilities.

'Yes, sir, I'd be glad to. How often do you want me to report in?'

'Every day. Sooner if you find something. We need to catch this man. It'll give you a taste of detective work. I'll make sure the college chancellor knows about you, so there won't be any problems.'

'Thank you, sir.' Sissons stood, gratitude all over his face. 'Really, thank you.' He saluted.

'Bring me some results as soon as you can.'

'I will, sir. I promise.'

As the door closed, Harper tried to recall the last time he'd seen a man so happy.

A note on Ash's desk: *Gone to see Cameron.* Well, he was more than capable of handling the grocer on his own. Perhaps he'd be able to dig some truth out of him.

It gave him time to put the final touches to the weekly crime figures. Do his divisional superintendent's duty.

A surprise; they were some of the lowest since he'd taken over the division. He checked the numbers once more, to be certain. What was behind it? It had to be this heatwave; the only possible explanation. Only one figure stood out. Murders. A pair of them. He was copying everything out in a good hand when Sergeant Tollman appeared in the doorway again.

'Sorry to bother you, sir, but everyone else is out. We've had a report just come in. A family back from holiday. They've been burgled. From the sound of it, your man's been at it again.'

Harper sighed. 'Give me the details.'

Most burglars were lazy; they took advantage of an open window or an unlocked door within easy reach. This fellow was someone special, someone different. By the look of it, he'd shinned three storeys up the drainpipe and edged along a roof, before swinging down to be able to enter through the second storey window that hung open now.

'They swear it was locked when they left last week, sir,' the constable said.

'They always do. What did he take?'

With the family gone, he'd have free rein of the place. No way of even knowing when it happened.

'Some jewellery. Money they had tucked away for an emergency. Not that much, really, sir.'

'Make sure you get good descriptions of the jewellery. We can circulate that.' He stood and stared at the back of the house. This burglar relished a challenge. In a curious way, it was impossible not to admire him. A climb like that took some courage. 'Talk to all the people in the area in case they saw something.'

'No lights back here at night. It's black as pitch,' the constable said. 'This is my beat, sir. I know every inch of it.'

'Nobody nosying around during the day?'

'I'd have noticed, sir.' He sounded offended. 'Or somebody in one of the other houses would have said something.'

'Ask them, just to make certain. You might jog a memory or two.'

'Yes, sir,' the man muttered.

Inside the house, he let the homeowner bluster and blow. Of course he'd made sure all the windows were closed before they left. You couldn't be too careful these days. Harper checked upstairs. The catch was so loose he could have blown it open. How could any burglar know that, though? He stared at the ginnel running behind the garden. Nothing you could spot from down there.

'What do you do, sir, if you don't mind me asking?' He was already quite sure of the answer. He just wanted to hear it.

'I have a private income.' The man sounded faintly embarrassed. 'And I lecture at Yorkshire College from time to time. Geology and natural sciences.'

'Thank you, sir.'

Young Sissons would need to be very quick off the mark. They couldn't take any more of this.

'What about the things that were taken, Superintendent? Some of those were my wife's keepsakes.'

'The constable will take all the details, sir. We'll do our best.'

FOURTEEN

Get Tollman to make sure Sissons puts his skates on, Harper thought. He hoped the lad was up to the job. But the expression on the desk sergeant's face pulled him up short.

'Inspector Ash wants you in Harehills, sir. As soon as you can get there.'

A hackney dash up Roundhay Road, the horse flecked with sweat as they darted through traffic in Sheepscar, galloping along the street until the driver pulled up at Harehills Parade. A bright sun burned down through the haze, but there was no striped awning in front of the grocer's today. Just a constable standing guard at the door and shopkeepers gathered round in their aprons, chattering to each other.

Harper barged his way through. The bell tinkled as he entered the shop. Inside, all the mix of scents overwhelmed him.

'Upstairs, sir.'

He went through the velvet curtain that separated the shop from the rest of the building and climbed the steps. The inspector was waiting by the door to a living room, his face grim.

'It's not pretty.'

Flies were buzzing everywhere. Hundreds of them, thousands. Cameron's face was black with them. They were in the blood spatters on the floor, on the fragments of skull and the jelly of his brain.

The room was hot, the air so close it drew his breath away. Already the body stank with decay.

'Open the windows. All of them.'

It hardly seemed to help. Even as he tried to wave them off, the flies gathered again. It was going to need a post-mortem to make sense of this and put it in any kind of order.

Harper gazed around the room. Cameron had overturned a small table as he fell. Nothing else was disturbed.

'Go through it all for me.'

'When I got here, a few of the other shopkeepers were outside,' Ash said. 'Cameron hadn't opened up this morning. They thought maybe he was poorly. A couple of them had banged on the door, but there'd been no answer. Two of them had seen him when he was closing last night.'

Not long after Fowler had taken the letters for the Smiths.

'Did they say how he looked?'

'Tired, that's all.'

'Scared?'

'Not that any of them mentioned. I forced the lock on the back door and came up. Once you get those flies off him, it looks like he's been beaten to death. I checked the letters he takes in. They're all gone, every single one of them.'

'Right,' Harper said. 'You're in charge here. I'll send some men out to help you.'

'Very good, sir.'

Harper stood in the office, staring at the map again. He'd added three more pins, all with red flags. One for Hester Reed, another for Jeb Pearce out in Roundhay. Now a third for Douglas Cameron.

His head ached. Dear God, what was happening here?

The telephone rang, the bell loud and shrill. Still staring at the map, he reached for the receiver.

'Tom? Have I caught you in the middle of something?' No mistaking that voice: Chief Constable Crossley.

'We've got another murder, sir.'

'So I've heard. And a burglary.' A small hesitation. 'I need you to drop by. I wouldn't ask, but it's quite important.'

That wasn't a word the chief used lightly.

'Of course, sir. I'll be there shortly.'

'Thank you.'

Too much traffic on the Headrow. He had to thread his way between vehicles as they crawled slowly along the road. The Town Hall clock read one as he climbed the steps, the stone lions glaring silently at him.

At least Crossley's office was hushed and cool, the windows open wide to look down on Great George Street.

'There's no point in beating around the bush,' the chief began. 'I had a deputation of councillors in here first thing this morning. They feel you're not doing a proper job at 'A' Division. They're demanding I replace you.'

Harper felt a weight in his gut, hard as a stone. From the summons, he knew something was coming. His mouth was dry, chest tight. He swallowed hard. He didn't want to ask the questions, but he had to know.

'How do they think I've failed, sir? And might I ask who they are?'

'They say you haven't caught this burglar, for one. I know this new burglary makes five so far. They seemed to believe you haven't done a thing about it. As to who, it's May, Howe, Wilson, Hart, and Thomas.'

Five of them. More than he'd anticipated. Too many.

'You know that Councillor May has no love for me, sir,' Harper said. 'I put his son in jail a few years ago.'

'I'm very well aware of that. I listened to them because I'm obliged to, Tom. Then I told them I thought you were an excellent policeman and I had no intention of dismissing you, or whatever it is they want.'

A flush of relief roared through him; he realized he'd been holding his breath.

'Thank you, sir,' he said gratefully.

'It's no more than the truth. I stand up for my officers. I'd be a poor leader if I didn't. I just want you to be aware they have their knives out. May and Howe are important figures on the council. Remember May's on the watch committee.'

'Not a chance of forgetting that, sir.'

'Don't put a foot wrong. That doesn't just mean wrapping up the burglaries soon. The murders, too. You said there was another.'

'I was just up at the scene.'

'I'd like a report on my desk in the morning. On everything, and what you're doing.' He stopped and offered a small smile. 'Watch yourself, Tom. I'll do everything I can for you.'

'Yes, sir.' Harper stood. 'And thank you again.'

In the corridor, he leaned against a marble column and gulped in air. Thank God for Crossley. Five of the bastards. May he could understand: the man would jump on any chance to bring him down. But the others? He didn't know them at all. Had May browbeaten them? Perhaps he had something on them; that was possible, given the way the man worked.

The chief was on his side, but there was an unspoken warning in his words, too – he could only do so much. The more May and his mob pressed, the harder it would become to defend him. So he'd better make sure the man had no ammunition.

Slowly, he went down the stairs, holding on to the bannister and feeling his legs shake a little. Halfway along, he stopped so suddenly that the man behind almost bumped into him.

Councillor Howe. Every bit as corrupt as May. He'd made his fortune in property. On the planning committee, shady deals involving his son-in-law. Property was at the heart of these killings. Maybe he just had a clearer idea who owned the North Leeds Company. He glanced at his pocket watch. He couldn't stop to think about that now. He needed to be at the mortuary.

'That's not one of the most pleasant bodies you've given us, Superintendent,' Dr King said.

It had been a sweaty, clammy walk over to Hunslet, a press of people crowding the bridge, bodies ripe from the day's warmth. After that, the chill of the mortuary felt like balm, the moisture cooling quickly on Harper's skin.

But his mind was thorny. The only link they had to the Smiths was dead, a group of councillors wanted his scalp, and maybe a few shadows were clearing.

'What killed him?'

'A blow to the back of his head,' Lumb answered. 'A very hard one. If it had been cricket, I'd say someone was aiming for the boundary. Smashed his skull. Death was very likely instantaneous. I don't believe he was expecting it. There was no indication he'd struggled.'

That matched what he'd seen in the room. He saw the doctors glance quickly at each other.

'You look like there's more. What is it?'

'Whoever did it broke most of the bones in the corpse's hands afterwards,' Lumb said. 'He stamped on them. I found heel prints on the skin.'

'Are you positive it was after death?' He remembered what they'd done to Jeb Pearce before they threw him into the quarry.

'According to the report, he was found above his shop,' Lumb said.

'That's right. Cameron lived there.'

'Superintendent, if those injuries had been done while he was alive, people would have heard his screams a hundred yards away.'

'I see.'

'The work on his hands was done for the sheer pleasure of it,' King added. 'I don't know who you're dealing with here. But between this and the quarry murder, I'd say he's a sadist.'

'They,' Harper corrected him. 'Two of them.'

'Then I wish you all the luck in the world in finding them,' King said. 'And I hope this is the last body you bring me, Superintendent.'

'Cameron's keys are missing,' Ash said. 'They must have taken them and locked the door behind themselves.' The windows in the office at Millgarth were wide open, but all they brought was thick, heavy warmth. 'They took their time, no doubt about that.' The inspector fanned himself with his hat. 'No robbery, though. The day's takings are still on the table. As if they're saying they don't need it.'

'Exactly the same as Hester Reed,' Harper said. 'They left the money and took the keys there, too, remember?'

'The sooner we find this pair, the better it's going to be for everyone, sir.'

'No doubt about that,' he agreed with a sigh. 'But with Cameron gone, how do we find them? Any ideas?'

Ash shook his head. 'I wish I did, sir.'

'Charlie Reed's suicide opened up a real can of worms. And if it hadn't been for Billy, we might never even have known anything about it. How can something like this go on and we don't have a clue?'

'It's an odds-on certainty that there are plenty of things happening under our noses and we don't have a clue. We can't stop what we don't know.'

'If people would tell us . . .'

'Come on, sir. Talking to a copper isn't the way for some of them. They're too scared, or they think they can take care of it themselves . . .' He shrugged. 'Getting these two off the street might help.'

'What about it, Mr Walsh? Are we any closer to them?'

'Honestly, sir, I feel like I'm banging my head against a brick wall. If we didn't know they were real, I'd think we'd made them up. The best I can come up with are rumours. Nobody knows a pair of brothers of that description. Doesn't matter what name you give them. The criminals haven't met them. No word back from other forces yet, but it's early days.'

'You all know what the inspector and I found today. These two love to hurt. If you get any leads on them, I don't want you pursuing it alone. They're too dangerous.' He paused. 'If there's one piece of good news, they've painted themselves into a corner. For the moment, they don't have an accommodation address for their companies. The Post Office is going to hold everything sent to Cameron's and let us know if any of those customers put in changes of address.'

'Easy enough for them to find somewhere else, sir,' Ash said.

'I've given orders for the men on the beat to visit every shop offering those services. If they try to find somewhere else, we'll know.' He looked at their faces. Worn, beaten down by work and heat. 'Go home, rest, sleep, if you can in this weather. We'll find something tomorrow.'

Ash lingered by the door after the others left.

'I put the word out about Nicholson to a few people I know, sir. Heard back from them today. I thought you'd like to know.'

Harper leaned against the desk. 'Go on. It must be good.'

Ash rubbed a hand across his moustache. 'He's a very clever chap, by all accounts. Left school at eleven, apprenticed as an engineer, got himself promoted. Then he invented some sort of process to improve the brakes on railway engines. I don't understand it.'

'Carry on.'

'Decided he could make more money if he had his own works. He'd married well and his father-in-law put up a lot of the money.'

'A lot?' He picked up on the words. 'Not all?'

'No, sir. That's where it becomes interesting. The rest came from Tosh Walker.'

Well, well, well. Walker was finishing up a sentence in Armley Gaol. He'd been given seven years for taking young girls and letting rich men abuse them. Another two years tacked on for fighting. Ash and his wife had adopted one of the little ones Tosh had snatched, and the police had torn his empire apart. When he was finally released, he'd come out to a pauper's life.

'How did he become involved?'

'I haven't discovered that yet. But Nicholson's business was successful. His main client was Hunslet Engine, and you know how big they are. Seems he had ambitions to expand at one time, but never followed through.'

'Why not?'

'No idea, sir. In the end, he received a very good offer for his works and sold up a couple of years back.'

'Any other criminal connections?'

'Mr Nicholson is a respectable gentleman these days. Tosh was paid back years ago.'

'And then the Smiths appear when Nicholson's looking to buy the quarry. He must attract bad company.'

'I thought you'd want to know, sir.'

'I do, thank you.' Curious, but did it mean anything? The boundaries between good society and crime grew more blurred every year.

'There's one other thing, sir. I hear a few of the councillors are gunning for you.'

Harper gave him a sharp look. He hadn't mentioned it to a soul. How could Ash know? The conversation with Crossley had been private. But he seemed to hear every whisper in the force.

'Not much point in me saying anything if you already know.'

'We're behind you, sir. All of us.'

'Have you told the others?'

'It only seemed fair.'

After a moment, Harper nodded. They were his men. They were all a part of this.

'I'd better tell you, sir, I'm looking into the gentlemen involved. Very, very quietly,' he added before Harper could protest. 'They'll never hear about it.'

'You'd better make sure they don't. It's making me think that perhaps May or Howe are behind this North Leeds Company.' He paused for a second. 'Maybe both of them.'

Ash grinned. 'I'll find out, sir. If they are, we'll nail them to the wall.'

Alone, Harper sat at his desk. The men were with him. That gave him heart. With help like that, he could beat May and his cronies. He picked up a nib, dipped it in the inkwell and took a sheet of paper. Time to write another note to Billy, then his report for the chief.

FIFTEEN

There was more paper as he walked through the door upstairs at the Victoria. Wadded into balls, tossed across the table, scattered over the floor. One blank sheet on the table surrounded by small, torn scraps of notes.

'What happened here?' Harper hung up his hat and started gathering everything.

'I'm trying to come up with these recommendations for the Guardians.' Annabelle sat at the table, a pen in her hand. 'The way things need change after the Redshaw case.'

'Not having much luck?'

She gave a deep sigh. 'I know what I want to say, but I can't make it come out right.'

'Give it time.'

She reached up and took his hand. 'The sooner the better, that's all. Before they forget about it.'

'I know you. You won't let them. What happened with that relief officer?'

'I read him the Riot Act. We'll see what happens there,' she said darkly. He pitied any man who felt the rough side of her tongue.

'What have you done with Mary?'

'She's over at Maisie's. Can you collect her and bring some fish and chips back? The time got away from me.'

'In a minute,' he said. That caught her attention. 'The chief called me in today.'

He told her about the councillors' demands, seeing her mouth set and her eyes harden. No mention of the North Leeds Company.

'I know men on the council, too.' Her eyes were blazing. 'So do you. If they want to push this, we'll see they have the devil's own fight on their hands.'

Harper smiled. 'I'm hoping it won't come to much. I just want you to be prepared.'

'May's as crooked as they come. Howe's not far behind. Who's going to listen to them?'

'They have influence. Anyway, no need to worry about it for
now. I just wanted you to be aware. In case . . .' Of what? Rumours,
innuendoes? Accusations?
'If anyone says a word, I'll bite their head off.'

It was an evening for play, not books. A light breeze was blowing;
still warm, but a good time to be outside, to feel it on his skin.
Collar and tie off, Harper walked up to Jews' Park with Mary, the
only open grass anywhere near the Victoria. As she ran and played,
he sat on a bench, watching and letting his mind wander until he
was aware of a shadow close by. Harper turned his head and saw
a smiling face.
'I was looking out of my window and I thought, that must be
Tom Harper.'
'Moishe. It's good to see you.'
He meant it. He'd grown up with Moses Cohen in the Leylands,
their old houses just a stone's throw away from here. Cohen was
broad around the waist now, his hair receding, eyes half-hidden
behind thick spectacles. He owned the tailor's shop on the other
side of North Street, running it with one of his sons, the large family
living in the rooms upstairs.
'You're looking well.' Cohen settled on the bench with a contented
sigh. 'Prosperous.'
'You look good, too.'
An eloquent shrug. 'I make a living.' He beamed. 'I'm a *zayde*
now.' A grandfather. 'Isaac and his wife have a girl. Rachel. Born
last month. Before all this heat.'
'Congratulations. That's Mary.' He pointed her out. 'Can you
believe she's seven now?'
'They grow so fast, my friend. Before we can even blink.'
It was true enough. Life changed, things slipped away. He only
lived a quarter of a mile from here, but this was the first time he'd
seen Moishe since . . . it had to be two years, when he'd ordered
a new suit.
'Business good?'
'Good days, bad days. Not like you. Always steady work.'
'Too steady.' Harper sighed. 'Long days.'
'But better than rolling barrels at the brewery?'
He laughed. That had been his job after he left school. Hard,

physical work for years, until he was old enough to apply for the force.

'Anything's better than that.'

'Not anything,' Cohen said quietly. 'Isaac is talking about enlisting if this war comes.'

'What? Why?' He couldn't begin to imagine that. Certainly not with a new baby.

'Says he wants to show that Jews are patriots, too. I told him he was just scared of being a father. If you want to be patriotic, I said, sew a few uniforms, don't go and die fighting Dutchmen in South Africa.'

'Is there anything I can do?'

'Bang some sense into him with your truncheon.' Cohen sounded weary to his core. 'I'm tired of arguing.'

Mary ran up, breathless. 'Da, Da, a boy over there took a ball from a girl so I made him give it back.' A rush of words that his hearing took a moment to follow. She was grinning, proud of herself. 'I said you were a policeman and if he didn't do it you'd arrest him.'

Harper heard Moishe begin to laugh; he couldn't stop smiling himself.

'That might not be the best way to do it,' he told her carefully. 'Do you remember Mr Cohen?'

'How d'you do, sir?' She gave a very quick curtsey, then dashed off again.

'A few more years and she'll be bringing boys home . . .' Cohen said.

'Don't remind me. I pity any lad who tries to take her on.'

He let her play a little while longer, then called her name. Time to go home. Moishe put a hand in his pocket, drew out a penny and solemnly presented it to her.

'For a young lady,' he said. 'But don't spend it until tomorrow.'

Wide-eyed, she nodded. 'I won't, sir. Thank you.'

'And you, Tom, come and see me. You're due a new suit and I have a cloth that will be perfect for you.'

'I promise. Look after yourself. And your son.'

Cohen clicked his tongue. They shook hands.

'One of the girls over there said their cat has just had kittens and she said we can have one when they're old enough if we like.' A torrent of words and a hopeful look.

He took a deep breath. 'Why don't you ask your mam in the morning?' With any luck, she'd have forgotten all about it by then.

Plenty of people were still promenading as Billy Reed and his wife strolled up Flowergate. She had her arm tucked through his, chattering away about the day at the tea shop. The takings were tucked away in a bag, ready to bank in the morning.

He let her talk, barely hearing what she said. He had too much on his mind. That morning, the night constable had reported a possible arson behind a shop on Baxtergate. Quick and crude; Reed had seen that immediately. He knew fires, he'd been an investigator with the Leeds brigade. This was amateur work, it had burned itself out before it could do any damage. But at the height of the season . . . that was enough to worry him. For now, though, he'd keep quiet. No sense in causing a panic yet.

They turned on to Silver Street, and the shade from the houses felt deliciously cool. Just right, he thought. A pair of girls were playing with a whip and top outside number seventeen, still wearing their school pinafores. Sisters, by the look of them; the same black hair and dark eyes.

He'd noticed them once before and never given them a thought; just two children. As they neared, the older one looked up and asked, 'Excuse me, sir, but are you from Leeds? Only someone told me you was, that you was a policeman.'

'That's right, luv.' It was Elizabeth who answered. 'We're both from Leeds. Have you been there?'

The girl glanced at her little sister. 'We're from Leeds, too. Only we live here now. Our ma died, and our pa couldn't keep us.'

'I'm sorry to hear that. I have children, too. How old are you?'

'She's seven, missus, and I'm ten. Eleven next week.'

'Do you like it in Whitby?' Reed asked.

'I think so,' the girl answered. 'We like to play on the sand and Mrs Lyth is good to us.' She gestured at the house behind her. 'But we've only been here a fortnight. We don't know no one yet.'

After their father couldn't keep them, they'd ended up in the Leeds Workhouse all through the winter and spring, the girl said. Then they'd been told that a woman would look after them and they'd been brought on the train to Whitby with three other children.

She gazed up and down the street. 'It's not like the Bank.'

Reed laughed. This was about as different as he could imagine. Good, clean air, clear skies, the sea in the distance. He looked at the pair, thinking that Annabelle might have helped make the decision to send them here; she was on the Board of Guardians. Still, they were better off in Whitby. There might be a future for them here.

'What are your names?' Elizabeth asked.

'I'm Catherine Bush,' the older one said. 'People call me Cathy, but I like Catherine better.' She smiled at her younger sister. 'She's Charlotte.'

'I'm Mrs Reed, and this is my husband.' She smiled down at them. 'You enjoy playing while you can.'

'Yes, missus. Thank you.'

In the house, Elizabeth unpinned her hat, looking thoughtful.

'Poor little things. It can't be easy for them, living somewhere new. That older one, she's sharp, isn't she?'

'Very,' he agreed.

'And if she's almost eleven, she'll be leaving school. She's going to need a job, and I could use a hand at the tea shop. What do you think, Billy?'

He grinned at her. 'It sounds like it was meant to be.'

A restless, prickly night. Harper fell asleep quickly, but as soon as he dropped off, the dreams began. People tumbling from the skies to land on jagged rocks that broke their bodies. Men chasing him as he tried to hide in the shadows. Every time, he'd jerk awake covered in sweat.

Finally, a little after four, he gave up and slid out of bed. The streets were silent as he walked to work, still too early for the knocker-up. The lights were on at Millgarth, but even in the police station there were the hushed voices of the small hours.

An early edition of the *Post* lay on the front desk: *Leeds Boils!* was the headline. After so many days of it, that hardly seemed like news. There'd be more of the same weather today. Saturday, payday, and men would be out drinking tonight. Tempers would spark. There'd be blood on the streets later, no doubt about it. The constables would have their hands full, and the cells would be packed with people.

But there was nothing he could do to change human nature.

His eyes felt gritty. In his office, Harper searched out the thin book that listed all the councillors, their addresses and responsibilities. Know your enemy. He'd read that somewhere; it seemed like an excellent idea. Howe was on the planning committee, of course. He'd probably arranged that himself. Two of the others who'd gone to the chief – Thomas and Wilson – served on there, too. How many pies did they have their fingers stuck in? Hart he knew; he was on the watch committee that oversaw the police. May's protégé, he'd do anything the old man wanted. And May himself . . . not just the watch committee, but also planning. Well, well, well. When had he forced his way on there?

For a moment, he considered writing a note to Crossley. No point: the man was an excellent politician as well as policeman. He'd already know exactly what every councillor did.

Harper sat back and stared at the map of Leeds he'd put up on the far wall. Pins for murder, pins for property. Plenty to bring in good rents for the North Leeds Company year after year as the building boom carried on sweeping through the city. More money to be made in putting up the houses. It took capital, but men like Howe weren't short of a few bob. He'd have been able to spend five thousand to acquire thirty-five shops. So would May.

He opened the book, checking the names again. Both May and Howe were lawyers, although God knew where they'd find the time to practise. They'd know how to hide ownership of places.

Arrest the burglar. Put the Smiths in jail. That would shut them up. Catching the Smiths would put the fear of God in them. But he was nowhere close to that.

May was dirty. It had been a joke for years, the envelopes changing hands, the favours done. And Howe was as bad, with his nepotism and the curious deals that tucked a few pounds in his pockets. Somehow, though, they'd remained untouchable. Time for that to change.

He needed evidence. Irrefutable proof. Easier said than done, especially with everything else going on.

A tap on the door. Harper glanced at the clock, surprised to see it was after six, the sun already high and hazy.

'Come in.'

Sissons, looking neat in his shirt and tie and carrying a leather attaché case that bulged with books.

'You look just like an eager student.'

'Yes, sir. Thank you.' The man gave a wide smile. 'I thought I'd blend in like this.'

'I'm sure you will. Have you learned anything helpful yet?'

'I'm still finding my feet, sir.' He gazed down, embarrassed by the admission. 'But I've had a chance to watch and listen a little.'

'Any candidates for the burglar?'

'Three that I've found so far.'

Three? That was more than he'd expected. 'Tell me about them.'

Instead, Sissons unlocked his case and brought out a sheet of paper, everything written down in a careful copperplate hand.

'I thought it would be easier this way, sir.'

'Very good.' He glanced at the report. Carefully put together. The man had been busy. 'I need you to be quick. There was another burglary. I'm sure you heard.'

'I did, sir.'

'We don't have the luxury of time.'

'Yes, sir. Of course.'

Harper picked up the constable's report. 'Now, what made you pick out these men?'

SIXTEEN

Another murder. Another bloody murder. He could hardly believe it. Billy Reed sat in his office, staring out of his window down to the River Esk. Harper's letter lay on the blotter, a brief summary of what Leeds police had managed to discover.

And here he was, miles away. No evidence, that was what Tom had written. No idea who the brothers were; nobody knew them. He could feel the frustration in the words. Three dead and they were getting nowhere.

All he could do was read about it in hurriedly written letters. Far off and helpless. He lit a cigarette and hoped today wouldn't bring another report of a fire.

'Did anyone whisper any secrets to you yesterday?' Harper asked.

'I wish to God they had, sir.' Walsh sighed. 'Just more of the same. Blank looks and people shaking their heads. These two might as well have dropped from the sky.'

'Well, we know that didn't happen. They started out somewhere. Anything back from the other forces yet?'

'We're still waiting to hear from a few, but none of them seem to know the Smiths by any name, sir.'

'I did some checking on older deaths in Harehills,' Ash said. 'There's only one that might be their doing. But people said the chap had a dicky heart for years.' He shrugged. 'Not a chance of proving anything.'

Brick walls everywhere.

'Pass the description Hester Reed gave us to all the beat bobbies. Let's see if that brings anything.' He didn't expect it would, but he was growing desperate.

'Yes, sir.'

'Cameron.' He turned to Ash. 'Any sign he had a close involvement with the Smiths?'

'Not that I've been able to dig up, sir. I told you about his past. Seems that once he passed his wild years, he applied himself to the grocery trade. Then his uncle lent him the money to buy a shop and he turned up in Harehills. Everything paid back, fair and square. Unless I've missed something, he was exactly what he appeared to be.'

Another possibility vanished. Every way they turned, they were stymied.

'Nicholson. We know how the brothers were aware of the quarry. But he had brushes with two lots of criminals . . . if I believed in coincidences, I'd call that unfortunate.'

'It could just be that, sir,' Fowler said. 'After all, they were years apart.'

'It's possible,' Harper agreed. 'But do some digging. You're good with papers and forms. Take a look.'

'Yes, sir.' He pushed the spectacles up his nose. 'I'll get on it.'

'Nicholson will be back from holiday tomorrow,' Ash said.

'I hadn't forgotten. I'm sure he'll be at the quarry Monday morning. We'll pay him a visit.' He glanced round the faces. 'You know what to do. This pair are leading us a merry dance. It's about time we made the music stop.'

*   *   *

He chafed. But there was nothing he could do out there that others weren't already handling, and he had responsibilities in the office. Rotas, leave requests. A constable came to see him fumbling over his words as he explained that he wanted to join the army and fight in South Africa. The chief was right: they'd need plenty of specials if they were going to keep Leeds safe. If not . . . he didn't want to think about that. It might not be his concern, anyway, if May and his friends had their way.

Out for his dinner. Not to the usual places, the cafe at the market or White's Chop House. Instead, he wandered over towards the grand offices of the assurance companies and banks, fanning himself with his hat as he walked. Into the Guildford, then the Green Dragon, finding the men he wanted off in the corners where they spent most of their days. You didn't last long as a detective without building a web of contacts. And you didn't rise in the ranks without people owing you favours. It was time to pull in a few of those. Quiet words over a drink, setting things in motion. Walking up the Headrow, he glanced back at the Town Hall. What did they think, that he'd roll over without a fight?

Saturday afternoon and town was packed. The work week was done, people shopped in the market, going up and down the streets and gazing at window displays. Saturday afternoon and still he had nothing. His men had been in and gone again. Not a word to report. Harper banged his hand down on the windowsill, so hard that the glass rattled in the frame.

The only ray of hope was Sissons and the people he'd identi-fied. Harper had telephoned Newcastle and spoken to a detective sergeant. But he'd just transferred from Carlisle; he didn't know anyone yet.

'I'll check, sir.' The smallest of hesitations. 'It might be Monday before I know anything. It's Blaydon races this weekend, and every-one's out there. We have a rash of pickpockets who work the track.'

No doubt they did. But it would be popular duty, too, a chance for a bet and a few drinks. He'd have to wait, and hope the burglar decided to take a few days off.

Then, finally, some good news.

'I stopped in at the Post Office.' Fowler was breathless, as if he'd run all the way. 'The Smiths put in a new address for their post.'

'Where?' Harper was already walking towards the door and reaching for his hat.

'Harehills Lane, right up towards the cemetery.'

The workhouse loomed large at the top of the hill. Over the years it had grown and grown. More building was going on as they passed, an addition to something or other, courses of bright red brick rising into the air.

The place they wanted lay just around the corner, a shop at the end of a terrace so new that the soot had barely touched it yet. The bell tinkled as Harper opened the door. A grocer, the same as Cameron and the Reeds, the same smells of spices and meat, the exotic and the familiar.

The couple behind the counter were older, probably man and wife. He was big, burly as a miner, a white moustache hanging over his top lip. She was thickset, her body heavy inside her gleaming apron.

'I'm Superintendent Harper with the police. This is Detective Constable Walsh.'

'Joe Mercer,' the man replied warily. 'This is my missus.'

They looked like a couple who'd spent their lives saving and scrimping for the dream of having their own business. Everything in the shop was pristine and exact. They had pride in this place.

'I understand you take in post for people.'

Mercer nodded. 'Doesn't bring in much, but some folks like it. It's not illegal, is it?' A hint of worry in his voice.

'Nothing like that, sir. Not to worry.' Harper smiled. 'We're interested in a new customer of yours.'

'Which one?' the woman asked. Her voice was a hard rasp. 'We only have a few so far.'

'The Harehills Development Company.'

'A lad came in yesterday,' Mercer said. 'Paid two months in advance.'

'How old was he?'

The man glanced at his wife.

'Young. Sixteen, seventeen, something like that,' she said. 'Trying to look like he was someone important in his suit. What's he done, any road?'

'It's the people who own the company that we're after,' Harper told them. 'Did he say when he'd come back to pick up the post?'

'Soon,' Mercer answered. There was real fear in his voice now. 'We only had the first delivery for them this morning.' He inclined his head towards a series of pigeonholes on the wall. 'What have they done?'

'Just of interest to our enquiries, sir.' It was safer if the man didn't know too much. 'Did the boy say if he'd be here today?'

'Didn't ask. We're open until late.' Most business came in the evening, after the workers had finished their shifts.

'I see. Excuse us a minute, sir.'

Outside, in the thick air, Harper looked around. Traffic moved up and down the road, carts plodding, the bell of the tram giving a warning as it moved along the rails.

'I want you to spend the rest of the day here. When that young man comes for the post, bring him in. If he doesn't show his face today, back here on Monday. Cuff him, haul him down to Millgarth. He's our best chance of getting to the Smiths.'

'Yes, sir.'

'From the look of those two, you won't need to lift a finger. They probably like everything just so. You'll be sitting in the back, drinking tea.'

Walsh grinned. 'Worse ways to make a living, sir.'

As he walked to the tram stop, Harper could feel the tingle in his fingers and the tightness in his chest. Very slowly, it was all beginning to move. Arrest that boy and they were on the way. Exactly the boost they all needed.

Harper stopped at Millgarth to check for any messages and put a quick shine on his boots. Couldn't turn up at King's leaving party looking like a ragamuffin. He'd just stuffed the polish into a drawer when he heard the timid knock on the door. Sissons. He'd been so full of the Smiths that he'd forgotten about the burglar. Damnit.

'Sorry to disturb you, sir, but I thought you'd want to know what I've found. I came by earlier but you were out.'

'Come in and sit down, Constable,' Harper said. 'And I hope you've got something good for me.'

'I might have, sir.' Sissons blushed brick red. 'I think so, anyway.'

He hadn't managed to identify any more Geordies, but he'd been able to discover more about the names he'd found.

'I don't know if you've been in the college, sir, but it's not that big, and it's empty on a Saturday afternoon. All the staff have finished for the week.'

'Only the students left.'

He nodded. 'Not too many of them and they're mostly in the library. So I could wander around a bit. I took a look in the office there.'

'Wasn't it locked?' Harper raised an eyebrow.

'Yes, sir.' Another, larger blush. 'I, ah . . .'

'Go on.' Was there a single copper who didn't have lockpicking skills? Just as well they were usually honest men.

'I had a chance to look through the files.' He unbuckled the attaché case and brought out two pieces of paper. 'I wrote this up from the notes I made.'

'Very resourceful, Mr Sissons.' He looked through. Two employees, one student. One of the men was almost fifty; he wasn't about to start climbing up drainpipes. That left a pair of possible candidates.

'You've had the chance to observe them all?' Harper asked.

'Only a little, sir.' He sounded wary.

'Have you gone through everyone? Even the cleaning staff? They can hear a great deal; no one ever notices them.'

Sissons stood at attention and lifted his chin higher. 'Even them, sir.'

'Is there one person who stands out to you?'

'Yes, sir. This man here . . .' He pointed to a name on the sheet. 'Carl Dunn. I'd say he fits the bill perfectly.'

'Excellent work,' the superintendent told him, already expecting the blush that came. 'I'm sorry to tell you, but your time at the college is over.' The lad tried to hide his disappointment, but he couldn't manage it. No matter; they had a lead to follow. 'However, from tomorrow you'll be working the case from this end. In plain clothes.'

'Sir?' He looked confused.

'You said you wanted to be in CID, didn't you?'

'Yes, sir, but—'

'Consider this a trial. Keep on doing a good job and you'll be a detective constable. No more money and longer hours. But you'll be working directly for me, and Mr Ash will teach you all you need to know. What do you say?'

'Yes, sir. Thank you.' He practically shouted his answer.

'Then report here first thing tomorrow.'

'Of course, sir. Thank you,' he said again.

At least one person would go home happy tonight, Harper thought. They were drawing closer to the Smiths. Now he could almost smell the burglar. Maybe Lady Luck had decided to smile on them for once.

At half past five, he walked down the stairs of Hunslet police station, into the smell of carbolic soap. This time, though, the rooms were crowded with the living, all there for Dr King's leaving party. Old faces and new, chattering away until Chief Constable Crossley presented King with a clock for his mantelpiece.

Harper slid out. It would carry on for hours yet, everyone drinking and talking, and he was in no mood for a celebration. Too many things pressed on his mind. By seven he was home, wearily climbing the stairs at the Victoria and opened the door to the sitting room. He stopped. Annabelle was on the settee, head in her hands, shoulders moving up and down as she sobbed quietly.

'What is it?' He came and wrapped his arms around her. 'Where's Mary? Is she all right?'

She sniffled, trying to smile as she took a handkerchief from her sleeve and wiped her eyes.

'She's fine. I left her over at Maisie's. I asked if they'd look after her for a while.'

'Has anything . . .? You look . . .' Lost, he thought. Yet there was something else, too. Happiness. He couldn't make head nor tail of it.

'I needed to make a few calls this afternoon.' It was something she'd begun when she was first elected as a Guardian, checking on those in the ward who were receiving relief. 'Ellen was out, so I took Mary with me.' She took a breath and rubbed her red eyes again.

'Go on.' He kept a tight hold of her, as if she might vanish if he let go.

'The last stop was Mrs Perkins. She has three daughters, the oldest is just Mary's age. Husband ran off as soon as the youngest was born. The house is always bare, and they might as well be wearing rags. But she's doing her best by those girls. Mary played

with them while we talked. When we got back here . . .' Her voice
faltered. 'She said, "Mam, they don't have any toys, do they?" Went
into her room and came back with one of her dolls. Marched me
down there and handed it over, solemn as you please.'

'All off her own bat?'

She nodded. 'I swear, I didn't say a word. You know, Tom, I
didn't think I could love her any more than I do, but . . . I just
needed to be on my own and have a little cry.' Annabelle gave a
wobbly smile. 'Must be going soft in my old age.'

He didn't say anything. He was just a copper who tried to do a
good job, a father who did his best to love his family. Behaviour
like that was all Annabelle's influence, everything she'd taught their
daughter. Mary was going to grow into a remarkable woman. By
God, he was a lucky man.

Later, after they'd walked down hand-in-hand to collect their
daughter, Annabelle said: 'I had a letter from Elizabeth Reed this
morning.'

'I remember Aunt Lizzie,' Mary said.

'I'm sure you do, all those cakes she fed you when we were in
Whitby,' Harper said, ruffling her hair. 'How's her business?'

'Rushed off her feet, she says. She dropped a note because she
met two of our girls.'

'Our girls?' What did she mean?

'From the workhouse,' Annabelle explained. 'Turns out they're
boarded out just down the street from her and Billy.'

'I had no idea you sent them that far.'

'It's a church group that arranges it. Two sisters. Made me think
of Ada and Annie Redshaw.'

Too late for them to go anywhere. He squeezed her hand.

'The older one's set to leave school,' Annabelle continued. 'Elizabeth was asking about her, to see if she should take her on in the
tea shop. I'll check the records on Monday. Small world, though,
isn't it?'

'Sometimes,' he said. 'And sometimes it seems huge.'

'Had a bad day?'

'A very frustrating one. We might have had a break, though.'

Soon, he thought, willing the telephone to ring with news. Let
it happen very soon. Get that lad down to Millgarth and let the dam
break.

'You can play with me, Da,' Mary told him. 'That will make you feel better. Mam says it always works for her.'

'Don't you be so forward,' Annabelle told her. 'Maybe he just wants to relax.'

But Harper was already on his feet, moving around the table and roaring like a monster. A few seconds later he was chasing his daughter across the room as she laughed. It always worked; she was right.

SEVENTEEN

Sunday morning and Leeds was quiet as he walked from Sheepscar. Barely six and already the day had some heat. Would this weather ever break, he wondered.

'I take it the lad never showed,' Harper said to Walsh.

'No, sir. I waited until they closed.' But he had a broad smile on his face.

'Back there on Monday.'

'I will, sir. I think you'll be pleased, though. We've finally got a line on the Smiths.' No wonder Walsh was grinning, Harper thought. 'It came through first thing. I heard back from a copper in Manchester with a good memory.'

'Let's hope it's worthwhile.'

'Oh, it is, sir. This sergeant had dealings with them when they were still juveniles. You won't believe it, but their names really are Jack and John Smith.'

Harper shook his head; sometimes truth was a damned sight stranger than imagination. But he could feel it, the tide was definitely beginning to turn. 'Juveniles?'

'In and out of trouble more or less from the moment they could walk was how he put it,' Walsh said. 'By the time they were fourteen or fifteen, they were big lads and there was plenty of intimidation and violence involved. The thing was, he told me, they were clever with it. Not school clever, they left when they were nine. But their brains worked, if you know what I mean.'

Harper nodded. That fitted with what they knew.

'When I told him what they were up to now, this copper was

impressed, but he wasn't surprised. He arrested them when they were eighteen. Protection racket. One shopkeeper had enough of it and came forward. When the Smiths found out, they beat him up. But they did it right as a couple of constables were coming along. Ended up doing three years. He's going to send us photographs.'

Those would be useful for identification. Circulate them to every man on the beat.

'What about since their sentence?'

Walsh shook his head. 'He heard they left Manchester after they were released, but he doesn't know where they went.'

'How long ago was that?'

'Eight years, sir.'

'And they seem to have come up for air here a year or so ago.' Harper tapped his pen against the blotter. 'We need to fill in that gap.'

'I'll do what I can, sir.'

Walsh left the office. But Fowler remained.

'You look like you have something on your mind.' Harper sat back in his chair. 'Is something wrong?'

'No, sir,' the sergeant began, then halted. 'That is . . . you've read about what's going on in South Africa.'

'I know, war's coming, and very soon by the look of it. I don't see what that has to do with us.'

'Well . . .' Fowler started again. He looked nervous, unsure of himself.

'You might as well spit it out.'

'A friend of mine is in the army, sir. Has been for years. A clever bloke, been promoted a few times. He's offered me a job.'

A job in the army?

'He wants you to be a soldier?' He couldn't picture Fowler on parade or traipsing through the bush with a rifle.

'No,' the sergeant replied quickly. 'That is, yes. But it's not what you think. He's in intelligence. Reckons I'd be a big help to them.' His face reddened with pride. 'I'm good with crosswords and codes and things like that, you see, sir.'

This was the last thing he'd expected. But a conversation like this could only mean one thing.

'I take it you're going to accept his offer.'

'Yes, sir, I'd like to.'

Harper exhaled slowly. This was the very worst thing that could happen now. 'I can't say I'm happy to see you go. I'm sure you know that. We have a good squad.'

'We have, sir.'

'But if this is what you want . . .'

'It's the challenge, you see. I might not have another chance like it.'

'Of course.' He was still a young man, he wanted to test himself. That was understandable. Just a shame he didn't feel he could do it here.

'Like I said, sir, it's only for the duration.'

How many men had said that over the centuries? And how many of them had returned?

'Then you have to go.' Off to serve Queen and country, how could he say anything different? 'When do they want you?'

'As soon as possible, sir.'

'I'd be grateful if you'd stay until we catch the Smiths. I need you for that. We're getting closer. You heard Walsh.'

Fowler smiled. 'I'll be glad to do that, sir. I want to see it wrapped up, too.'

They stood and shook hands.

'Just one thing,' Harper said. 'Make sure you come back safe.'

'I plan on it, sir. Thank you.'

After the door closed, he sat and clenched his jaw. Dammit. He had good men, the best he'd ever known. Why did this bloody war have to come along and change it all?

'Well, Mr Sissons, how was your first day as a detective constable?' He'd paired the man with Ash, digging into their burglary suspect.

'Very good, I think, sir.' He stood to attention. Fingertips pressed against the side of his trousers, staring straight ahead.

'You can relax. There's no need for that in here. We're not formal.'

'Yes, sir.' He didn't move. Never mind, the lad would learn in a day or two. He'd been the same at the beginning, wanting to obey every rule to the letter.

'What have you discovered about our friend?'

Ash took over. 'We went through to see if he had any record here or in Newcastle, but he's clean. Found out where he's living and went for a stroll round the area. Woodhouse, not far from the college. Decent digs. He's married, his wife grew up in Leeds.'

That might explain the pull here, Harper thought.

'There's more, isn't there? You have that look in your eye.'

'He's a member of a climbing club, sir.' The sentence gushed out of Sissons's mouth.

'I'd say that makes him a very likely candidate, wouldn't you?'

'Yes, sir.'

'What does he do at the college?'

'A clerk, sir. He has access to plenty of information and talk in the office.'

'And how old is he?'

'Twenty-nine.'

'Very good. His name's Carl Dunn, I think you said?'

'That's right, sir. He and his wife rent rooms on Raglan Road.'

'Let's dig up everything we can on her, too.' If this man was the burglar, his wife had to be involved.

'Very good, sir.'

'What do you think of him?' Harper asked after Sissons had gone and the door was closed.

'A natural when it comes to finding information, sir,' Ash told him. 'Just point him in the right direction and let him go. Like one of those clockwork toys the children enjoy so much.'

'That's a start. How is he on the rest?'

'He's been on the beat for four years, remember, sir. If he can survive that, this should be simple.'

'Let's see how he does on the burglar.'

Annabelle hurried out of the kitchen as soon as he walked into their rooms, a jubilant smile on her face. Mary stood behind her, strawberry jam smeared around her mouth.

'That bobby of yours, Cartwright. He came through for me. Sent a message this morning.'

'He found the Redshaw woman?'

'Not even a mile from where it all happened.' She turned and saw Mary. 'Honestly. The state of you. Go and wash that off your face. We were making a cake,' she explained. 'Someone decided the filling would be just as good inside her.'

'It's excellent news about the woman.' No surprise, though. Cartwright probably went through everyone he knew until he found her. Annabelle had that effect; her passion infected people so they were eager to help. 'When are you seeing her?'

'Already have.' She folded her arms. 'Juliana Cooper.'

Juliana. A fancy name. But those cost nothing, about the only thing in this world that didn't. A hope for fortune and grandeur. He knew how often that worked, though; he'd seen too many Augustinas, Marguerites and Florentines who didn't have two brass farthings to rub together.

'Did she give you her side of the story?'

Annabelle's mouth turned down, the triumph gone in a flash. 'Poor woman looks like she's been trying to drink herself to death since it happened. Mr Cartwright found her in a doss house. Penny a night and you can guess what that gets you.'

He didn't need to; he knew. As low as anyone could go, short of sleeping in a doorway.

'In a bad way?'

She nodded. 'Did you know she left her husband and kiddies for Redshaw? After his wife died and he needed someone to look after his daughters. She gave up her own children for those girls.' He could hear her disbelief. 'She loved those lasses, Tom. Him, too, come to that, though God knows why. He wouldn't stop boozing and gambling, even after they lost their room. She used to take in washing so she'd have money to feed Ada and Annie. Then she hurt her arms and couldn't do it any more, and he still wouldn't hand over his pay packet.'

Another man who couldn't see beyond himself. He'd arrested dozens of them when he was on the beat. Maybe two of them had eventually changed their ways.

'She was at the end of her rope when she threw them out,' Annabelle continued. 'She had a ha'penny left and he was jingling the coins in his pocket.' She stared at him. 'Now she blames herself, of course. Always women who carry the guilt, isn't it?'

Redshaw would hang for what he'd done; Harper had no doubt about that. But this woman would have to live it all over and over, every single day. That was a worse sentence, with no reprieve.

'What did you do?'

'I listened, then I hugged her and gave her two shillings.'

'She might just drink it away.'

'That's her choice, isn't it?'

Mary came out of the bathroom, her face clean and bright, and

Annabelle put on a wide, brittle smile. 'You look better,' she said.
'I suppose you'll want some cake with your tea, too.'

'We baked it,' Mary reasoned. 'That means I worked, so I've
earned some. It's like my wages.'

God help them, Harper thought and looked at his wife again,
seeing the grief just below the surface. God help them all.

Monday morning and the seagulls were crying loudly; the fishermen
must be home with their catch.

'There's a letter for you,' Reed said as he picked up the post
from the mat. 'It looks like Annabelle's writing.' One for him, too,
from Tom Harper.

Elizabeth hurried through from the kitchen, pinning her hat in
place on her hair, and slit open the envelope.

'Oh, that's lovely,' she said with a wide smile. 'She says Catherine has excellent reports for conduct and classes.' She folded
the paper into her reticule and kissed him on the cheek. 'I need
to hurry and open up.'

As the door closed behind her, he read the letter from Tom.

> *Dear Billy,*
> *I wish I could say we were on the verge of arresting the
> Smiths. We don't even know how to find them. I'm positive
> they're guilty of another murder – Cameron the shopkeeper.
> We talked to him, I'm sure you remember.*
> *Everything has become more complicated as I look into who
> really owns all these properties. I don't want to put anything
> on paper, but it will be tricky to prove anything against the
> people I suspect. They have a lot of influence.*
> *I shall let you know when we're close to an arrest, if you
> want to be here. After all, without you, who knows when we'd
> have found out about any of this?*
> *Tom*

He definitely wanted to be there. The sergeant was back from
holiday now. Surely the chief constable would grant him a couple
of days' leave for that. First, though, he needed to find his arsonist.
No more fires, but always the worry of another that might do some
serious damage.

Five minutes alone with each of the brothers to see how tough they really were. He thought he'd left that part of himself behind, but . . . this was different. This was family.

Monday morning and the streets were bustling. A soft, hot breeze from the south had sprung up overnight. It fluttered the papers on Harper's desk. He glanced at the clock again. Just two minutes since the last time he'd checked. The day was crawling along.

The photographs had arrived from Manchester. One of each brother, taken when they were charged twelve years before. He had them on his blotter, his eyes coming back to stare at them. Smooth, youthful faces, still too young to shave properly. But there was hatred and anger in their eyes, and behind that, the spark of intelligence. Dark hair, the light glinting off the pomade. A dangerous pair.

Later today he'd have copies made and given to every copper on the beat.

Harper was hungry, but not about to leave the office in case Walsh came back with the Smiths' lad. Instead he tried to work, forcing himself to concentrate, head jerking up every time he heard a door close.

But it was Ash who returned first, close to three o'clock, wiping the back of his neck with a handkerchief.

'Still very close out there.'

'I'll be glad when this summer's finally over,' Harper said. 'Happier still when we have a few people in the cells.'

He was desperate for results. Something concrete. Putting men in the dock would keep the council wolves at bay. He was about to say more when the door crashed open and a young man wearing handcuffs stumbled in, Walsh right on his heels.

'Brought you a present, sir. A pity he didn't really like his invitation, though. Called me all manner of names on the way here.' He pushed the lad on to a chair. 'You bloody well stay there.'

The boy stared at him, defiance bright in his eyes. He had a handsome, mobile face, spoiled by a flame of red spots across his cheeks. He took in the room, gaze resting for a moment when he saw the map and understood what it represented.

'What's your name?' Harper asked.

'In't done nothing wrong, have I?'

'I don't know. Have you?' He brought his face close enough to smell the sourness on the lad's breath. 'I asked your name.'

'John Brown.' He smirked.

'Is that right? Let's turn out your pockets and see if you can prove that.'

He struggled, but with Ash gripping his shoulders, he never had a chance. A comb, some change, and an empty wallet.

'Right, Master . . . Brown. It has to be master, you're nowhere near twenty-one.' He nodded at Walsh, who left the room. 'Who do you work for?'

'You already know, don't ya?'

'Tell me, anyway.'

'The Harehills Development Company.' He held his head straight. With his hair cropped close, the light glinted off his scalp.

'What do you do there?'

'This and that. Filing, collect the post.'

'An office boy.'

The boy tilted his chin. 'I'm working my way up.'

'Who are your bosses?'

'Two of them. Brothers, in't they?'

'Name?'

'Smith.'

Harper sighed. He walked round behind the lad and took hold of the chair, swiftly jerking it back on two legs as Brown's cuffed arms flailed helplessly. No pussyfooting. No wasting time. He wanted some answers. Further and further, until the boy was staring straight up at him and gulping.

'Let's get this straight. I've brought you in here to give me some answers. And you're going to be happy to cooperate. Yes, sir, no sir, three bags full, sir. Do you understand?' Harper let the chair fall another inch, staring at the young man, keeping his voice steady. 'Do you?'

The boy nodded quickly, face on the edge of panic.

'What's your name?'

'Mark Walker,' he replied after a moment.

'Very good, Mark. If you work, there's an office. Where is it?'

'It's not—'

'Where?' A sudden jerk, the chair was upright, then back again. 'I thought we agreed you were going to cooperate.'

'Barrack Road. Across from the barracks.' He swallowed hard, looking as if every word hurt him.

'Were they there when you left?' No answer. He let the chair tip a little more. 'Were they?'

'Yes.'

'And what do you know about them?'

'Nowt.' He shouted the word. 'I just take care of the office, like.'

'Has he mentioned his previous yet, sir?'

Harper turned his head. He hadn't heard Tollman enter. The old sergeant filled the doorway.

'No. He must have forgotten that.'

'Mark Walker. Three months for stealing a woman's bag. We know his uncle, sir. He's related to Tosh.'

'Is that right?' The second time Tosh's name had come up. Once with Nicholson and now with the Smiths. 'The apple doesn't fall far from the tree, does it?'

'Me laddo here absconded before he'd finished his sentence,' Tollman said. 'Very lucky you found him.'

'Mark, Mark . . .' Harper shook his head. 'And here you are, back to enjoy Her Majesty's pleasure again. I'm sure they'll want to keep you a while longer this time, until you really feel at home.' He rocked the chair back and forth, letting it teeter on two legs before steadying it again. 'Now, do you want to tell us about the Smiths?'

It was property. That was all Walker knew. The brothers were hard cases. He liked that, they didn't take any guff. But he didn't understand about the business, the ins and outs of it, and they didn't even try to explain.

'Who put up the money for everything?' Harper asked. He tried to make the question sound casual.

'Don't know, do I?' Walker answered, and it sounded like the truth. The cockiness had vanished from his voice. He was scared now, hunting around for a way out. Anything at all.

'Whose names have they mentioned?'

'No one's. Not when I'm around. I just do the little jobs for them.'

'Where do they live, Mark?'

He shook his head. With each minute, he seemed more and more like a child.

'Dunno. They never told me.'

'Take him down to the cells. We'll hand him over later.'

The lad opened his mouth to speak, then closed it again. Not an ounce of fight left as Walsh led him away.

The others were waiting in the office.

'Barrack Road,' Harper said with a smile. 'Gentlemen, shall we?'

Three of them, armed with truncheons, squeezed into the small police wagon alongside two hulking bobbies.

'Park down on Roundhay Road,' Harper ordered the driver. 'I don't want them to see us coming.'

At the barracks, a platoon of soldiers was marching up and down on the square as a sergeant roared out his orders. On the other side of the street, buildings had gone up higgledy-piggledy. Small shops and anonymous fronts.

The one they wanted stood on its own, small, squat and worn, the blind lowered in the front window. The superintendent gave his instructions, waiting for everyone to get in place, front and back doors covered.

Harper could feel his heart beating too fast, thumping loudly in his chest. So close. Put the Smiths behind bars and everything would crumble. He knew they wouldn't go without a fight; he'd seen the damage they'd done to Jeb Pearce and Douglas Cameron. Go in swift and hard. That was what he'd told his men. Don't give them a chance.

'Should all be ready now, sir,' the uniform said.

Harper nodded, brought the whistle to his lips and blew. Shoulders battered against the doors, a crack as the wood gave, then flew wide open.

He rushed in, truncheon raised and ready. Just a single room with three desks. Empty. No staircase, nowhere to hide. And no bloody Smiths.

His knuckles were white. He panted, disappointment flooding through his body. Harper walked around, touching the walls, the chairs, the papers. Close enough to taste them. To smell them. But they weren't here. *They weren't bloody here.*

'They've got the luck of the Devil, sir,' Ash said.

'Looks like they have.' The constables were standing by the door, waiting for orders. Walsh was leafing through documents.

'We have their whole business here, sir. Looks like everything.'
'Pack it up and take it all back to Millgarth,' Harper told him.
'Let's ruin their week. If they want to complain, they can come
down and see us.'

Outside, he leaned against the wall to catch his breath. He could
leave the others to do the donkey work. At least they could shut
down this office; that was something. A start. But not enough.

The soldiers on guard duty at the barracks were staring, caught
by the whole scene. Harper marched across the street and showed
his identification.

'Did you see two men leaving before we arrived?'

'About a quarter of an hour ago, sir.' The private stood at attention, eyes sharp, voice clear and deep. 'Locked up and strolled off
that way.' He pointed towards Chapeltown Road. 'Have they done
something?'

'Suspicion of murder.' He waited a moment, letting the words
sink in as the soldiers stared at each other. 'I need to see your
commanding officer.'

Everything was quickly arranged. Two bobbies would keep watch
on the office from the gatehouse, ready to run out soon as the Smiths
returned. If they needed help, the soldiers would wade in. There'd
be no escaping from that.

Back out on the road, Harper began to walk, Ash at his side. He
needed to think, to work off his frustration. He'd come so close to
having them. But not close enough. Not yet. Down on Roundhay
Road he was tempted to go home to the Victoria. Instead, he turned
in the other direction.

It was as if nothing bad had ever happened at the quarry, no body
ever found on all the chips and fragments of rock. The shank of a
warm afternoon and workers were hammering and chiselling at stone,
walking casually over the ground where Jeb Pearce had lain dead a
few days before. Harper stood at the gate, taking in the scene.

A pair of men came out of the hut. Waters, the foreman, with a
sheaf of papers in his hand. Next to him, someone prosperous, who
listened and then pointed towards the cliff. Nicholson, it had to be.
Back from holiday and checking on his business. Waters spotted
the policemen and leaned towards the other man, speaking softly.
A nod, then the fellow came forward.

'I'm Nicholson.' A quick handshake and introduction. He was wearing a well-cut tweed jacket and plus fours, socks and stout boots. Hardly fashionable, but practical for a place like this.

'I know Inspector Reed talked to you in Staithes, sir, but we'd like to ask a few more questions,' Harper said.

'Of course.' His face was serious, full of concern. 'As I said to him, it's a terrible business.' He led them towards the far corner of the quarry, away from the rock face, into a small clearing hidden by the shade of some trees. Away from the sun, the air felt cooler and fresher. A hint of breeze made the leaves shudder.

'The men come down here to eat their dinner,' Nicholson said. 'We won't be disturbed.' He took a deep breath and exhaled slowly. 'How can I help you? I told the inspector everything I know last week. But I'm happy to do whatever I can.'

Nicholson looked as if he hadn't slept well for the last few nights. Rumpled, strain showing on his face, dark circles under his eyes.

'We're looking for information on the Smiths, sir. You've dealt with them.'

'I have. I told Inspector—'

'Reed, yes.' Harper produced the photographs of the Smiths. 'Is this a good likeness?'

'Close,' he said after he inspected it. 'They're older now, but yes, it is.'

'How were your dealings with them?'

'They were business-like, seemed to know what they were about,' Nicholson said after a little thought. 'They came out and inspected the quarry. I told Inspector Reed, though, it all came to nothing. They wanted too great a return on their money.'

'Did the negotiations advance enough for you to learn where they bank, by any chance?'

'Yes.' Nicholson looked surprised by the question. 'Beckett's, the same as me. Why?'

'Just more information, that's all. And the address you have for them is the grocer on Roundhay Road?'

'That's right. The inspector seemed to know all about it.'

'We all do, sir,' Ash told him. 'The grocer was called Cameron.'

'Yes, I've seen the sign.'

'Someone killed him.'

'I see.' His face grew pale. 'Was it . . .?'

Harper nodded. 'We're certain it was. That makes him their third victim.'

'Tell me what I can do to help you,' Nicholson said.

'Who put you in contact with the brothers?'

'I was looking for a loan to buy this business. The banks had refused, they thought it was a risky venture. A friend of mine told them about it.'

'Who was that, sir?'

'David Howe, the councillor.'

Councillor Howe. Well, well. Another link. Harper made sure his face showed nothing.

'How did he come to know them, sir?'

'I've no idea. I never asked.'

'When you were starting out with your engineering works, I believe you had an investment from Tosh Walker.'

Nicholson reddened. 'Everything was above board. I had no idea he was . . . who he was. I paid him back, and that was the end of it.'

Harper smiled. 'I'm sure it was fine. How did you come to him?'

'Through a friend of my father-in-law, actually. Another councillor. Mr May.'

'Thank you, sir.' Howe, May, the Smiths. Like a web. He needed to find the brothers and drag the truth out into the daylight. 'We'll catch them, I promise you that. But in the meantime, if there's any contact from the Smiths, tell us. You can telephone me at Millgarth.'

'What did you make of that?' Harper asked as the tram rattled through Harehills.

'I think we need to dig deeper into our friends on the council, sir,' Ash said. 'Much deeper.'

'What did you do with everything you took from the Smiths' office?' he asked Walsh. The station was busy with the shift change, the night men assembling, the day patrol looking relieved as they went off duty.

'That empty room at the end of the corridor, sir. There's a ton of papers.'

'Let's hope they tell us something.'

'We should know all about their dealings by the time we've finished. Fowler's looking at everything right now. I'm going to give him a hand. Doesn't get them under lock and key, though.'

'Soon,' Harper said as Walsh left. He prayed he was right.

'You've heard what Fowler's going to do?'

Ash nodded. 'I tried to dissuade him, but his mind's made up.'

'Maybe this war won't last long.'

'That's what they say about every one of them, sir. And they're always wrong.'

'We're going to need a sergeant.'

'Walsh is ready for promotion,' Ash said.

He considered the idea. The young man had learned a great deal in two years. He had a strong eye for detail, and his initiative had grown.

'Yes,' Harper said. 'Do you think Sissons can cut the mustard after we wrap up the burglaries?'

'I like him. A little while in here should toughen him up.' Ash grinned. 'I can take him under my wing.'

'That's all settled, then.' Easily and simply. About the only thing that was likely to be.

EIGHTEEN

The rooms above the pub were stuffy, no breeze at all. Harper heard a loud voice from downstairs in the bar, a man on the verge of anger, and he tensed, ready to go and help. A few seconds and it faded away; Dan was in control of things.

He leafed through the paper. More articles on South Africa. Crossley was right, it was inevitable now. Everything was in motion and no one wanted to stop it. Britain needed its battle. Posters had gone up around the city, urging men to volunteer as special constables. If enough came forward, they'd be fine. Surely, the fighting couldn't last too long. A trained army against an unorganized group of Dutch farmers? Maybe Ash was wrong and it really would be over in a few months.

Before coming home he'd gone back to the pubs he'd visited a couple of days before. More hushed words in quiet corners, tiny nuggets of information. May's brother ran a building supply company; Howe was their biggest customer. He also bought most of his stone from Nicholson. It was like a club where everyone knew everyone else and traded favours. But no mention of any North Leeds Company.

'You've been quiet all evening,' Annabelle said.

'Thinking,' Harper told her. 'These cases. And Fowler's told me he's joining the army.' He almost spat the word.

'A soldier? Him?' she asked in amazement.

'In intelligence. They approached him, he says.'

'You've always known he was bright as a button.'

'Doesn't make losing him any easier. I might have found someone to bring along, but . . .'

'You'll have to break them in to your ways?' Her mouth curled into a grin.

'Something like that,' he laughed. Sissons impressed him. He was bright, resourceful, very observant. But no one could be a proper replacement for Fowler, and the lad would need to grow up quickly. 'Anyway, you haven't had much to say, either.'

'Same as you.' She shrugged and pushed herself off the settee and fanned herself. 'I'll make us some lemonade.'

He followed her into the kitchen, watching as she deftly squeezed the lemons, adding water and sugar to the jug. A quick taste and a nod before she poured glasses for them both.

'Would you take a look at something for me?' she asked.

'Of course. What is it?'

'A few ideas that might stop anything like Ada and Annie Redshaw happening again.'

She produced some folded papers from the pocket of her dress. Almost shyly, he thought. That wasn't like her. He read as he sipped the drink. They were good proposals, he thought. Some of them very good. But . . .

'Do you think the Guardians will go for all this?' he asked once he'd finished. A few of the suggestions were quite radical. Harper had seen the staid old men who made up most of the board. He couldn't see them backing this. Especially if it came from a woman.

'As it stands?' Annabelle asked. 'Not a chance. There are two or three who hold a lot of influence, though. I thought maybe I could

sweet talk them a little . . .' He stared at her and she reddened. 'I
know,' she told him. 'I *know*. I don't like it. But if a little flattery
and flirting can get them to support this, it's worthwhile, isn't it?'

'For the greater good.'

'Quoting philosophy at me now, Tom Harper? But yes, I suppose
that's it. For the children. They're the ones who matter.'

'Then do it.' He wrapped her in a hug. 'I'm so proud of you.'

'I haven't done anything yet.' She picked up the papers and
stuffed them back in her pocket. 'It might all fall flat.'

'It won't.' If it did, she'd have tried. And she'd try again.

'Did I tell you I dropped Elizabeth Reed a letter? She'd been
asking about that girl. Catherine Bush.' It took him a second to
remember who she meant: the one from the workhouse who was
boarded in Whitby. 'I told her she ought to give her a job. Good
reports all the way through. It's her sister who's always been a bit
of a problem, apparently.'

'What—' he began, but the harsh bell of the telephone cut
him off.

'It'll be for you,' she told him. After dark, who else?

The duty sergeant's deep voice boomed through the wires. 'I'm
sorry to bother you, sir, but Mr Ash says you're needed urgently.'

Harper felt the hair prickle at the back of his neck. 'Where?
What's happened?'

'Someone's tried to rob Mr Nicholson. The inspector said you'd
know who that was.'

'I do.' Thoughts and questions were already pouring through
his head.

'He's shaken up but not badly hurt. At the infirmary—'

Harper cut him off. 'Send a hackney for me.'

'He's with the doctor now, sir.'

Ash met him at the front door of the hospital, and they strode
through the corridors. They both knew the place too well, footsteps
echoing off the walls as they walked, the grim, harsh stink of carbolic
catching at the back their throats.

'Are we certain it was a robbery?'

'Looks like it, sir,' Ash replied after a small hesitation. 'Or it's
meant to. Wallet gone, watch and chain, gold tie pin.'

'Any injuries?'

'I only had a glimpse, but he doesn't look too bad. The beat constable was called to a disturbance in a ginnel off Swan Street, the one that leads through to the old courts. Nicholson was on the cobbles. According to his report, people heard someone shouting for help. When they arrived, they saw two men running off. Someone went and found a bobby . . . that's it.'

'*Two* men?' Harper asked. 'They were sure about that?'

'Haven't spoken to them myself, sir, but yes.'

A brief word with the physician. No bones broken, no real damage that he could find.

'Some bruising and he took a bad tumble,' the doctor said, 'but it's all on the surface. We're keeping him in tonight as a precaution, but he should be completely fine in a day or two.'

Nicholson was sitting up in the hospital bed. He looked older than the man Harper had spoken to that afternoon, as if the years had suddenly touched him and made him frail. Thin arms above the blankets, with the bruises beginning to show. Scraped knuckles. The cuts on his face had been cleaned, but he'd have a matching set of black eyes in the morning.

'I hadn't expected to see you again so soon.' His voice was thick, as if his tongue was too large for his mouth; the words came out heavy and slurred. But his eyes were lively and clear.

'What happened, sir?' Harper asked. 'Just take your time and tell us.'

He'd left the Leeds Club, strolling to the cab rank at the top of Briggate, cutting down Swan Street, behind the music hall. Suddenly, something was thrown over his head and he was dragged into the shadows where two men punched him.

'Two, sir?' Ash interrupted. 'You're positive about that?'

'Yes.' Nicholson nodded then winced at the movement. 'They didn't speak. I was trying to call out, but the . . . thing over my head muffled it. They took what they wanted, then ran off as soon as they heard other people coming. Gave me a last kick and that was it. Then someone was asking how I was.'

'Do you always go that way to catch a hackney, sir?'

He nodded and winced at the pain. 'I do. Routine.' Anyone watching him would know. Nicholson turned his head slowly. 'Was it the Smiths?'

'Hard to be certain,' Harper told him. 'But I'd say it was.'

Why, though? Because he'd talked to the police? How could they even know?

'Good job I'm a tough old boot,' Nicholson said. He tried to smile.

'You rest,' the superintendent said. 'Inspector Ash will come by in the morning to see if you've remembered anything more.'

'There's nothing more to remember. I couldn't see them, they didn't speak.'

'Maybe something will come to you.'

'Talk to the men on the beat,' Harper said as they stood out in the warm darkness. 'Find the names of the people who helped. Get someone to speak to them in the morning.'

'We know who's responsible, sir.'

'And we still have absolutely no evidence,' he said. 'Exactly the same as before.'

They started back to Millgarth. Monday night, nobody with money left from payday, and the town was quiet. They didn't talk; there was nothing worth saying.

At the station, Harper unlocked a drawer in his desk and took out a folder.

'I've been talking to a few people myself and putting together a file on May and Howe. Just so you know.'

Ash left the room. A moment later he returned, a small notebook in his hand, eyes twinkling with amusement.

'Snap, sir. Perhaps we should put them together.'

'This stays between us. Don't even tell Fowler and Walsh. I don't want to involve them yet.'

'Very good, sir.'

'What about Nicholson? Why would they do it?' He chewed his lip and stared at the inspector. 'Could it have been a simple robbery?'

'They wanted to put the fear of God in him, sir.' He paused. 'There's something else in there, too.'

'A warning to us, you mean? For raiding their office.'

'That's my guess.'

'Then they're scared,' Harper said.

'We know what they look like now, sir. Every bobby on the force will have copies of the pictures tomorrow.'

'How could they know we'd talked to Nicholson?'

'Someone at the quarry?'

'Take another look at everyone who works there.'

He sighed and stretched back, trying to ease the kinks in his neck, sitting up quickly as a thought struck him.

'Maybe they have someone on the force. Here in Millgarth. They seem to know what we've been doing every step of the way.'

Ash frowned. 'I'll have a word with Tollman in the morning. If there's anything, he can ferret it out.'

'Good.' A copper being paid by the Smiths . . . it would explain so much. 'How are things coming along with all those papers we took from their office?'

Ash shook his head. 'Fowler and Walsh are trying to put everything in order, but they don't have the training for this, sir. And while they're stuck in that office, they can't be out doing their real jobs.'

'Leave it with me.' He looked at the clock. Close to midnight. 'We might as well go home. We're not going to find any answers tonight.'

Ten in the morning. The monthly meeting of division heads with the chief. He sat with the other superintendents in Crossley's office, quietly sweltering in the warmth. Brian Patterson's face was slick with sweat, and John Curtis from 'D' Division looked ready to fall asleep.

Harper felt as if he'd only had a few minutes' sleep. His eyes stung when he blinked and his tongue felt furred as he listened to the drone of voices.

It was the same as ever: poring over crime figures and trying to make sense of the changes. After four years he'd learned to adjust to the boredom of it, to switch off his mind. The chief saying his name made him jerk up his head.

'Sorry, sir, I missed that.'

'The murders, Tom.'

He told them, seeing interest stir on everyone's faces. This was meat, something tasty for them all. He finished by telling them about the attack on Nicholson.

'We have photographs of the Smiths when they were younger. From the police in Manchester. I'll make sure you have copies.'

Nods and murmurs. They all knew what it was like. The constant battle to keep crime in check in a city that was growing and changing.

As if he needed a reminder of how fast things moved, he heard the roar of a motor car as it passed along Great George Street. The future. They had to keep pace.

'A quick word if you would, Tom,' Crossley said as the meeting ended.

The room seemed hushed with just two of them.

'How are all your investigations coming along?' The chief poured another cup of tea from the pot.

'These papers . . . we need someone who can make sense of them, sir. Someone who understands figures.'

The chief spooned sugar into his cup, stirring it slowly. 'I'll take care of that.'

'Thank you.'

'Councillor Howe came to see me before the meeting.'

'I see.' He could feel his body grow tense, every muscle tight. 'What did he want, sir?'

'The same thing as before.' He took a sip of the tea. 'I think it was just a reminder that they won't let it drop. They want your head.' A pause and a smile. 'They're not going to get it.'

'I appreciate you giving me the nod, sir.'

'If you can solve one or other of these cases, that would ease the pressure.'

'We're doing everything we can, sir.'

Crossley raised a hand. 'No criticism intended, Tom. But the sooner these are over, the quicker we'll neutralize them.'

'Yes, sir.' What else could he say? They both knew the answers already. For now he wasn't going to mention any possible connection between the councillors and the North Leeds Company. No point until he had proof. 'One other thing while I'm here, sir.' He explained about Fowler and Sissons.

The chief's face clouded. 'I hate to lose an experienced detective like that. But I suppose it's an opportunity for him.'

'I think the new man will work out.'

'Very good. Just keep doing what you've been doing. I'd like the burglar, but I really want this pair of killers.'

'So do I, sir. More than you can imagine.'

'Mr Nicholson was discharged from the infirmary this morning, sir,' Ash said. 'He's under orders not to do much for a few days.'

'How did he look?' Harper asked.

'Stiff and bruised. But he left under his own steam. A bit frightened, maybe.'

'Hardly surprising. Let's keep an eye on him.'

'We will, sir.'

'One more thing. The Smiths have their account at Beckett's Bank. We need to cut them off from their money.'

Ash grinned. 'You can leave that one with me, sir. I'll have that arranged in two shakes of a lamb's tail.'

How? Harper wondered as the man left. But he had no doubt it would happen.

Were they doing everything they could? Harper stood by the open window. Still hot out, and no relief in sight, according to the newspaper. The summer that wouldn't end.

He'd studied the file on the Smiths, searching for mistakes, small things they might have overlooked. But they'd done it all properly. Every t crossed, every i dotted. A thorough investigation, everything step by step.

This pair killed at the first sign of risk. They took no chances, and they seemed to know what the police were doing. Having an informer at Millgarth would be a natural move. They were clever. If not them, then whoever was running it all.

It was a bloody cancer, and he had to cut it out.

Harper took out the folder on the councillors. He desperately wanted Howe and May to be the ones behind this. He'd relish the sweet revenge of arresting them. But simply wanting didn't make it true, though. He wasn't that blind. They were a corrupt pair, they loved money. He'd discovered plenty about them; Ash had more. But still no direct link to the Smiths. And until he had that, he was going to tread very, very carefully.

A tap on the door followed by a short cough. Sergeant Tollman.

'Two gentlemen to see you, sir. Said Mr Crossley sent them. And that other thing Mr Ash asked me about: I'm looking into it.'

'Very good. Show them in, please.'

They were thin and stoop-shouldered, men who'd spent all their lives bent over a desk, a pair of gnomes wandering awkwardly in the daylight. Their skin had a grey pallor, both wearing glasses, hair

receding off their foreheads, wearing old-fashioned frock coats and
stiff wing collars. A pair of unloved bookends.

'I'm Andrews,' the one in front said. 'You have some papers . . .'

'That's right.' He led them down the corridor. 'Where are you
from?'

'We work in the council's finance department,' Andrews told
him. 'We've done work for Mr Crossley before. He said to tell you
that he trusts us.'

As soon as they entered the cramped room with its piles of paper,
the pair seemed to relax, as if they'd discovered a new home.

'If there's anything you need, let me know,' Harper said.

'We'll be fine, thank you, sir.' He was already at the desk, pulling
a sheaf of documents towards himself. 'Absolutely fine.'

He'd called off the watch on the Smiths' office. No sign of them
at all; they were too clever to risk showing their faces. Now they'd
vanished. All the constables on the beat had their pictures, but not
a peep of recognition.

Still nothing by six o'clock. Outside, people bustled about, on
their way home from work. He stared down at a sea of hats, bowlers,
caps, the colourful headwear of the women. Another day of frustration. The men were still all out there. Tomorrow, he'd do the same.
He'd thought their luck was changing. It seemed to have stalled.
Or perhaps Lady Luck simply wanted to tease them.

He caught sight of Walsh entering the detectives' room and
beckoned him through. Detective Sergeant Walsh. The rank would
suit him. A few words, a handshake and a beaming smile, and he
sent the man off to tell his wife.

Just as Harper was ready to leave, Andrews knocked on the office
door, face grave and pale as the angel of death.

'We've put the papers in order and gone through everything,
Superintendent.'

'That was very quick.' How had they managed it so easily?

'It doesn't take too long when you know your way around.' For an
instant, a smile flickered across his face, then it was gone again. He
extended a hand that held three sheets of paper. 'My report for you.'

'Give me the summary, please.'

'All their income is derived from the Harehills Development
Company.'

Harper nodded. He already knew that.

'From there, three-quarters is passed to another company, the North Leeds Company.'

'Any indication who owns that company?' He held his breath, hoping against hope.

Andrews shook his head. 'It's not in the papers, sir. The money goes to a lawyer, Mr Dryden.'

No luck at all.

'Money came into the Harehills Development Company to set it up and buy properties,' Harper said.

'That's correct. Several thousand pounds.'

'Where did it come from?' That was the heart of the matter, the real nugget of information to sift from all those piles of paper.

'From the North Leeds Company.'

And Dryden was using the law to stop him discovering who owned *that*. All that work and they had absolutely nothing new. He still didn't know who was giving the orders. At least the papers would be evidence once they had the Smiths. The net was closing. But slowly, too bloody slowly.

'Thank you,' he said finally.

Solemnly, Andrews placed his report on the desk.

'We've compiled a list of every company they do business with.'

'You've done it all extremely quickly and efficiently.'

'Thank you, sir. There is one other item you might find useful, sir. Just a small thing in the notes, but the Smiths have a house in Hyde Park.'

Suddenly the man had Harper's complete attention.

'Whereabouts?'

'I'm sorry, Superintendent, I searched but that information wasn't in there.'

'Thank you, Mr Andrews. I'll take it from there.' A solid lead. They could track that down and the pair wouldn't be expecting them. He took out his watch. The city offices would be closed for the night. 'Walsh, Fowler,' he called out, 'You're going to the Town Hall first thing in the morning.'

Annabelle had another evening meeting; he couldn't keep track of them all. Mary was eager to play, even if her ideas of enjoying

herself seemed strange to him. She wanted to be tested on her
spelling and arithmetic. After an hour he finally asked, 'Don't you
want to play a game?'

Her eyes widened and she smiled. 'Skittles, Da.'

NINETEEN

'She's very quick, Billy. I only need to tell her something once
and she has it.'

Elizabeth settled in the easy chair with a contented sigh.
It sounded as if Catherine Bush's first day working at the tea shop
had gone well, Reed thought. Good; his wife needed more help.
She came home exhausted every evening.

The job had been simple to arrange. Elizabeth had gone to the
Catholic Society supervising the girls. They were overjoyed, especi-
ally as Catherine's employer was the wife of a police inspector.
Two signatures and it was settled.

He poured a cup of tea. Elizabeth barely looked awake, just
enough to stroke the back of his hand and smile. They worked and
worked each day, and by the time they were done, they barely had
the energy to enjoy any time together.

Reed lit a cigarette and thought about the telephone call he'd
received during the afternoon. The rasp of Tom Harper's voice down
the line.

'We're getting there, Billy. Slowly but surely. We got all the
Smiths' papers and closed their office.'

'Do you have *them*?' Never mind the papers.

'Not yet. Tomorrow we should have an address for them.'

'What about evidence for murder?'

He sensed the hesitation. 'We will. And we'll discover whoever's
behind all this, too.'

'Do you know who that is?'

'I have an idea. But . . .'

No, Reed thought, Tom had nothing to connect all the dots and
make the full picture.

'Who is it?'

'No names, no pack drill,' Harper had replied. 'Not until I'm sure.'
He was clutching at wisps. He'd need more than that. And anyone
who could testify was dead.

At the top of the hill he gazed down over the estuary. There had
been no more fires. Every morning he woke with dread of another.
His sergeant and constable knew; they searched, too. Don't tell anyone,
he'd ordered them. Not a soul. If word spread, there could be panic.

Maybe it was a holidaymaker who had gone home now, he hoped.
Or a drunk. Maybe. But he daren't take that chance. He'd keep
looking.

'That's where we stand, gentlemen,' Harper said. Fowler and Walsh
sat at their desks. Ash leaned against the wall, and Sissons stood
nervously in the corner.

'I can't believe they worked their way through all that in three
hours,' Fowler said. 'I was going cross-eyed from looking at it.'

'Much good it did, anyway,' the superintendent said. 'For those
of you who haven't noticed, we have a new member of the squad.
Detective Constable Sissons. He's been looking into our burglar.'
The young man reddened as everyone turned to stare at him.
'He'll be working with Mr Ash. The rest of you know what you
need to do. I'm going to be joining you out there. Constable, this
is Sergeant Fowler and *Sergeant* Walsh.' He saw Walsh beam with
pride.

Sissons had been the first to arrive. Young and eager, unsure of
himself and where to put himself in the office. He'd feel at home
soon enough. For now, though, he was the outsider, the one with
something to prove.

'What else have you learned about this couple from the college?'
Harper asked.

He took out his notebook. 'I've done what I can, sir. I already
told you about the man. Carl Dunn, born and raised in Newcastle,
somewhere called Jesmond. Always worked as a clerk, loves to
climb.'

'Carry on.'

'It turns out his wife is a qualified teacher.'

'Is she now?' A professional woman and a burglar's accomplice?
Well, stranger things had happened. 'What have you turned up
about her?'

'Her name's Agatha. She grew up in Chapeltown, parents moderately well-off. Went to St Hild's in Durham to train. It's a very highly thought-of college, apparently.' He thumbed through a couple of pages of writing. 'Did well there. She's an avid climber, too, even started a club for the girls. Met her husband through the sport.'

A pair who loved climbing. More and more interesting. 'How did they end up in Leeds?'

'She had a teaching position in Newcastle after she took her certificate. I talked to the headmistress where she worked. Excellent at her job, apparently. Good with children, absolutely unflappable. The head was sorry to lose her when they married. Mr Dunn had a reasonable job, he'd been there five years. Then he gave in his notice without any warning. I talked to someone in Newcastle police. The Dunns left Newcastle six or seven weeks ago.'

The same time the burglaries stopped there, and shortly before they began here.

'Good work. How long did that take you?'

'Most of the day, sir. The hardest part was tracking down the headmistress and persuading her to talk.'

'Does Mrs Dunn have any kind of job down here?'

'No, sir. Not that I've found.'

Harper wanted to be outside these four walls, to be hunting the Smiths. He couldn't; for now, he needed to be here, to wait and give orders. He chafed at his desk, swearing five minutes passed for every one the clock showed. The windows were open wide, but his office still felt like a furnace.

Every time the door opened, he raised his head, hoping some of his men had returned with answers. Nine o'clock passed, ten, eleven, midday, one. Nothing. He tried to work on the papers that needed his attention, but it was impossible to concentrate. Finally he gave up, standing and staring out at the flow of people around the outdoor market.

Finally. Familiar voices. He rushed through to the detectives' room.

'Well?'

'They own a place in Hyde Park, right enough,' Fowler said, pushing the spectacles up his nose, and Harper couldn't help but wonder how the man would fare in the rough country of war. 'Took us four hours of digging, sir.'

'Whereabouts is it?'

'Brudenell Mount. Quite a respectable area. They bought it six months ago. Joint ownership, sir. Both brothers.' Walsh read from his notebook. 'Paid cash. The previous owner was Councillor Howe, although he'd been renting it out for a few years.'

One more link to close the circle. At this rate, he'd make it into a noose to go around all their necks.

'Do you want us to go in, sir?'

'Not yet.' He'd been far too hasty with the Smiths' office. A little patience and watching and he could have caught them there. This time he'd move a little more cautiously. 'I don't want you questioning the neighbours. Nothing to arouse suspicion. Just watch the house. Back as well as front, if you can. If you see them, don't try and arrest them. That's an order. You've seen how dangerous they are. We can get men up there quickly enough.'

'Yes, sir.'

Hyde Park was a few miles from Harehills, on the other side of Leeds. No one there was likely to recognize them. A safe spot for a bolt hole. Harper could feel the tingle in his hands. This time they were going to have them. Now all he needed was good news from Ash and Sissons and his day would be complete.

'Superintendent Harper.'

The voice was a bellow, the sound of someone used to giving orders and being obeyed. He stood at the entrance to the office, Tollman looking helpless behind him.

The man was as big as the noise he made. A hefty paunch held in by an expensively-cut suit and waistcoat, jowls sagging on his cheeks, and a double chin that shook as he spoke. Small, dark eyes that seemed to absorb the light.

'Councillor May.' Harper stood, slowly extending a hand to a visitor's chair in his office. 'You should have let us know you were coming. What can I do for you?'

'I'm on the watch committee.' He glared, fire in his eyes. 'I don't need an invitation to see how one of the divisions is spending the public's money.'

'Of course not. Tea?'

May waved the idea away. He remained standing, a heavy, looming presence in the room, eyes moving slowly around until his gaze settled on the map.

'What's that?'

'Related to a case.' He wasn't about to offer a word more than necessary.

The councillor snorted. 'These murders?'

'Yes.'

'Something else you're wasting time and good brass over. What's happening about the burglaries? I've got people telling me they're terrified to go out.'

Harper didn't believe a word. May could conjure outrage from the empty air. He loved nothing better than stirring a crowd by appealing to its prejudices. Nobody named, just a wink, a nod, a hint; he knew how to work them. He despised the police, insisting he was on the watch committee to keep them in check.

This was the first time since Harper became superintendent that May had stirred himself into Millgarth. And it wasn't a friendly visit.

'We're working on that. We have some suspects.'

'Some suspects?' He shouted out the question. 'What good is that to honest people who are scared they'll come home to find all their valuables stolen?'

Harper gritted his teeth and forced himself to smile. 'As I said, Councillor, we're making progress.'

'Not enough.' He moved around the room as if he owned it, picking up a piece of paper, glancing at it then putting it down again. He seemed to fill all the space, to take all the air. 'In case you don't already know, a number of us feel you shouldn't be in this job.' A lower voice now, more intimate and threatening. 'We've taken our concerns to the chief constable.'

'So I've heard.' He wasn't going to show any trace of fear. He wouldn't give May that satisfaction.

'We're going to keep on with it until he replaces you, Harper.' The words came out in a hiss.

Harper stared at him. 'That's your privilege.'

'I've been on the council for a long time. Plenty of people owe me favours.' May gave a thin, hard smile. His eyes glittered with hatred. He took a step closer. Harper could smell his breath, whisky and red meat. 'That's how politics works. And when you're ready, you collect them. It's easy to ruin a career. Just like that.' The snap of his fingers sounded like a gunshot.

'I can't stop you trying.' The man was goading him. Harper bunched his fists, but he didn't move. He wasn't that stupid. Hitting a councillor? Instant dismissal, no appeal.

'I know you can't.' The dark smile returned for a second and vanished again. May loved the sound of his own voice. 'And I'll win. Do you know why? Because I have power and you don't.'

He extended his hand. Without thinking, Harper took it, and May dragged him close. A whisper that fed like poison into his ear. 'I know men in this city who could make you disappear for five pounds and give me change for the pleasure of the work. Think on that, Harper. Imagine how your godawful, jumped-up wife and little girl would feel when you never came home.'

A hard squeeze of the hand, a final, bitter look, and May was gone, only the stink of him trailing in the air. Ten seconds later, Tollman appeared.

'I'm sorry, sir. He barged right through, and I couldn't exactly stop him, could I? Not with him being . . .'

'It's doesn't matter, Sergeant. You can't keep a councillor waiting.'

'There's something else, sir.'

'Not right now.' He turned, taking a deep breath. 'A few minutes, please.'

Bluster and righteous fury. That was all anyone would have heard. Christ, had he imagined it all? He replayed the words in his head. A councillor threatening a police superintendent with murder in his own office? Things like that didn't happen. He knew he should feel *something*. Anger. Fear. He should be flaming. Instead he was strangely calm, as if he was standing apart and observing it all. May thought he'd already won the war. He was wrong. Battle was just beginning.

Finally he began to move, to put one foot in front of the other as if he was walking out of a dream and back to everyday life. Harper stopped at the front desk.

'You had something to tell me?'

'You wanted to know if the Smiths might have someone on their payroll here, sir.'

Harper smiled. 'I haven't forgotten.'

'I've come up with two possibilities.'

'Tell me about them . . .'

'Tollman said you had a visitor this afternoon,' Ash said.

'Councillor May. He thought he could intimidate me.'

'Did he succeed, sir?'

'He threatened to have me killed.'

'What?' For once, Ash looked astonished.

'Right where we're standing. Pulled me close and whispered it.'

'Have you told the chief?'

Harper shook his head. 'What can I say? Nobody else was here, there's no evidence.'

'To be sure he knows, sir.'

'What's the point? Anyway, I've told you now. May seems to believe he can have my scalp. He wants revenge for his son.'

'He's bitten off more than he can chew,' Ash said.

'Our friend the councillor seems to believe the world revolves around him.'

'I believe it's time he had a fall from grace, don't you, sir? Him and the North Leeds Company.'

'Long overdue,' Harper said. 'But first let's make that connection to the Smiths. I'll tell you what Fowler and Walsh have discovered . . .'

'One last thing, sir,' Ash said after he'd finished. 'I took the liberty of calling in and having a word with the manager of Beckett's Bank.'

'What did he have to say?' He'd met the man at a do once. A prig, a stickler for everything just so.

'The Smiths no longer have access to their accounts, sir. Business or personal.'

He was astonished. 'How did you arrange that?'

A wink. 'All done with a handshake, sir.'

He laughed. Freemasons. The brotherhood. Quite a few coppers were members. But no one had ever approached him; they knew he'd refuse.

'Very handy.'

'Didn't you have a meeting today?' Harper asked. He was at home, jacket on the peg, collar and tie gone, but he didn't feel any sense of ease. Everything kept worrying at him. The Smiths. The burglar. They were so close. For once he wanted the telephone to ring and bring him some news.

And the looming snake behind it all, Councillor May. He'd tried to shake off the words. No one would dare to have a copper killed like that. But the idea had wormed its way into his head.

'Mr Hardcastle,' Annabelle answered. She was in her day dress, plain brown cotton, high at the neck and three-quarter sleeves. Working clothes. 'You've met him, older, bald, half an acre of grey side whiskers. He's the leader of the Conservatives on the Guardians.'

'Did he survive the encounter?'

'He was a little surprised that a lady would treat him to luncheon.' A wicked grin crossed her face. 'But he listened to my proposals and he didn't reject them straight off the bat. I'd say that's something.'

'It is.' More than he expected. It didn't mean he'd go for them, though. 'What next?'

'I have the pleasure of entertaining one of the Liberals. Don't worry, I know they won't fall over and accept everything. A little would be a start.' She stared at him. 'What's wrong with you, anyway? You look miles away.'

He told her. Not about the cases, but May's visit, every word he spoke, seeing her grow angrier and angrier.

'He said that?' She was on her feet, arms folded, stalking around the living room. 'He really said that? That he could have you killed?'

'Yes.'

'Have you told anyone?'

'Ash. It was done in whispers. It would be my word against May's.'

'I'll kill him myself.' He'd never heard her sound so angry. 'I'll see him swing.'

'He called you jumped-up.'

'I don't care what he says about me. It's you I'm worried about.' She burned with a cold, determined fury.

'He won't win. We're making sure of that.'

'It's not about winning, is it, Tom? It's about you staying alive.'

TWENTY

'A quick word, sir,' Tollman said as Harper walked into Millgarth. Another close morning. Half past six and already
the shirt was sticking to his back, the white cuffs covered
in smuts. God only knew what it would be like by two.

'What is it?'

'Constable Osborne,' the sergeant said as he followed Harper
into his office and closed the door. 'I'm fairly certain he's the one
giving information to the Smiths.'

'How certain?'

'I'd stake my pension on it.'

That was good enough for him; Tollman was no gambler. 'Is he
on duty today?'

'Yes, sir. I told him not to cover his beat, that you wanted to
see him.'

Harper glanced at the clock. 'How long has he been waiting?'

'About half an hour, sir.'

Long enough for the worry to build.

'March him in. Let's see what he has to say for himself.'

The man tried to show nothing, standing straight, facing the
wall ahead of him. But fear was in his eyes as they flickered around
the room.

'How long have you been on the force, Constable?' Harper
asked.

'Three years, sir.'

He turned to Tollman. 'Good record?'

'Fair, sir. More slipshod lately. Late a few times, caught away
from his beat once.'

'What do you have to say for yourself, Osborne?'

The guilt rolled off him in waves.

'I'm sorry, sir. It won't happen again.'

'Why did it happen at all?' Harper asked.

'I've had some problems at home, sir.'

'Problems a little money might help, perhaps?' The police were underpaid. A man on the beat barely earned enough to survive. The surprise was that more of them didn't turn bad.

'Sir?'

'Do you know who the Smiths are, Constable?'

A fragment of hesitation. 'I know plenty of people called Smith, sir.'

'Brothers. Jack and John. Ever met them?'

'I don't think, so, sir.' He was a poor liar, sweating now, drops glistening on his skin. But he didn't dare move to wipe them away.

Harper stood. He wanted to face the man as he damned himself.

'Sergeant Tollman believes you're on the take, that you're the Smiths' man here.'

'No, sir!' But there was no power behind the denial.

'How much do they pay you?'

'Nothing, sir. I'm not like that.'

'How much?' Harper insisted. No answer. 'How did they get to you?'

Osborne swallowed hard. 'It was my wife, sir. She was poorly and she needed to go into hospital. We didn't have the money. They heard and offered to lend it to me.'

'We have a fund for that type of thing. Why didn't you come to us?'

'Pardon me, sir,' Tollman interrupted. 'He's borrowed twice before. He's been slow paying it all back.'

'I see. Go on, Constable.'

'They said I could keep the money if I slipped them word about things here.' He looked almost relieved to let the truth pour out. 'Gave me a little whenever I told them something. I didn't think it would do any harm, sir, and we needed the money, since my Esme can't work now.'

'You know what you've done, don't you?'

'Yes, sir.' He hung his head. 'I'm sorry, sir. I really am.'

'I'm not going to prosecute you,' Harper told him after a moment, seeing the relief, 'even though you've harmed our investigation.'

'Thank you, sir.'

'How did you get the information to them?'

'If I had anything, I'd write it down. There was a place, by one of the gravestones at the church on Kirkgate. I'd leave it under a stone there.'

Tollman looked at the constable with disappointed eyes.

'As of this minute, you're no longer a member of Leeds City Police,' Harper said to Osborne. 'I'm going to put a bad reference on your record. Hand everything to the sergeant and get the hell out of my sight.'

Tollman marched him out. One two, one two. The superintendent stood, breathing slowly. One more avenue closed to the brothers. Office gone, informant gone, bank account closed, their house under observation. It was just a matter of time now. And the sooner it all happened, the better. Before anyone else died.

First, a talk with Fowler. The sergeant had arrived, unshaved, his clothes rumpled, looking weary to the bone.

'Walsh and I are taking it turn and turn about to watch the Smiths' house, sir,' he said. 'I drew the night duty.'

'Any sign of them?'

'Nothing. No lights during the evening, didn't see any movement behind the lace curtains.'

Were they even there? Or still one step ahead?

'We'll give it a little while longer. I'll stop and take a look this morning.'

'Very good, sir.'

Harper raised his voice, speaking to the whole room. 'In case you're wondering how the Smiths seemed to know what we were doing, they had a man here. A man on the beat. I dismissed him. We're almost there. Let's get to work. Fowler, you go home and sleep.'

'Happily, sir.'

'Mr Sissons, let's take a walk.'

Raglan Road was a little north of Yorkshire College, veering off Woodhouse Lane at an angle, tucked behind the open gymnasium area across from the moor. Neat terraces of three-storey villas, the bricks all blackened by soot drifting over from the factories.

'Which one is it?' Harper asked.

'Thirty-six, sir.'

The house had a glossy black front door, exactly the same as its neighbours. A front garden hardly bigger than a postage stamp, the grass withered from the heat. Donkeystoned steps. No sign of anyone as they passed, walked to the next corner, then crossed the street to the shade of an oak tree. Hidden enough not to be seen, but with a clear view of the front door. Just being out of the sun felt wonderful, Harper thought, fanning himself with his hat.

'I'll warn you now, there's very little excitement in what we do. For the next several hours you're going to stand here and see who comes and goes from that house.'

'Yes, sir.'

'Report back to Millgarth at six. If you see them going out with climbing gear, call it in.' He pointed to the tiny police station at the junction with Clarendon Road.

'Yes, sir.' Sissons gave a tentative smile, not certain if it was a joke.

From there, it was a ten-minute walk to find Walsh in Hyde Park. Brudenell Mount was one street in a mass of them, acre after acre of grimy red brick. The kind of place where people could hope and start to believe they were making something of their lives.

'Any activity?'

Walsh had found a space, a small nook in a ginnel overgrown with weeds. He looked bored and uncomfortable.

'No, sir. My guess is that they've gone.'

'It's possible.' But where? The Smiths had run out of options. Harper pulled out his pocket watch. 'Give it until noon, then start talking to the neighbours. Don't go into the house, though. Not on your own.'

'Yes, sir.'

'If I don't hear from you, I'll send some men up this afternoon. Then you can go through the place.'

That brought a grin. 'Very good, sir.'

Back into town. His chest was so tight that every breath felt painful. It was all coming to a head.

The conversation with May kept playing in his head. He wanted to forget it, he'd tried to wrench it loose, but it clung on. Just words, they had to be, the man couldn't be stupid enough to do more. But they'd had their effect. As he walked, Harper kept glancing over his shoulder, straining his ear for footfalls behind him.

May wasn't going to win this one.

He made a circuit of the public houses, from the old Cork and Bottle on the Headrow down to the Royal Hotel by the railway bridge on Lower Briggate. Hurried conversations with a few more figures. About time they repaid their debts. By the time he reached

Millgarth, he felt a little better. Soon, perhaps, some solid evidence
against a pair of corrupt councillors. Maybe even that connection
to the Smiths.

Ash stood in the doorway. 'I've been thinking, sir, maybe you'd
like to buy me my dinner.'

The superintendent patted his pockets.

'It'll have to be the cafe over in the market. I don't have much
money on me.'

'That's fine, sir.' Ash grinned. 'They'll have the cottage pie today.'

They did, along with liver and onions and mashed potatoes. Tea
the colour of mud in large, cracked blue and white striped mugs.
But no ghost of Tom Maguire in the place any longer. One of the
few honest men he'd known, a socialist and union organizer, dead
before he was thirty in his bleak, empty room. Maybe he'd finally
moved on and found some peace. The man deserved it; the world
had become a darker place in the four years since his death.

Harper pushed his plate away and took a drink.

'What did you want to say that's better away from the station?
And why don't you trust the place?'

'It should be fine now we're rid of Osborne, sir. But better safe
than sorry.' His thick moustache twitched. 'I had a little time, so I
stopped to talk to a couple of pals of mine at the Town Hall.'

'Do you trust them?'

'We've known each other since we were nippers, sir.' He understood; those years meant loyalty. 'They had a few interesting tales
about our friends in high places.'

'How interesting?'

'Envelopes passed to building inspectors to sign off on new houses
that weren't up to snuff. Enforced contributions from any contrac-
tors who wanted to bid for work. Things like that.'

'Are they any worse than anyone else?'

'Probably not,' Ash agreed. 'But this is all the time, every time.
It's not even hidden.'

'Does it give us the North Leeds Company, though? That's what
we need. Something solid.'

'They mentioned a few names. I thought I'd drop by for a chat
with them this afternoon, if that's all right with you. After all, it's
police time.'

'You're looking into possible crimes,' Harper told him in a bland voice. 'What could be wrong with that?'

The inspector grinned. 'I thought you might feel that way, sir. But with everything else going on . . .'

'We have that covered for now. But I might need you about three.'

'I'll make sure I'm back by then.'

No word from Walsh. He dispatched Ash with three large constables to Hyde Park. It was time to go into the Smiths' house. They'd flown, he could feel it. But there might be some clue inside. They were on the run now. He had to find them and finish this off.

The telephone call came just after four. Tollman had brought him a cup of tea and he was working through the papers on his desk, waiting for word. Harper snatched at the receiver.

'Yes?'

'Superintendent, sir?' A voice he didn't know.

'Who is this?'

'Woodhouse station, sir. I've got a message for you from Inspector Ash. He says he wants you out here as soon as possible.'

TWENTY-ONE

The front door hung off its hinges, a uniformed constable keeping an eye on the neighbours who'd gathered.

As soon as he was inside, Harper could smell it. Unmistakeable, an iron tang in his nostrils. Blood.

'Cellar, sir,' Walsh called from the kitchen. 'Watch yourself, it's a bad sight.'

Someone had hung an oil lamp over the stairs. Gingerly, Harper clambered down, one hand steadying himself against the cold brick of the wall. With each step, the stench grew stronger. By the time he reached the bottom, it was overwhelming. He put a handkerchief over his nose.

It wasn't bad; it was horrific. Worse than Jeb Pearce or Douglas Cameron. The body on the floor was naked and bruised from head to toe. Wrists tied behind his back. Lying in a wide pool of blood where he'd been gutted, all the organs pulled out. A mass of flies buzzed and whirled around. White maggots were curled in the wounds that covered the flesh.

Ash was there, squatting near the body.

'I'd say he's been dead since yesterday, sir. He must have been lying here the whole time we were watching the place.' His voice was grim, full of shadows and dark corners.

'One of the brothers?' The way the face was beaten, every feature obliterated, he couldn't begin to guess.

'It might be, but I wouldn't have a clue which one. Walsh is going through the house to see what he can find.'

This was savage. Not anger. Complete, methodical, destruction.

'The build and hair colour's right for the brothers,' Ash said as he stood. 'The wagon's on the way to take him to Hunslet. Both the doctors are out today. Post-mortem first thing in the morning, sir.'

Harper stared at the corpse. Then he asked the question that had bothered him since he saw the body.

'If it's one of the Smiths, why would he do this to his brother?'

Ash ran a hand through his hair, making it stand on end. 'I really don't know the answer to that one, sir.'

Billy Reed walked along Church Street. Past Elizabeth's tea room, filled with holidaymakers, a few more queueing outside. She'd be in the kitchen, wiping the sweat off her face as she cooked up the meals. He spotted Catherine Bush, clearing away some plates, but the girl was too busy to notice him.

The tide was out, people set up on every scrap of sand, sitting on towels and deck chairs to take in the sun. Another beautiful day. The owners of the hotels and guest houses were blooming with happiness; it was the best summer they could recall. Every room was booked until the end of August.

The tea room was packed every day. Elizabeth was raking in money, but the long days were leaving her drained.

'Never mind, Billy love,' she'd said last night. 'Another month and it'll ease up. It's the way things are, we have to make our money while we can. Winter will be dead, you know that.'

He climbed the hill of Henrietta Street, pausing at the top where it petered into the grass of the cliff, and stared out at the water. A few fishing boats, out late in the day, bobbed like corks. Off in the distance, a steamship moved in a stately manner over the North Sea.

No word from Tom about the case. He'd expected something by now. He scoured the papers every morning, going down to the railway station to buy the *Yorkshire Post*, but nothing.

At least no one had tried to start any more fires here. Reed still spent his days checking, walking all over the town, peering in the alleys and the ghauts. But nothing. He was beginning to believe that the danger had passed. Part of him hoped that was true. Yet a tiny piece hoped it would continue and give him some real police work to do.

Almost seven by the time Harper returned to Millgarth. He could still smell the blood, taste it on his tongue. The brutality of what he'd seen lingered as he walked into Millgarth and through to his office.

Sissons sat, patiently waiting. Of course; he'd told the lad to report back at six.

'Constable,' he said. 'You probably heard. There was some other business.'

'I did, sir.'

'You could have written up a summary and left it on my desk.'

The young man blushed. 'I'm sorry, sir. I didn't know.'

He'd learn. Bit by bit, he'd learn.

'What happened with the Dunns today?'

'She went out for two hours this morning. At least,' he added cautiously, 'I think it was her, unless the landlady's renting out more of the house. I came back here when Mr Dunn returned from work.'

'I see.' Harper sat. He was thinking how to organize his men tomorrow. The Hyde Park murder would need everyone he could spare. Burglary seemed nothing in comparison. No, he decided; let Sissons stay on Raglan Road. 'What time did Mrs Dunn leave?'

'Thirty-two minutes past ten, sir. She came back at twenty-seven minutes past twelve.'

The lad was certainly precise.

'Up there again in the morning. I'll come by about half past ten. If she goes out again, we'll have a word with the landlady and try to search their rooms.'

'Yes, sir. I thought I'd stand watch for a couple of hours tonight, if you don't mind, sir. I was reading the file. The burglaries seem to happen not too long after dark. I might be able to catch them on the way to something.'

'Very enterprising,' Harper agreed. Good to see him showing initiative so quickly. 'Do that. If they go out, follow and observe, that's all.'

'Yes, sir.'

'If they stop and he begins to climb, find help. I don't want you trying to handle it all yourself.'

Sissons looked hurt. He wanted the collar. But this was going to be done properly, with no risk.

'Yes, sir. Of course.'

Hurriedly, Harper wrote up what they knew about the Hyde Park killing. Something to bring the chief up to date in the morning.

Ash was in charge, and he had Fowler and Walsh with him. He didn't expect any quick news. And if there was, he decided as he took his hat off the peg, they could telephone him at home.

There was a tiny, welcome breeze on the open upper deck of the tram. Harper sat and watched the city go by. After he alighted in Sheepscar, he looked around. May would never make good on his threat, he told himself. He'd never dare. Still, he scurried across Roundhay Road, checking behind himself, then into the safety of the Victoria. He needed to get over this. It was no way to go on. Nobody was lying in wait to attack him.

'You should see me Mam.' Mary rushed up as soon as he was through the door, excitement glowing across her face.

'Why?' he asked as he picked up his daughter and rubbed noses with her. So big now, too heavy to keep doing this.

'She means this,' Annabelle said as she came through from the kitchen, wiping her hands on a towel. A perfect black eye, the bruise already livid.

'What happened to you?' He could feel the hackles rising. Someone had hurt her. May, he thought. He'd gone after her instead.

She shook her head. 'Don't worry, it looks worse than it is.'

'She's been in the wars. Someone took a swing at her.' Mary's voice was bloodthirsty and eager.

'Hush, you,' Annabelle said softly. 'Your da wants to know what happened. It was my own fault. I was showing the child care inspector around. He had a complaint on Rosebud Walk, so I went with him. Came round the corner and there were two women ready to go at it hammer and tongs. Already taking off their blouses so they wouldn't get them mucky.'

'What did you do?'

'Muggins here thought I'd break it up.' She shrugged. 'One of them turned and took a crack at me. Soon as they realized, they were all apologies, of course. But I'll need plenty of paint and powder for a few days.'

'Does it hurt, Mam?' Mary asked.

'Tender,' she admitted. 'My pride came off worst.'

'Do you want me to do anything about it?' Harper asked. 'Officially, I mean.'

She shook her head. 'I should know better at my age. Let them sort it out themselves. Anyway, least said, soonest mended.'

He put his hand under her chin and tilted her face towards the light. She'd taken a good blow, but no real damage. Very gently, he kissed her eye.

Harper leaned against the wall, oblivious to everything else, staring at the corpse on the slab as if he could will identity into the body and make it one of the brothers. Lumb cleaned the corpse, working methodically, grumbling softly to himself. The old police photographs of the brothers lay on the desk. The doctor lifted a magnifying glass and studied them closely, not saying a word as he compared the images and what lay in front of him. The superintendent looked at Ash and raised an eyebrow.

The belly had been split open along its length, from chest to pelvis. The ambulancemen must have stuffed the guts back inside. The doctor removed them again, examining them as he pulled them out, sometimes nodding to himself.

Finally, Lumb turned.

'Two things I can tell you,' he began. 'If you want a cause of death, he was beaten until his heart stopped.' His gaze flickered to the policemen. 'Even worse than that man from the quarry.' He waved a hand at the evisceration. 'The rest was done afterwards, thank God.'

'Is he—' Harper asked.

'One of these brothers?' The doctor pursed his lips. 'It's possible,

that's as far as I'll go. These photographs are old and the face . . .
you can see it for yourselves.'

'Twelve years old,' Ash told him. 'The pictures are twelve years
old.'

Lumb nodded. 'The basic features don't change, but there are no
identifying marks I can find. Whoever did this broke every bone in
the face with a heavy piece of wood; there are splinters in the skin.
It's intended to look like rage, but my guess is that it was deliberate.
A very effective way of concealing someone's identity.'

'So there's no chance of discovering who he was?'

'No,' Lumb replied sadly. 'I'm afraid not.' He looked around
them. 'I'm sorry, gentlemen.'

Harper nodded and walked out without a word. Dammit. The
brothers were still one step ahead.

'Sir.' Ash caught up with him on Hunslet Road. 'What do you think?'

'You heard the doctor.' He could hear the harshness in his own
voice. 'Impossible to know. That's exactly what the Smiths want.
My gut tells me they're both still out there.'

'I have to agree, sir.'

The brothers had found someone who resembled them and
battered him until he died. Destroyed his face until it wasn't even
human, then cut him open and spread his insides around the cellar.
That went beyond brutal. It was evil.

'They're not men,' Harper said. 'No man could do that to
someone else.'

'We'll find them, sir.'

'We'd better. We can't let those two run around any longer.'

There'd been little at the house on Brudenell Mount. A few
clothes in the wardrobes, some crockery and food left in the kitchen.
Nothing to indicate where they might have gone. Fowler and Walsh
had talked to the neighbours; the Smiths were quiet, keeping to
themselves. No loud arguments, barely any noise. No one had
noticed them leave. Everyone was stunned by the killing. If they
ever learned the full truth of it, they'd be horrified.

'What about our other business, sir?' Ash asked.

It was linked, he felt that, but . . . he shook his head.

'We need these two first.' He took out his pocket watch. Quarter
to eleven already. 'Whatever you feel you have to do, I'll back you.'

*   *   *

The hackney dropped him off by Woodhouse Moor. Sissons was waiting, staring intently at the house on Raglan Road.

'Did they stir last night?'

'Doused the lights and in bed just after ten, sir.'

'Has she gone out this morning?'

'Yes, sir. Same as yesterday, half past ten again on the dot. Shopping basket over her arm.'

A creature of habit. No better chance to take a look inside.

The woman who answered the door had a severe face, grey hair pulled back into a tight bun, staring at them with disapproval.

'We'd like to ask you a few questions about your tenant,' Harper said, and produced his card. 'Leeds City Police.'

The woman sniffed. 'Why? What's he done?'

'Nothing that we know,' Harper told her with a smile. 'We think he might be able to help with our enquiries, that's all.'

'I thought there was something about them.' She gave a sour look.

'How long have they lived here?'

'Near enough two months.' She spoke as if each word cost her threepence. 'Been on time with the rent so far.'

'Anything odd about them?'

'He's all right, I suppose,' she said grudgingly. 'She always has her nose in the air, as if she's too good for everybody.'

'I'd appreciate a quick look in their rooms.'

She swooped on his request. 'I thought you said they hadn't done anything.'

'I don't know that they have,' Harper told her. 'This will let us find out.'

A moment's hesitation, then she turned and led them up the stairs.

'Off every Sunday with all that stuff,' she complained. 'Climbing. What sort of a thing is that? And for a woman, too.' At the door, she produced a set of keys. 'I heard her leave a few minutes ago.'

A sitting room, bedroom, tiny kitchen.

'Be quick,' he warned Sissons. 'Make sure you leave everything exactly as you found it. Look in the bedroom. See if you can find any pawn tickets.'

He had to trust the lad to perform a fast, thorough search.

Ten minutes. Time enough to sift through all the obvious hiding places and a few unusual ones. Nothing at the bottom of a jar of sugar or in the packets of this and that. Nothing attached to the bottom of drawers in the bureau. Harper stood back, making sure it seemed undisturbed. Sissons appeared, shaking his head.

'Their climbing gear is there, but everything else seems normal, sir. No stolen jewellery, I didn't find any money or anything else.'

Maybe it wasn't the Dunns behind the burglaries, Harper thought. No, it *had* to be, the fit was too perfect.

The landlady was waiting on the landing. She turned the key in the lock.

'I'll give them their notice as soon as she comes back. I'm not standing for this in my house. Having the police in, it's bringing shame on the place.'

She was a small woman. Harper towered over her. He stared down into her face until her expression turned fearful.

'Don't,' he said quietly. 'Not a word. We were never here. Everything is fine and normal. Can you manage that?'

A last, tiny flicker of defiance, then she nodded.

'Thank you,' Harper told her.

'You handled her very well, sir.' They were sitting in a cafe at Hyde Park corner.

Had he? The landlady's indignation was all a front, anyway. He'd spotted the threadbare runner on the stairs, the air of neglect around the house. She needed the money lodgers brought in, and the Dunns offered steady rent. It had all registered in his mind without a conscious thought.

'Experience, Mr Sissons. You'll learn. As soon as you've eaten, I want you at Brudenell Mount. Sergeant Fowler will tell you what to do. This murder is the biggest thing on our plate right now.'

'Yes, sir.' He took out a packet of cigarettes, then thought better of it in front of the superintendent.

'But tonight you're back watching the Dunns.'

Harper felt weary as he walked back into town. This summer felt as if it might go on forever. Somewhere up there the sun was shining, but all they felt was the heat.

The Smiths were both alive, hiding, waiting out there with nothing to lose. More men would die if he didn't find them first.

Killers, burglars; he had to catch them all. It was his job, his responsibility. Even the punch Annabelle had taken. He'd taken Tollman aside as he walked into Millgarth that morning.

'There was an incident on Rosebud Walk yesterday.'

'Was there, sir?' The sergeant looked at him questioningly. 'I didn't hear anything.'

'Take my word for it. That's Conlon's beat. I want him to have a talk with the two women involved. Tell them he's keeping his eye on them.'

'Of course, sir.'

That should be enough.

At his desk, Harper picked up his pen and began to write. Maybe putting it all on paper would help him find a way through.

Dear Billy . . .

TWENTY-TWO

R eed crumpled the letter and tossed it across his desk. It sounded as if the whole thing had become a pig's ear.

Tom's problem. He had enough of his own in Whitby. The arsonist had tried to strike again. Another amateur job. No damage done beyond a little scorching on the back wall of a business on Church Street, quickly spotted and doused. No clues beyond a pair of spent matches. But he was still here. He'd try again, and again. And soon enough he'd do some real damage.

Sissons looked exhausted, Harper thought as the young man entered the detectives' room. It was always the same. The longer hours, the standing around. Even after years on a beat, it came as a shock. Never mind; soon enough it would be completely normal to him.

'Did the Dunns go out last night?'

'For a stroll, sir. Half an hour, that's it.'

'Whereabouts?'

'Along Blackman Lane near All Souls' Church, sir, then back around Blenheim Square and the streets by there. I couldn't really follow, there weren't enough people for me to stay out of sight. But

Mr Dunn was walking with a bit of a limp, as if he'd twisted his ankle.'

Well, well, well. Two of the burglaries had taken place there. Were they scouting their next victim? But he wouldn't be able to climb like that, would he?

'I want you there again tonight,' he ordered. 'If his ankle's bad, I don't expect much, but you never know. If they go out with a bag, keep as close a watch as you can.'

'Yes, sir.'

Fowler and Ash were talking, Walsh completing a report.

'Do we have any idea at all where the Smiths have gone?'

'None, sir,' Fowler told him. He hesitated. 'Are we positive that body isn't one of them?'

'No, we're not. But someone took a lot of trouble to make sure we couldn't find out from the face. What does that tell you?'

'Something to hide,' Fowler replied. 'Or disguise.'

'Exactly. So we're going to assume they're both alive. Walsh,' he said, 'did you ever establish any link between Jeb Pearce and the Smiths?'

'No, sir. Then other things came up.'

'Go back over that. We know there is one. Maybe it can tell us something.' He spoke quickly. 'Fowler, you and Sissons are going out to beat the bushes today. They're on the run. That's hard to do without anyone knowing.'

The sergeant grinned and pushed the glasses up his nose. 'Yes, sir.'

'If you get a sniff of them, I want to know. Don't go in. We've seen what they can do.'

'What about me, sir?' Ash asked after the others had gone.

'We need to review everything.'

He raised an eyebrow. 'Everything, sir?'

Harper walked across to the map of Harehills and stared at the pins and lines. 'What have we missed? There has to be something.'

'It was all going smoothly for them until Mr Reed's brother committed suicide. We hadn't heard a word about what the Smiths were doing before that. As far as we know, they hadn't killed or hurt anyone.'

'As far as we know,' Harper repeated.

'If we hadn't come on the scene, they'd likely have forced Mrs

Reed out and we'd have stayed none the wiser. Things started to fall apart after we appeared. That's when the murders began.'

'To make sure there'd be no one to testify.'

'Precisely, sir. They've been on the run since the beginning.'

They were still running now. And still killing. He glanced at the map again. Where are you, you bastards?

'I want the men on the beat showing those photographs to everyone. Somebody must have seen them.'

'Very good, sir.'

There wasn't much more he could do for now. Not about that, at least.

'I thought you'd like to know, sir,' Ash continued. 'My friends at the Town Hall have given me some papers. Records of some very dubious payments made to Councillors May and Howe about a few building contracts and requests for planning permission.'

'Put them in the file.'

A grin. 'Already done, sir.' A small hesitation. 'How's Mrs Harper's black eye?'

Harper chuckled. 'You heard about that?'

'Conlon told me. The woman who did it is mortified. She's going to apologize, once she plucks up her courage.'

'The bruises are already starting to fade. Annabelle reckons it's her own fault for getting in the middle of things.'

'Funny, really. We keep an eye on the men, but it's the women who can do the damage, isn't it, sir?'

Harper walked up George Street, glad to be outside. Across Vicar Lane, the elaborate entrance to the new County Arcade was taking shape. A few months and it would be open for business. Ready for the new century. More shopping, more of the old courts gone; so few of them remained now. His own past was vanishing right before his eyes, all the streets where he'd walked a beat as a constable. Poor places, cramped, dirty, infested with cockroaches and rats. But they'd been cheap, and home to plenty of families. Where had they all gone?

'I'm glad you're back, sir,' Tollman said before Harper had taken two steps through the door. 'We've been looking everywhere for you.'

'Why?' He started to feel a tightness in his chest. 'What's happened?'

'The chief constable's here, sir.'

'How long?'

'About a quarter of an hour. I showed him through to your office. Took him a cup of tea,' the sergeant smiled. 'And a slab of that fruit loaf PC Hogg's mother makes.'

Harper grinned. 'That should keep him occupied, anyway. Thank you.'

Crossley was still chewing the cake, standing and studying the map on the wall.

'It's a very bad business, isn't it?'

'A pity we can't find out who really owns these properties,' Harper said.

'That's the law, Tom. We're never going to win that battle.' He put the plate down on the desk. 'I read the report on that body in Hyde Park.'

'It was the worst I've ever seen, sir. I thought Jeb Pearce was bad, but this . . .'

'Do you have *any* line on them?'

'No. We don't. Not a single clue. Everyone on the beat has their pictures, but . . .'

'Put the word out to the newspapers,' Crossley told him. 'Let's see what that brings us.'

A flurry of useless tips, the same as always. The chief knew it as well as he did. But Harper understood. They were desperate.

'I'll write something this morning.'

'Very good. Now, what about the burglaries? What progress have we made on that?'

'We've identified a suspect. Married. We searched their lodgings when they were out, but we didn't find anything. He and his wife are both rock climbers.'

'Perfect candidates.'

'The new detective constable is spending his evenings watching them. We're ready. As soon as they try something, we'll have them.'

'Make sure you do.' Crossley frowned and pinched the bridge of his nose. 'Councillor May and two of his disciples came to see me yesterday. They're trying to put pressure on me about you.'

'You saw my note about Councillor May coming here?' He'd

never mention the threat to Crossley. No point, when it was his word against May's. And he wasn't about to say a word about the file in his drawer. Not until he was good and ready.

'I did. For what it's worth, I told him to get out of my office.' His mouth hardened. 'I won't be cowed by a man like him.'

'I hope you didn't tell him that, sir.'

Crossley smiled. 'I'm not that foolish yet, Tom. If you can wrap up the burglary case, that should shut them up for a while.'

'We will, sir. It's probably the first time I've ever wanted someone to go out and commit a crime.'

'And on these Smith brothers . . . if there's anything you need, let me know and you'll have it.'

'Thank you, sir. After we find them, we're still going to need solid evidence against them.'

'Get them behind bars and we'll find that.' He stood. 'The first intake of special constables starts training on Monday. You'll be getting your share once they're ready.'

'Yes, sir.'

At the door Crossley turned back, glancing at the plate. 'Do you feed that cake to all your guests?'

'Only the special ones, sir.'

'You should try it on your suspects. It might increase your confession rate.'

Walsh was grinning as he hung up his hat and settled on his chair with a sigh of relief.

'I found that link between Jeb and the Smiths, sir.'

'Then tell me about it. I need some good news today.' He ran a hand through his hair. The hours had passed too slowly, every minute taking an age to go by.

Walsh opened his notebook. 'I finally managed to track down a friend of Jeb's. He's been working down in Sheffield. Came back two days ago. Seems Jeb had been doing one or two jobs for the Smiths. Keeping an eye on people, that sort of thing. He had the bright idea that he could blackmail them and make some real money.'

'Poor bloody Jeb. He was the eternal optimist, wasn't he? He should have known better than to try anything with that pair. Did your man have any other information?'

'One little nugget, sir. Jeb used to meet the brothers at Beckett Street Cemetery. There was a grave the Smiths would visit.'

That meant something. Harper placed his elbows on the desk and leaned forward.

'I don't suppose he knows which one?'

Walsh smiled. 'As a matter of fact, sir, he does. Jeb was curious and they went up there one day. Eight people mentioned on the headstone. Most of them are called Johnson, all died the best part of thirty years ago.'

Around the time the brothers were born. Who was in that grave? Parents? Grandparents? The cemetery stood across the street from the workhouse . . .

'Let's go and see,' Harper said. 'There should be someone around to go through the records.'

It took an hour of searching before they stood on a patch of dried brown grass and staring at the carving on the stone. Johnson, Emmeline and Charles. Both died in 1873. Five more with the same surname, their dates of death earlier, all of them children gone before they were two years old. Finally, someone named Christine Bonner, whoever she might be.

'Doesn't give us any explanation, does it, sir?' Walsh said.

'I'm not so sure.' Harper looked over his shoulder. Across the street, the workhouse loomed large and forbidding. 'You go back to work.'

A police superintendent and the husband of a Guardian; they did everything but have a brass band playing for him. The workhouse master brought out the ledgers for 1873. The entry was there, neatly written: *Admitted November 14, two orphaned boys, John and Jack Johnson, aged four years. Uncle a widower with children, unable to take them.*

'Can we trace their time here?'

Sometimes all the records and attention to paperwork was a blessing. The brothers had been a handful. Aggressive, often beaten by the teachers, bullying other boys. At the age of nine, they'd been recommended for emigration to Canada. The rough life out there might hammer some discipline into them.

One final note was clipped to the page, the ink fading to brown. On the way to the ship in Liverpool, John and Jack escaped.

The police were alerted, but they were never found. Gone, forgotten among all the other children who passed through the place. But this pair had come back to Leeds.

It wasn't much, but for the first time he felt he really knew them. He had a proper taste of them.

TWENTY-THREE

'We spent most of the day in Harehills,' Fowler said as he returned with Sissons. 'Visited the shops this Harehills Development Company owns. The Smiths haven't been round collecting rent. People are wondering what's going on.'

'They're trying to keep their heads down.' Harper rubbed his chin, feeling the bristles. He needed a shave. 'That's good. Let's keep them running.' A moment's thought. 'I'd like you out with Sissons tonight, keeping watch on our burglars. They must be about due to strike again.'

'Yes, sir.'

'If they set foot outside with a bag, telephone me at home. I'd like to be there when you catch them.'

He hadn't forgotten May's threat. He couldn't. Only words, maybe, but they still lurked inside him. To have him killed. As he climbed down from the tram in Sheepscar, Harper's eyes darted around, alert for anyone. He crossed the street quickly, then through the doors of the Victoria as he realized his heart was thumping. He was going to feel this way until the case was done.

He didn't carry a truncheon, but he had one weapon in his pocket, a woven leather cosh filled with lead shot that he'd confiscated from a street robber. Easily hidden, and handily dangerous. If they came for him, he'd give them a fight.

Annabelle was staring at her face in the mirror, adding a little more powder around her eye. The bruise was fading, the rainbow of colours growing dull.

'I had an appointment at the workhouse this afternoon,' she

said. 'I swear, half the women looked at me and assumed you'd done it.'

'I hope you set them straight.'

'I told them you beat me black and blue on Mondays, Wednesdays and Fridays, and red and green on Tuesdays, Thursdays and Saturdays, with Sundays off for good behaviour.' She saw his face fall and turned. 'Course I said what happened, you daft ha'porth. It gave them a good laugh. I hear you were up there yourself. Digging into records or something.'

'Mam,' Mary called out, 'why do they call it a shiner?'

'Because it glows in the dark.'

'Does it?' Her eyes sparkled with interest. 'Does it really?'

'No, it's just a word. Where did you hear it, anyway?'

'Billy Westow. He says his dad gives his mam shiners all the time.' Annabelle looked at him.

'You tell Billy that his da shouldn't do that, and he'd better not do it, either,' Harper said.

'I already did,' Mary answered. 'I told him if he tried it with me, I'd punch him on the nose.'

Annabelle rolled her eyes.

Home. A complete madhouse. But nowhere else he'd rather be.

Later, in bed with his arm around his wife, Harper asked, 'What about your meeting with the Liberal on the Guardians?'

'I've put it off till next week. Better if I look normal again. There's a third man I'd like to talk to, as well. But he's Temperance, so you can imagine how he feels about me owning a pub.'

'You'll convince them.'

She snuggled closer. 'Probably not. But if I can persuade them to go for one thing, that'll help. Something for Annie and Ada. Just *one* thing, Tom. I've asked the chairman to convene a meeting of the board so I can put my ideas forward. That's not a lot, is it?'

No, he thought. It wasn't, and sometimes small victories were the only ones possible. But he needed something bigger.

'Mr and Mrs Dunn took a stroll again last night,' Sissons said. Just a few days on the squad and he was already looking more comfortable, starting to belong there. 'The same route as the night before. He was still limping a little.'

'They kept stopping to look at houses,' Fowler added. 'Interesting, though. They were always ones with no lights burning.'

'Were they carrying anything?' Harper asked.

'No, sir. Looked like they were selecting their next job,' Sissons said. He glanced at the sergeant. 'We're sure of it. They took more time over everything than the night before. Probably just waiting until he's healed.'

'Or he might think someone's watching and he's putting it on for effect. We'll have the pair of you out again tonight. I'll join you.' He could feel the prickle of excitement. And if it wasn't tonight, it would be the one after. Just a matter of time until the Dunns were in custody. 'In the meantime, I have another job for you. You're both good with records and details. Find out about a family named Johnson. The parents died back in seventy-three. Surviving twin boys called Jack and John. They were put in the workhouse. I want to discover what happened with the family. We already know where the brothers ended up.'

'Glad to, sir,' Sissons replied, smiling.

'Where do you want me, sir?' Walsh asked. He seemed relieved to have escaped a day sorting through papers and fusty documents.

'We've cut the Smiths off from their account at the bank and we know they haven't been showing their faces to collect rents. Where's their money coming from? Find me the answer to that.'

'I'll do my best, sir.'

'The chief was here yesterday,' he told Ash after the others had left.

'Tollman mentioned it, sir.' For a moment, there was mischief in his eyes. 'Said he gave him some cake.'

'Mr Crossley's probably still chewing. May went to see him again. The chief more or less threw him out.'

'What do you want me to do, sir?'

'We need more ammunition against them.'

'We've gathered a fair bit already, sir.'

'But still no link between them and the Smiths.'

'If it exists.'

'It's there,' Harper said. He was convinced. 'It makes sense, it fits. I can feel it. If we could find out who runs the North Leeds Company . . .'

'You know we're hammering our heads against a brick wall there, sir. Their lawyer will never tell us.'

'I know, I know.' He exhaled loudly. 'Sometimes I think the best thing we could do for justice is get rid of all the attorneys.'

'I doubt there's a copper alive who'd disagree, sir.' He gave a small cough. 'By the way, I'm hoping to meet a friend who has a position in the Clerk of Works office. He has a few stories to tell.'

'We need *evidence*.'

'We have it in the file. Enough to give to the chief, sir. That should keep Mr May off your back.'

He'd love to believe that. But he knew about men like May. If they couldn't find revenge one way, they'd have it another.

Harper had a stop of his own to make. Over to the brand-new Metropole Hotel, a stone's throw from the railway station. Another sign of the money in Leeds. But all the elaborate facings on the brickwork and the cupola from the old Cloth Hall couldn't stop soot from turning the brickwork black. Just a year old and already it looked like it had been planted there for decades.

Seth Myers was sitting in the restaurant, an empty plate and a jug of coffee in front of him. He was a ponderous man, straining at the seams, cheeks hanging in jowls, chins merging with his thick neck. Every movement seemed to make him break out in a sweat as he waddled his way around Leeds. This was as much of an office as he had.

He looked ridiculous, but his mind was sharp and precise. Myers made a living selling information, everything he heard tucked away in his head and ready to be passed on if the price was right.

'Rare to see you in here, Mr Harper,' Myers said. He had a soft, high voice, more like a woman than a man, coy and striking.

'That's because I don't often need to speak to you.' He sat across from the man, took an empty cup and poured himself some coffee. A few years before, Myers had found himself in trouble, owing money he didn't have. For once, someone had been too clever for him. Harper had helped. A visit from a policeman and all the worry dispersed like smoke. It left Myers with another debt, but this was one he'd be able to repay.

He was the man who could shine a light on the shadows, the one who knew all the darker secrets. Harper had saved the best for last.

'You look like a man with something on your mind, Superintendent.'

'Two things, if you want to know. Councillor May and Councillor Howe.'

'I see.' He brought out a packet of cigarettes, lit one and began to cough, spitting into a handkerchief. 'They're powerful men in this city.'

'For God's sake, Seth, don't waste my time with the bloody obvious. If you can't do better than that, I might as well leave now.'

Myers kept a steady gaze. 'Give me an idea of what you want, Mr Harper.'

'The stuff hardly anyone knows. With proof, or tell me where to find it.'

Myers smoked, then rubbed his hand across his mouth. 'Can you come back tomorrow?'

'Yes. And if you can find a link between them and some brothers called Smith, everything between us will be square. I need facts, though, not rumours.'

Fowler and Sissons were collating their papers, a small stack of them, putting everything in order. Harper leaned against the desk, waiting.

'We've managed to find a few things, sir,' the sergeant said as he pushed the spectacles up his nose. 'Would you like to take a guess where Mr and Mrs Johnson lived?'

'Harehills.' It didn't need a genius to think of that.

'The father was a cobbler. Not a very good one, from all reports, he never had much business. Liked to drink what he earned. His wife took in washing.' Fowler shrugged. They'd all heard the story a thousand times. Children in those families were lucky to survive. Judging by the gravestone, most of them hadn't.

'The death certificates on both parents say pneumonia, sir,' Sissons told him. 'It was October, so they probably couldn't afford to heat the house.'

So common. So mundane. And a pair of killers had grown out of that. When the brothers were small, they were the type of children Annabelle would have been fighting to protect. Now her husband was going to put them on the gallows. Life playing its cruel jokes.

'We went up to their old neighbourhood,' Fowler said. 'A few people still remember them. The father was surly, drunk half the time. Pawned some of the boots people brought in for him to mend. Not very popular.'

'Have the brothers been seen up there?'

'I showed the photographs around. Nobody recognized them.'

One point bothered him. 'If they didn't have any money, how did they afford a headstone?'

'Mrs Johnson had burial insurance, sir,' Sissons said. 'Paid it every week, on the nose, always made sure there was a penny set aside. Doted on her children. Fed them before she'd take a bite herself. That other woman on the gravestone was her sister.'

It was common enough. People wanted some memorial, something to say that they'd lived and died and spent some time on this earth.

'Good work.'

The information filled out the image, added colour and shade to what he'd learned. Jack and John, a pair of boys who still idolized and mourned their mother, not seeing that they'd grown into the kind of men she'd despise.

'Any leads on where they're finding money, Mr Walsh?'

'It's definitely not the shopkeepers, sir. I visited more of them, and nobody's seen hide nor hair of the Smiths. No robberies that could be them. All I can think is that they have some squirrelled away.'

'They have another place,' Harper said. 'A bolt hole we don't know about yet. Sissons and Fowler, you're going back to the planning office tomorrow.'

The sergeant grinned. 'The clerk will be sick of the sight of coppers.'

'He loves the company.' Harper smiled. 'You've all done an excellent day's work.'

'What did your pal in the Works office have to say?'

The chop house was busy, alive with the constant low hum of voices as men dined after work. Prosperous people with content faces, tucking into their food.

Ash chewed a piece of lamb, picked out some gristle, then said: 'He's promised me some information on Monday, sir.'

'I went to see Seth Myers today,' Harper said.

'I wasn't aware you knew him.'

'He owes me a favour. I decided it was time to collect.'

The inspector raised an eyebrow. 'Anything interesting?'

'I'll find out tomorrow.'

'We're going to have a very thorough file, sir.'

'There's still one piece I want to find.' The link to the Smiths. 'What if we can't, sir?' Ash put down his knife and fork. 'What if it's not there?'

It was a fair question. He was hoping against hope for the evidence. If he couldn't find it, what would he do with all the information? There was enough in there to damn May and Howe.

'You could pass it to the chief constable, sir.'

'We'll see. Do you want some pudding?'

A still, warm night, no breeze to stir the leaves. Soot smuts hung in the air; they were part of the landscape of Leeds. He found Sissons standing under the tree, eyes fixed on the Dunns' window. A light glowed inside. Behind the curtain he could pick out the shadows of two figures moving around.

'Have they stirred outside at all?' Harper asked.

'Not since I've been here, sir. But they're busy enough.'

There was nothing to do but stand and wait. A detective's lot in life.

'Are you enjoying plain clothes so far?'

'I am, sir.' He still sounded enthusiastic. 'Better than being on the beat, if you know what I mean.'

'I do.' He'd felt that way himself. Even after all these years, he still did. 'One thing about this job, you'll always have something different. Even if it's not always entertaining.'

'Honestly, I don't mind this, sir. Gives me a chance to think.'

'What do you think about, Mr Sissons?'

'This and that, sir.' The lad sounded so earnest it was hard not to smile. 'Believe it or not, I conjugate Latin verbs. It fills the time and it keeps me alert.'

Harper chuckled. He'd never have predicted that answer. Still, to each their own.

'Keep your eyes open and learn from the others. They're good. Just don't get cocky, or I'll see you're gone before you know it.'

'Yes, sir. Of course.' Even in the darkness, he was certain the lad blushed.

'Are you in lodgings?'

'No, sir. With my parents in Beeston.'

'What does your father do?' Talk passed the time. And a good way to know the man.

'He works in a coking plant. I have two sisters, they're both pupil-teachers. One of them's going to qualify soon.'

He could hear the pride in the man's voice. 'And you like to study, too.'

'Yes, sir. Those couple of days at the college made me think.'

'You're not going to leave us?'

'No, sir.' Sissons sounded shocked at the idea. 'Definitely not now. But I would like to study classics properly sometime, sir.' A hint of a smile. 'I know it'll never happen, but . . .'

A man with intelligence and ambition. He'd work out well.

Close to half past eleven, the light in the room went off and Harper tensed. Ten minutes later, the Dunns still hadn't emerged. The only sound was a drunk bawling a song outside the Cemetery tavern on Woodhouse Lane.

'They've gone to bed,' Harper said finally. 'Find Sergeant Fowler and call it a night.'

'Yes, sir. Goodnight.'

The quickest way to the Victoria was cutting down the hill, then a short walk to Sheepscar. He set out at a quick, steady pace, thinking hard. Either the Dunns were preparing to flit or they were getting everything ready for a burglary. Tomorrow, he decided. And they'd catch the couple in the act.

He was on Meanwood Road when he heard them. A boot scuffling and kicking a stone behind him. If he hadn't been alert, still all too aware of May's threat, he might never have noticed. Soon enough even his poor hearing could pick out more. Two men, no more than twenty yards behind. Neither of them speaking. He slid the cosh out of his pocket, feeling the weight of it in his hand. The prickling of goose pimples on his arms. It was going to happen. He'd be ready for it.

Harper slowed a fraction, letting them gain ground on him. When they were about five yards away, he stopped suddenly and turned. The men halted, haloed under the gas lamp. Not the Smiths. He'd never expected that; they were too sly to risk attacking a policeman. These men were both stocky, years of labour showing on their bodies, wearing old jackets and shirts without collars. Their caps were pulled down low and they had kerchiefs covering the lower part of their faces.

'Can I help you?'

For a moment they stood absolutely still, unsure what to do now. Not professionals, that was obvious. Then one of the men charged towards him. A stupid move. He had his head down like a rugby player aiming for the try line. Too easy to sidestep at the last second and bring the cosh down hard on his head. The man crumpled on the pavement.

His friend wavered, looking around for an escape, before he turned and started to run. But he was too slow. Harper was already on him. A sharp blow to the hip sent him crashing to the ground, howling with pain. A second to the knee meant he wouldn't be going anywhere.

Harper stood, panting hard. If they were the best May could afford, he had nothing to worry about at all. That fear niggling inside had been for nothing. He dug through his pockets until he discovered the police whistle and began to blow.

TWENTY-FOUR

'I want them taken to Millgarth. Keep them in the cells overnight.'

'Yes, sir.' Two constables had arrived, heavy footsteps echoing off the buildings as they ran.

'Of course, sir,' one of them said doubtfully. 'Only that one, don't you think he needs a doctor? He's spark out.'

The other attacker was still moaning, curled up like a small child. Harper nodded sharply. 'Have them both checked.'

'Are you all right, sir?'

'Never better,' he replied with a smile. 'I'll fill out my report in the morning.'

He felt as if he was walking on air. After building it all up in his mind and imagining the worst, it had been nothing. Over in a moment. The walk home only seemed to last a few seconds. That sense of victory was still there as he unlocked the front door of

the Victoria and crept up the stairs. Everything in darkness. He
eased Mary's door open, standing and watching her as she slept,
before tiptoeing away.

Annabelle stirred as he slid into bed. A small grunt, but nothing
more. Harper lay, staring up at the ceiling and waiting for the
adrenaline to drain out from his system. Then he'd be able to rest.
All the danger he'd imagined had turned out to be hot air. Never
mind a teacup, it wasn't even a storm in a thimble. May was all
bluster. He could be broken.

Two folders sat on his blotter. Harper opened the top one. Harold
Bowling, aged forty-two. A few years as a boiler stoker in a factory
that ended after he broke his arm. After that, a history of convictions
for assault and robbery. The photograph showed a round, belligerent
face, cropped hair and aggrieved eyes.

The other was Ben Deighton. In and out of prison since he was
twelve. Affray, theft, violence, he'd done it all. Squat, thick features,
a broken nose and dull expression.

'Drag them up to the interview room,' he ordered.

'I'd like to be there, if you don't mind, sir,' Ash said. 'I arrested
Deighton a time or two. It'll be like a family reunion.'

'The more, the merrier.'

He'd managed almost four hours of sleep after his mind finally
slowed, and woke refreshed and curiously content. Not a scratch
on him and it had all been done before he knew it. An anti-climax.
No battle, no fight in the men who'd come for him. Harper knew
he should have felt more: fury, outrage, overwhelming relief. But
there was nothing.

They were a sorry pair. Bowling with a grubby bandage around
his skull, Deighton holding on to his friend and limping heavily.
Pushed on to the chairs, they looked sullen and defeated. Good, he
thought. Men like that always talked. Ash stood by the door, arms
folded, looming over the men like death.

'We know you attacked me,' Harper began. 'Let's take that as
read. What I want to know is who hired you to do it.'

'Nobody,' Bowling answered. 'Saw you and thought you was an
easy mark.'

'That's a good start. You've got the lie out of your system. Now,
why don't we try the truth instead?'

'He offered me a pound to help him do you,' Deighton said.

'Is that right? A pound for five minutes' work. Quite a bargain.' Harper slammed his hand down on the desk. 'Looks like you weren't up to the job. Either of you.'

'He's lying. It was him as offered me the money,' Bowling protested. He tried to stand, but Ash's large hand pushed him back down.

'Blaming each other. I'd say that's progress, wouldn't you, Inspector?'

'Always a pleasure when thieves fall out, sir,' Ash agreed.

Not much more than a grain of sense between them. Breaking them down wouldn't take long. Come up with the right names and he might achieve something.

'True, in't it?' Bowling said. 'He offered me the pound.'

'Didn't.'

'Shut up,' Harper barked, and the room fell silent. 'Someone offered you both money.'

No answer. Ash put his hand on the back of Bowling's neck and Harper saw the man shudder a little.

'The superintendent asked a question. It's polite to answer.'

'Ask him.' He jerked a thumb at Deighton.

'Well?' Harper asked. The man seemed to squirm on his chair, grimacing as he moved.

'This bloke I know. He come up to me in the pub.'

'When? Where?'

Deighton swallowed hard, his Adam's apple jumping. 'Night before last in the Palace. We was having a drink, him and me.' He tilted his head towards Bowling. 'Said he'd give us a fiver for a job. Good money, that.'

'Who was he?'

'Charlie.'

'Charlie who?' Ash leaned over them, his voice filled with menace.

'Cutter,' Bowling said. 'Got a scar here.' He ran a dirty fingertip down his cheek. Harper glanced at the inspector, seeing him nod then leave the room. He could believe this story. It tasted like truth.

'Why did Charlie Cutter want you to attack me?'

'Didn't ask. Not when he was offering money,' Deighton told him.

'Who was paying him?'

'Don't know. But he never said you was no copper. Just called you a gentleman.'

Inside, Harper smiled. The first time he'd ever been called *that*.

'Never mind. You'll have plenty of time in prison to think about it.'

'The word's out to the men on the beat, sir,' Ash said. 'We should have Charlie in here later on today.'

'I've met him before. He's hardly any brighter than those two.'

'Shouldn't be too hard to pry a name out of him, then.'

Another fire. At the back of a building on Grape Lane this time. The same method as before, with the same results. A scorched door, but no damage done. Twigs and paper heaped together, three matches to start the blaze. No paraffin, nothing at all to help it along. Done by someone who didn't have a clue. But who? And why? There was nothing to connect this place to the last small fire. They appeared to be utterly random. No rhyme, no reason, and that worried him more than anything.

Reed had been out patrolling every day, along with his sergeant and his constable. But there was a limit to how much ground three people could cover. He'd been reluctant, but after the second fire he'd warned shopkeepers to stay alert. Not much more he could do, except be ready as soon as anyone spotted smoke. So far they'd had two false alarms: someone burning rubbish in his garden and a call to the smokehouse where they were turning herring into kippers. But it was better to waste the time than miss something. He needed to find the firestarter before they got lucky. And he had no clues at all.

It was filling his days. At least he had the real police work he'd been craving, and it kept his mind off the lack of progress in Leeds. Billy had received another letter from Tom Harper, but it just said the same thing in different ways: the investigation was barely inching ahead.

He realized it all seemed so distant now. He had a devil of his own to find before someone died.

'Sir!' Walsh's shout jerked his head up from the piece of paper in front of him. Recruitment figures so far for special constables. It was encouraging. The first intake was training, a second forming.

Leeds would be covered once the fighting in South Africa began. They'd definitely need the men: already close to fifty police officers had gone, and more would join them as soon as war was declared.

'What is it?'

'We've had a good sighting of the Smiths.'

Harper was on his feet, chair scraping over the floor. He felt the electricity running through his body.

'Where?'

'Hunslet. A corner shop. Two men came in to buy cigarettes. The shopkeeper recognized them from the photographs. As soon as they left, he sent someone to fetch a bobby.'

'I want that area flooded with men. Everyone we can spare. House to house in the streets all around.'

'Very good, sir.'

'You're a sergeant now. You can supervise.'

Walsh beamed. 'Glad to, sir.'

'I want to know everything you find. And if you discover where they are, send for me. You understand?'

'Absolutely, sir.'

He was going to be there when the brothers were captured, to snap the cuffs on them himself and hear the lock click shut around their wrists.

'What are you waiting for?'

He'd barely gone before Tollman put his head round the door.

'Just wanted to let you know, sir. They're bringing Charlie Cutter in.' He frowned under his moustache. 'He might be a little the worse for wear, if you know what I mean.'

'I don't care if he's been put through the bloody mangle. Tell me when he's here.'

Yes, he thought. The tide had definitely turned. He was going to win this one and he was going to do it soon.

Charlie looked battered. The shoulder seam on his jacket was ripped, the sleeve hanging off. Blood and bruises on his face, and the white scar on his cheek seemed to glow. Wrists cuffed behind him as he sat with his back straight in the interview room.

Finally, as Harper stood and stared at the sorry figure, the dam seemed to burst and the feelings raged through him. All the anger, the bile, the frustration at the cases that still stood unresolved.

'Simple question,' he said. 'Who paid you to have me attacked?'

'Don't know what you're talking about,' Cutter replied.

Harper grabbed him by the hair, jerking him up to his feet, and slammed him back against the wall. Before Charlie could react, the superintendent's hand was round his throat, pinning him in place and very slowly squeezing. The man was choking. He didn't care. It would be so easy to throttle the life out of him now. Simple to put it down to an accident, resisting arrest. No one would question it. For one quick moment, the satisfaction of it seemed to overcome him. But then he'd never hear the name. And he knew whose name he wanted to hear.

'Are you a little deaf?' Harper hissed.

'No.' Cutter had just enough breath to speak and try to shake his head.

'I was starting to wonder, Charlie, since you didn't answer my question. Do you want me to repeat it?' A nod. 'Who paid you to have me attacked?'

'Can't say.' The words struggled out of his mouth. Harper's fingers tightened a little on the man's windpipe.

'I didn't catch that.'

'I can't say.'

'Oh, you can,' Harper told him. He brought his face close, seeing the panic rise on Cutter's face. 'And you're bloody well going to. I get very nasty when people try to hurt me.'

Without warning, he let go. Cutter staggered forward, gulping down air.

'Do you want another go at answering?'

'He'll kill me.' He. That confirmed it wasn't the Smiths. Which left . . .

'Who?'

But Cutter just pushed his lips together and stared ahead.

'Who'll kill you, Charlie?' he said. 'Who'll put you in your grave?' Nothing.

'It'd be a pity if a whisper went around that you'd told me.'

'You wouldn't.' There was panic in Cutter's eyes. The doubt was there now.

'What sort of bet would you put on that? Wager your life on it, would you?'

But whatever Harper tried, Charlie wouldn't budge. He was too

scared to give up the name. The inspector took a pace closer and
the other man flinched. He could intimidate, he could go from a
whisper to a shout, but nothing helped.

An hour and a half of it, until Harper was hoarse, his voice
rasping in his throat.

'Take him back to the cells,' he said with disgust.

A mug of tea tasted like balm as he swallowed and sighed.

'Any word from Hunslet yet?' he asked.

'No, sir,' Tollman replied.

Damnation. Maybe they were passing through, on their way
somewhere else? One step forward brought another going back.

By the time Fowler and Sissons arrived, his temper had settled.
He'd talk to Cutter again later. Let him spend a few hours behind
bars, not that it was his first time.

'You look like two gentlemen who've had a fulfilling day.'

If only that were true, he thought. They seemed exhausted and
dejected.

'Sorry, sir,' Fowler told him. 'We've been through every single
transaction for the last year. If they've bought another property,
they've hidden it well. The only place bought by brothers was the
one they had in Hyde Park.'

Another road that led nowhere.

'Give yourselves a break for a few hours. We're going to watch
the Dunns when it's dark. They'll do something tonight. I can feel
it in my water.' Another lie. But worthwhile if it gave them some
heart.

No rest for him, though. Instead, a walk through the sweltering
heat of town to the Metropole Hotel.

'What do you have for me, Seth?' Harper asked as he settled at
the table. He poured a glass of water from the jug. Lukewarm, but
better than nothing.

'Scraps, Mr Harper.'

'Let's hear them.'

The man was right. Bits and pieces, crooked deals that had put
money in their pockets. More weight, but not what he needed.

'The Smiths?' Harper asked, and Myers shook his head. 'The
North Leeds Company?' The same again.

Harper nodded, then left.

*   *   *

The clock had turned seven when Walsh returned. He looked dusty and rumpled, a serious expression on his face.

'We can't come up with any trace of them in Hunslet, sir.'

'How many men do you have working on it?'

'I managed to scare up ten bobbies. A few new recruits, a couple of those specials who've just started, too. They've been going house-to-house, fanning out from the shop. I had a word with the fella who runs it. He swears he'd never seen them before today.'

'Could be worth finding out who's new in the area.'

'I'm doing that, sir. Followed up on three so far.' He shrugged. 'All clean.'

'Keep going. It's the best thing we have at the moment. Who did you leave in charge out there?'

'Sergeant Dunkley from 'B' Division. He's solid. I warned him not to go in if he finds them.'

'Good.' He was going to have the pleasure of leading that, however long it took. 'Go and get some sleep. Another long day tomorrow.'

'And there I was thinking Sunday was the day of rest.' He grinned.

'You ought to know by now. Remember what they say: no rest for the wicked.'

'You'd think they'd make an exception for coppers. I'll see you in the morning, sir.'

At half past nine he turned off the gas to the mantle and put on his hat. He'd had another go at Charlie Cutter, question after question, every one of them answered by silence, until Harper slapped the wall with the palm of his hand.

'The men you hired will be spending plenty of time at hard labour for attacking a copper. You'll serve even longer.'

'Where's your evidence?' The first words he'd spoken during the session, and the first small spark of defiance.

'The testimony of two men.'

'Prove they're telling the truth!'

'And your own record.' Two convictions for fixing up something similar; that would be enough. But neither had been on a policeman. Cutter shut up. Not another word.

He wasn't going to find out who'd ordered the attack. So simple, so bloody simple, and he'd never know. Charlie was so terrified he'd rather do a year's hard labour than give up the name. Who in God's name could have that effect on him? He could guess.

'Penny for them, sir.' He turned and saw Ash waiting.

'Right now they're not worth a farthing. What are you still doing here?'

'I thought I'd come along with you tonight, if you don't mind. I quite fancy a little action, and I'd like to see how the new man is doing. And have the pleasure of nabbing the burglars, of course.'

'If it happens tonight.'

'We can try to propitiate the gods, sir.'

Harper stared at him doubtfully. 'Sometimes I don't have a clue what you're saying.'

The inspector grinned. 'Blame my Nancy, sir. It's all this stuff she has me reading. Right now it's *The Decline and Fall of the Roman Empire*, by some chap called Gibbon. Quite stirring.'

'You should talk to Sissons. He has a head for that type of thing.'

'Happen I will sometime, sir.'

They began the walk through town, up Eastgate and the Headrow, before turning on to Woodhouse Lane. All the raucousness of the night around them, shouting, crying, singing. Life.

The lights glowed in the Dunns' rooms, faint shapes moving behind the curtains. Half an hour and they snapped off.

'Go and tell Fowler,' Harper ordered Sissons. 'Be ready to move.' His gaze was fixed on the front door. But it didn't open. He kept utterly still, breathing softly, then Sissons was back.

'They slipped out the back and down the ginnel, sir. The others are behind them. Mr Dunn was still limping. Not as bad tonight, though.'

'Right. Let's go.'

As soon as he reached the main road, he could see them. Dunn was carrying a bag, the weight making one shoulder sag. He was moving awkwardly. But it was going to be tonight. Finally. Harper smiled. The man must be a good climber if he could attempt something with a bad ankle.

'Let's cross the road,' he said quietly. 'People never look that way.'

Fowler and Ash were dawdling. Impossible to miss them, though. Finally they vanished into a shop doorway. Good, Harper thought. Out of sight. But the Dunns never even glanced back, acting as if they were on another casual stroll.

All the way down past the college. No hurry, and eventually a turn on to Blackman Lane. Going back to the Blenheims. Exactly what he expected.

'Hurry up,' he said to Sissons. 'Run to the corner and keep an eye on them.' He waved his hand, trusting the others would notice.

By the time they'd all gathered, the Dunns were out of sight. Then Sissons seemed to materialize from nowhere.

'Second ginnel along on the left, sir. Couldn't see which house.'

'Good work. Fowler and Ash will go to the far end and work their way back down. You and I will start here.'

TWENTY-FIVE

For a large man, Ash could walk with surprising silence. He appeared out of the darkness and placed his mouth close to Harper's good ear.

'Fourth house from the end.'

'Mrs Dunn should be waiting in the yard. You two whisk her away. Make sure she doesn't have a chance to call out. Sissons and I will wait for the husband to come out of the house.'

He gave it a full minute, long enough, then began to move softly along the ginnel behind the houses. A strange street, Harper thought, the buildings towering to three grand storeys and a cellar kitchen, but still only a small yard of flagstones like any ordinary terrace.

Ash stood by the back gate. 'Hasn't come back down yet.'

'No problems arresting her?'

'Taken to the lock-up on Woodhouse Moor.' A moment's pause. 'You're going to get the shock of your life, sir. I'll just wait out here in case of any escape.'

Baffled, Harper led Sissons into the yard. Filled with shadows, there were plenty of places to hide. A light burned in the kitchen; he had to hope that none of the servants popped outside and spotted them.

Five minutes edged closer to ten. Finally, Sissons nudged him.

'I heard a scrape of something, sir,' he whispered. 'I think he's coming out.'

He hadn't noticed any sound. Harper strained his eyes, staring at the drainpipe that ran up the back of the house. Then he picked out a shape, something blacker against the dark bricks.

His heart was so loud he was astonished the burglar didn't notice.

Down, down . . . and at the last moment Harper emerged and locked a handcuff around one of the burglar's wrists. The figure turned . . .

For a moment, he was too astonished to speak. Ash had said . . . but never mind. Then Sissons was there, removing the bag.

'Mrs Agatha Dunn, I'm arresting you for burglary.'

She tried to pull away, but he was expecting that, giving her just enough room to fall as he yanked her back towards him. A cuff on the other wrist behind her back.

The servants were spilling out of the door, drawn by the commotion. Sissons opened the bag.

'Plenty of jewellery in here, sir.'

'That belongs to the mistress,' a maid said as he held up a brooch. 'She keeps it on her dressing table.'

But Harper barely noticed. He was staring at Agatha Dunn, still trying to overcome his surprise. It served him right for having assumed something. A woman could be as good a criminal as a man. He ought to have considered the possibility. With Dunn's bad ankle, the signs were right in front of his bloody eyes. More fool him.

Her thick hair was hidden by a cap, her body clothed in a tight-fitting black outfit, a pair of trousers and a top that clung snugly against her body. Like a circus performer, he thought. A high-wire act.

'Is there a skirt in that bag?' he asked.

'Yes, sir, cushioning everything so it doesn't rattle.'

'Pass it over.' The least he could do was make her decent.

She glared as he dropped the skirt over her head, then pulled off the cap. A sudden silence in the yard as everyone realized.

'That's your burglar, ladies and gentlemen. Sissons, take her to the station. With her loot.'

A few questions for the servants and he knew the facts. The owner of the house was a professor at the Yorkshire College. He and his wife had gone to the Grand Theatre, seats booked a week before. Easy for Carl Dunn to have heard something at work.

'Someone will come by in the morning and take statements,' he promised.

Ash was waiting out in the ginnel.

'I told you that you'd have the shock of your life, sir. Could have blown me over when Fowler came out with the husband.'

'Yes,' Harper agreed. He began to laugh. The signs had been there, if he'd had the wit to see: she loved to climb, she was good at it. He'd assumed it would be the man; without thinking, he'd taken it as given that she'd be the lookout. His own blindness. 'I think it's time to go home.'

'I'll walk down to Sheepscar with you, sir.'

'A bodyguard?' For a second, he bristled. May had shot his bolt with last night's attack. After a moment, he calmed. Better safe than sorry. For tonight, at least.

'I thought we could have a chat, sir, that's all.'

They began to walk. The night air was still warm and close. 'Something on your mind?'

'This business with the councillors, sir. What are we going to do? Charlie Cutter's too scared to give up a name.'

'I know.' Harper wiped sweat from the back of his neck. 'Believe me, I know. We still need to find out who's behind the Smiths.'

'They won't talk when we catch them, sir.'

Harper knew that, too. He'd realized it from the very first murder. The brothers wouldn't give them a thing.

'We haven't caught them yet,' he said. 'They've managed to run us ragged so far.'

'They're out of options and out of money now, sir. It's just a matter of time. We can sweat them once they're behind bars.'

He expected nothing. The link between the Smiths and the councillors was real; he knew that in his heart. But he wondered if they'd ever be able to drag it into the light.

They parted at the Victoria. They'd seen no one on the streets, heard no footsteps anywhere. All the way home he hadn't given a thought to the possibility of attack.

'Thank you.'

'All part of the duty, sir.' He nodded towards the light in the window upstairs. 'Looks like Mrs Harper has waited up for you.'

He wondered about that as he climbed the stairs. It wasn't like

Annabelle. She was sitting calmly on the settee, staring straight
ahead and brooding.

'Is something wrong?'

'Yes,' she answered simply as she turned to face him. 'I heard
what happened last night.'

He could hear the accusation in her voice.

'It was nothing that hasn't gone on before,' he said. 'You were still
asleep when I left this morning. When was I supposed to tell you?'

'You know who was behind it?'

'I do. I've spent half the day questioning the men who did it.
And they won't say.'

'Why not, for God's sake?'

'They're more afraid of him than of prison. But it's over now.
He won't try again.'

'Are you sure?'

'Yes.' He had no doubt.

'I worry, Tom. I'm your wife.'

'Look at me. I'm fine. They never laid a finger on me.' He paused.
'It's not just that, is it?'

'No, I suppose it's not,' she admitted. 'It's . . . I don't know.
Everything.'

He drew her to her feet and hugged her close.

'Come on,' he said softly. 'Tell me.'

'I finally had a cup of tea with that Liberal from the Guardians
today,' she said. 'Told him how I thought the rules should change
so we can protect children properly.'

'What did he say?' He had to ask, although he could already
guess the answer.

'He heard me out, all polite, then he said, "Madam, I appreciate
that the law means we can now have women elected to the Board
of Guardians. That doesn't mean I have to like it, or that I will act
on anything a woman suggests." Haughty as you like. Got up and
walked out. I about had my jaw on the floor.'

Some men would never change. And there was nothing they could
do about it.

'What now?'

'My best hope is the one who's Temperance.' He felt her breathe
slowly against his neck. 'I don't think I'll have his support. Still,
the chairman agreed to a meeting so I can put forward my ideas.'

Gently, he stroked her back.

'Let's go to bed. Maybe it'll feel better in the morning.'

It wouldn't and they both knew it, but the words were like a salve.

Another day. As Harper quietly locked the door of the Victoria, he wondered if he'd even rested. With the burglars in their cells, he should have felt some relief. Instead, he'd lain there, mind refusing to wind down as he made his plans.

Maybe he'd managed two or three hours. His eyes stung as he blinked; it was still early, long before the first tram, but he could feel the heat rising off the cobbles.

The milkman was on his rounds, cart parked on Sheepscar Street. As he passed, the horse glanced at him with a big brown eye.

The Dunns would have been transferred to Millgarth overnight. He'd leave the questioning for Sissons, with Fowler to help. The new man had done all the work; he deserved the experience, as well as the credit for the arrests.

Harper sighed as he looked at a small mountain range of papers waiting on his desk, his expression softening as Sergeant Tollman brought him a mug of tea.

'You're a lifesaver.'

'Can't have you parched, sir.'

The station came to life around him. The shift changed at seven, boots tramping up and down the corridors, constables lining up in the yard outside before going off to their beats.

Harper watched them disperse, lost in his thoughts. Arresting the Dunns had bought him some time; the councillors wouldn't dare come after him for a little while now. But they'd be circling, and back on the attack soon unless he managed to stop them.

'It's the strangest tale I've ever heard, sir,' Fowler began. He'd come into the office, Sissons hurrying behind him. Harper glanced out of the window. Half past eleven and he felt cooped up in this place.

'Tell me over some food,' he told them. 'I need fresh air.'

The cafe by the market. It was handy, it was quick, and as close to cheerful as anywhere else.

'Right,' the superintendent told them as their sandwiches arrived.

'We already knew they both like climbing, sir,' Sissons began.

Harper nodded. 'Apparently it all started as a game. They were out for a walk one night and saw a house with no lights on. Mrs Dunn challenged her husband to climb up the drainpipe to the roof. He did, and the next night she told him to do it again, then walk across the slates.'

'But she was the one who was the burglar,' Harper said.

'He challenged her to try it.' Fowler picked up the story. 'She made herself that outfit she was wearing last night. He egged her on and she discovered she enjoyed it. Mrs Dunn was willing to go further than him. She developed a taste for it.'

'Was all this in Newcastle?'

'Yes, sir. She'd do a bit more each time. In through an open window, walk around, take a little something.'

'And soon she was taking more?'

Sissons nodded. 'They started doing it regularly. He'd go off and sell what they stole, always in another town. Once the force up there began looking for them, they decided to move. Mr Dunn found a job down here, and . . .' He shrugged.

'What did they think? We wouldn't be as bright as the coppers in Newcastle?'

'I don't know, sir,' Fowler answered. 'But we proved them wrong.'

'They'll have plenty of time to think about that once they've been sentenced.' He chuckled. 'Unless they manage to climb the wall and escape.'

Fowler winced. 'Don't even think it, sir. Where do you want us now?'

'Back on the Smiths,' Harper said. 'We've won this one. It's well past time to wrap up the other.'

By three o'clock, the small victory felt like ancient news. One more added to the pile of cases solved. The Dunns had led them a dance, but the music had stopped, the band packed up and gone home.

When the telephone rang, Harper reached for it without thinking, holding the receiver to his good ear.

'A good job on the burglars, Tom.' The chief constable's voice came clearly through the line. 'Give my congratulations to your men.'

'Thank you, sir, I will. It's the new lad, Sissons; he did all the work.'

'Already paid for himself?'

'With change left over.'

The smallest of silences and Crossley said: 'You've bought yourself some time, Tom. For now, anyway.'

He didn't have to spell it out. Finish the job and find the Smiths and the councillors would be off the chief's back.

'We're doing everything we can, sir.'

'I'm sure you are. I'm not really ringing about that, anyway. As I said, *that* threat has receded. It's the other one that concerns me.'

'Sir?'

'The war in South Africa.' He heard the man's low sigh. 'I had a chat with a friend at the War Ministry yesterday. He says all hell is going to break loose in September. October at the very latest. After that we're only likely to have volunteers the army rejects.'

Not a wonderful prospect; Harper knew that. Too many men in Leeds were already small and malnourished. Ending up with the worst of those patrolling the streets was like offering a licence to crime.

'What can we do?'

'I'm putting in more advertisements and going out to talk to groups. We're going to lose some good police officers to this war, Tom.'

'I know, sir.' He thought about Fowler, champing at the bit to go off and do his part.

'Don't mind me, Tom. I just rang to congratulate you and let off a little steam. We'll muddle through. And don't you worry about May and Howe. I'll make sure they can't touch you.'

'Thank you, sir.' But May had already done more than that. He knew the councillor had paid Charlie Cutter. But some truths you could never prove, only take on faith.

Harper sat back for a moment, then reached for a piece of paper and picked up his pen.

Dear Billy . . .

TWENTY-SIX

No more fires. Good news, Reed thought as he walked around Whitby, but baffling. The constable looked after the areas where the holidaymakers gathered, and he handled everywhere else, checking all the yards and the areas behind buildings.

He'd seen nothing suspicious that morning. No indications of any fire for a few days now. The ones he'd seen had been so poorly made they didn't even look like serious attempts at arson. But they were. He knew they were.

At dinner time he returned to the police station. The second week of August and Whitby was all any visitor could hope. They still had blue skies with a few high clouds, calm sea and a gentle breeze. Perfection. No wonder the place was so popular.

'Letter came in the second post for you, sir,' Sergeant Brown said. 'I put it on your desk.'

'Thank you. No reports of anything?'

'Quiet all morning, sir.' He chuckled. 'I've even done the dusting.'

'I'll bring out my white gloves and check.'

Brown grinned. 'You do that, sir. Just don't tell my missus how good a job I did or she'll expect me to put on a pinny at home.'

Tom's handwriting. He read it through quickly. Good news that they'd finally caught the burglar, but no breakthrough with the Smiths, Billy saw. Just some wishful bloody thinking in Hunslet. He crumpled the sheet and tossed it in the bin. He had enough problems of his own at the moment. He didn't need Tom's, too.

'Hunslet,' Harper said. 'We've had men going through it since that sighting.'

'And we've come up with nothing,' Walsh told him.

'Are we likely to find them there?'

'Honestly, sir, I really don't think so. We've covered a wide area, gone through it all twice. If they were there, someone would have recognized them by now.'

'Pull the men out. No sense in wasting them.' He looked at the others. 'Any ideas?'

'We've established they're not in Hunslet.' Ash frowned. 'But it makes me think two things. They had business there, and they're probably not too far away.'

'Why not too far away?' Fowler asked.

'I saw a list of what they bought in the shop. A twist of tea, cigarettes, and some sliced meat. That sounds like someone on their way home.'

Clever. Harper hadn't even thought to check their purchases.

'Then where's home?' he asked. 'That's the big question.'

'I've been thinking about that, too, sir,' Ash replied. 'The shop's on South Accommodation Road, just by the Royal Oak.'

Harper picked up the idea. 'Down the hill from Cross Green.'

'No more than a hop, skip and a jump.'

'Walsh, shift the men to Cross Green. Same thing, showing the photographs, asking around.'

'Yes, sir.'

'If I might, sir.' Sissons spoke for the first time. 'I had a beat in that area for two years. I still know people there. I could go knocking on doors. They might be more open with me.'

'Excellent,' the superintendent agreed. 'Do that.' Anything that could give them an advantage, an edge.

'I'll go with him if you don't mind, sir,' Fowler said. 'I know someone out that way myself. Very observant chap.'

It sounded mysterious, but he agreed. What did they have to lose?

'We're betting everything on them being in Cross Green?' Harper said to Ash after the men had gone.

'It's as likely as anything, sir.'

Maybe it was, but . . . he pictured Leeds in his mind, all the neighbourhoods bleeding one into another. From Hunslet to Cross Green, then down into the Bank. Or the other way: Hunslet to Holbeck or Beeston. It was a gamble, and he didn't feel as if Lady Luck was offering her brilliant smile.

'I know.' He raised his eyebrows. 'I just hope your hunch is right.'

'We'll find out, sir.'

*   *   *

It was no more than a quarter of an hour's walk from Millgarth to Cross Green. He itched to be out there himself. No. Stay in the office and take care of the divisional work, he thought. He had good men running everything. Trust them to get on with it and do their job. But that didn't make waiting any easier. At twelve he slipped out to a cafe and gulped down a sandwich and a cup of tea before returning to the station. No word.

By six they still hadn't returned. What was going on over there? Finally, he forced himself to go home. They'd telephone if they found anything; in a hackney, he could be there in ten minutes. Stepping off the tram in Sheepscar, he realized he'd given no more thought to being attacked. The worry had evaporated with that one feeble attempt. Still, he patted his pocket and felt the reassuring shape of the cosh.

As he opened the door to the living room above the Victoria, Mary scrambled to her feet and ran to him, holding out a piece of paper.

'Mam said I should show you this.'

'You should say hello and let your da take his hat off first,' a voice called from the kitchen.

It was a story, about a doll named Dolly who came to life at night, causing mischief and moving things around when everyone was asleep, before becoming just a porcelain doll again at first light. No one where she lived could understand what was happening.

'It's very good,' he told her. 'Are you going to continue it?'

She stared up at him, puzzled. 'Why?'

'How will the family find out who really did it?'

'But they don't need to, do they?' she asked as if his idea made no sense.

'In your da's mind, they do.' Annabelle came through, ruffling Mary's hair. 'He's a policeman, remember? They like every mystery to be solved.'

'Do you want me to write more, Da?'

'That's up to you,' he said. 'Why don't you tidy up and wash your hands before we eat?'

They watched as she scampered off.

'Don't ask me where it came from,' Annabelle said. 'She just settled down with a pencil this afternoon. The next thing I knew, she handed that to me.'

'It's good.' He pushed a lock of hair from her cheek. 'How about you? How do you feel today?'

'Downhearted. Hardly surprising, is it?'

'No.'

'I honestly thought I could persuade him. Now I'm relying on a Temperance chap who's already made it clear he doesn't have much time for a woman who runs a pub.'

'Maybe you can change his mind. And you still have the meeting. When is it?'

'The day after I talk to the Temperance man.' Annabelle sighed. 'Do you think I'm a fool for even trying?'

'Of course I don't. And nor do you. You're just trying to do your best for the children. Maybe they can all see that.'

'The Temperance man can't see beyond the end of his nose.'

'If you don't speak to him, you'll never know.'

She smiled. 'You sound like me talking to Mary.'

'Why, Mam? Is he telling you to tidy your room up?'

They looked down to see her standing beside them.

'Little pitchers and big ears,' Annabelle said. 'Get yourselves sat down and I'll put the food on the table.'

'I'm not going to write any more on that story,' Mary said with a serious face as she wiped her plate clean with the last of her bread. 'I think it's just right as it is. But,' she added, 'I might write another one tomorrow.'

A little before nine, just as he wondered if he'd hear anything tonight, the telephone began to ring. He was on his feet immediately, raising the receiver to his good ear.

'Hackney on the way for you, sir,' the night sergeant told him.

'Cross Green?' Harper asked.

'That's the one, sir.'

Standing in front of the mirror, Harper attached his collar studs and tied his tie.

'Is this it?' Annabelle asked.

'I hope so.' He stared at his reflection. His face was growing older, the skin coarse and grainy. All the lines seemed to go deeper, as if they'd been carved into his flesh. The hair was thinner on his head, and more of it was grey. A very different man from the one who'd first put on a police uniform. 'I really hope so.'

Out through the pub, quiet on a Thursday night, and he waited on the corner for the cab to arrive. Then a rush along empty streets. People stood on their doorsteps, talking in groups, heads turning as the hackney rumbled past over the cobbles.

'We're there now, sir,' the driver called as he pulled up and Harper climbed down. By the coal shoots that marked the end of the mineral railway, not even a hundred yards from Ellerby Lane Mills, its broad shoulders outlined against the evening sky. The light was fading, a deep red on the horizon, as if all the factory chimneys of the West Riding were on fire.

'Have you found them?' he asked Ash. The others were with him, a pair of uniformed constables standing back, watching.

'Not yet, but we're close, sir. Two reports of them being seen on Timber Place in the last few days. It's just up the road.'

'How reliable are the people who told us?'

'One of them is the nosiest old biddy in the area, sir,' Sissons told him. 'Very sharp eyes. I think she remembers everyone who's ever set foot round here.'

Sometimes he could thank God for busybodies. They might make life loud and annoying, but they were there when you needed them.

'Didn't you say you have a friend round here?' he asked Fowler.

'He keeps a shop, sir. But it's up by the recreation ground. He's never seen them.'

'Do we know which house is theirs?'

'No, sir. But everyone reckons it's in a block of four terraced houses near the Methodist chapel, right before you get to Timber Terrace.'

'Is there anywhere to keep it under watch?'

'Three possibilities, sir,' Ash replied. 'There's the chapel and a school just down the street. Both of those would mean dragging out the caretakers; plenty of noise. But we'll be able to see the front of the houses that way.'

'What's the third idea?'

'Low Fold Mill. It's just down the hill. Good view from the top floor.'

'I want a man in there tonight.'

'I'll do it, sir,' Sissons volunteered.

'Someone will relieve you in the morning. I want a man in that chapel first thing tomorrow. That should cause less fuss than the school.'

'Very good, sir,' Ash answered. 'I thought you'd like to see the place.'

'I do.'

'Walk up there and turn down Grand Street. Timber Place is the second on your right.'

He stood at the corner, out of sight among the shadows. His fingertips tingled and he could feel the hair rise on the back of his neck. This was the place. He knew it. He *knew* it. The Smiths were behind one of those doors. They'd find out which one. And then they'd go in and take them.

'You see what I mean, sir?' Ash said after Harper had wandered back to the coal shoots. 'If we stick a man on the corner, he'll stand out.'

'I do. Who has this beat?'

'Me, sir.' One of the uniforms stepped forward. 'PC Storey, number 739.' An older man with a grave, concerned grace and a thin grey moustache. 'If you'll forgive me saying so, sir, all this standing around has put me behind. I'll have to explain it to my sergeant, you understand.'

That put *him* in his place, Harper thought. But the bobby was right. They had their rounds and people expected to see them.

'Just a few questions and you can be on your way. Has anyone moved into those houses on Timber Place recently?'

'Last would be about three months ago, sir. Number twelve. But I haven't seen them, so I don't know if it's your men or not. I don't know everyone on that street. As I told the inspector,' he added pointedly.

'How often do you go by there?'

'Every hour and a half, sir. It's a large beat.'

'From now on, I want you to make it every hour. And keep your eyes peeled. If you spot anyone or any movement out of the ordinary, or if you see one of the brothers, you let us know immediately. Understood?'

'Yes, sir.' He began to walk away, the slow, rocking gait of a beat copper.

'Constable.'

Storey turned. 'Sir?'

'If your sergeant has any questions or complaints, tell him to see me.'

'We're close now, sir,' Ash said.

'Yes.' He was thinking ahead, planning tomorrow. 'Walsh, you take over from Sissons in the morning. Fowler, you have the first stint in the chapel.'

'I'll pop and see the caretaker tonight and arrange everything,' Ash told him.

'Very good.' He was imagining how the day would go. A good force of men, battering down the door. The Smiths wouldn't give in without a fight. The police would have to knock them down and drag them out. 'Everyone make sure you have your truncheons. It's not going to be easy.'

Fowler joined him for the walk back to town. As they strolled, Harper had to chuckle.

'I don't need a bodyguard any longer. Our councillors tried and it didn't work.'

'We want to be certain, sir. It's on my way, I have to catch a tram. Besides, we're going through the Bank. Never know what you'll run into.'

True enough. He'd earned a few scars here over the years. But tonight he felt safe, like nothing could touch him. Things were finally coming to a head.

'We'll have them tomorrow, Sergeant.'

'I hope you're right, sir.' He pushed the spectacles up his nose. 'We've thought that before, though.'

'They're out of places to go. They don't have any choice.'

'I'll just be happy when it's all over,' Fowler said.

'So you can join the army?'

The sergeant straightened his back. 'I hope you can understand, sir. I love this job—'

'Then why go?' Harper asked. 'We need you here in Leeds, too.'

'Because the intelligence work will be something different, sir. Quite a challenge, too, from all my friend says.' He stayed quiet for a minute. 'I suppose that if I don't go, I'll spend the rest of my life wondering "what if" and feeling I should have done it.'

'You'll be welcome back when it's over. You know that.' But how many who boarded the boats to South Africa would come home? he wondered.

'Thank you, sir. For whatever it's worth, I think you've picked a good one in Sissons.'

'Seems that way so far. He might look like a lean streak of wind, but he has a good head on his shoulders.'

'He'll be fine once he gets his feet dirty.'

'I daresay,' Harper chuckled. 'You know we all wish you well, don't you?'

'I do, sir.'

At Millgarth they shook hands, as if they wouldn't be seeing each other again in a few hours.

Sheepscar was quiet as the late tram squealed to a halt. Harper alighted and looked around. Empty streets. No danger, exactly the way he'd told Fowler. That would come tomorrow.

'Billy?' The telephone line crackled. 'We think we've got them. The Smiths.'

'Where?'

'In Cross Green. I have men watching the place. We're going in later.'

Reed had heard it from Tom before. The same eagerness, the same hope. And afterwards, the same disappointment.

'I hope you find them.' It seemed like the diplomatic answer.

'You could jump on a train and be here in time. You said you wanted to see them arrested. For Charlie.'

He remembered what he'd said. He remembered every word of it. But day by day, as time passed, the feeling was starting to fade. Charlie's ghost was growing fainter. He wanted his revenge, but it had stopped overwhelming everything. He still cared, but the living meant more than the dead.

'I can't,' he said. 'I've got someone here trying to set fires. Pathetic jobs, but I need to catch them.'

He'd been out late the night before, walking around town in the darkness, eyes alert for any flame or smell of smoke. Nothing. He'd keep searching. That was his job.

'Any leads?'

'None at all. When you find this pair . . .' He let his words tail away, not sure quite what he wanted.

'I will, Billy.' Harper's voice was faint at the other end of the wire. 'And good luck.'

TWENTY-SEVEN

'Which is number twelve?' Harper asked.

'The last one at this end,' Fowler replied.

The attic room at the Methodist chapel gave a good view along part of Timber Place. High enough to look down into the houses. Nine in the morning, the sun trying to find a way through the smoke haze from the factory chimneys. Men had long since left for work. Most of the women, too. A pair of young children played with a ball on the pavement. A sorrowful air of desolation hung over the area.

But all the curtains were still closed at number twelve.

'If I thought someone really lived there, I'd say he'd worked the night shift,' Fowler said.

'We need to make sure. Don't want to be barging in on an innocent man.'

'You don't believe that any more than I do, sir.'

'No,' Harper agreed. 'I don't suppose I do.'

His eyes were fixed on the house and the ground around it. Waste ground to one side and behind, a heavy tangle of chest-high weeds that ran down to Low Fold Mills. But walls ran around it all; from all he could see, there was no other way out.

'I'm going down to the mill,' Harper said. 'Keep watching.'

Atlas Street, Grand Street, then across more empty ground. The mill was overwhelmingly loud, row after row of looms booming like thunder in the huge room. The women still seemed to talk to each other, mouthing words and reading lips as their hands moved without thinking. Even up the stairs in the office, with the door closed tight, he could hear the machines and feel the thrum of machinery through his body. What would it be like for someone with proper hearing?

'Anything to see from here?'

'Nothing at all, sir,' Walsh told him. 'Curtains closed at the back of the house, no one's been out in the yard. Sissons said there was no movement last night, but he did spot lights inside.'

'Good.' Someone was definitely there. Now he just had to hope they hadn't vanished in the darkness. But how could they know anyone was watching?

'Is there any other way out for them?'

'Just that gap next to the house we're watching, sir.'

They could be bottled in.

'Is there a back door to the mill? A way to get to that ground?'

'No idea, sir. You'll have to ask the manager.'

He couldn't hear a word as the man led him through the factory and into a store room. The noise buffeted him, pushing and pulling as he walked carefully between the looms. How could anyone stand it day after day? The women here must be stone deaf.

But the manager chattered away, seemingly oblivious to the sound. Finally, he closed the wooden door. Shelves lined the walls, all filled with bolts of finished cloth from floor to ceiling. It smelled dusty, catching in his nostrils and at the back of his throat and making him cough.

'You get used to it.' The man laughed. He had a thick, ruddy face, the back of his hands covered with wiry ginger hair. 'Get used to anything in a place like this. This is what you're looking for.'

A heavy door made of metal, two locks and a bar to hold it in place.

'Needs to be solid so no bloody thieves can get in. Them lasses out there are bad enough, they'll take owt that's not nailed down.' He produced two keys, worked them and lifted the bar. The door opened with a rusty shriek. Was everything so loud in this place, Harper wondered. 'There you are.'

A mess of high weeds. A collection of rubbish near the door. Old machine parts, empty boxes. Anyone coming out of here would be hidden.

'Is there another way through to this ground?'

'Just here and that little bit of ground next to the houses up there. There's a tiny little passage over there, but you'd need to be a kiddie to get through.'

So there was one more way. 'Very good. Thank you. I need someone to be here with the keys to this door at half past eight tonight.'

'I go home before then,' the manager said.

'Then leave them with someone else.'

'I—' He started to demur, then saw Harper's expression. 'Yes. Of course.'

A climb back up to the top floor.

'We'll go in this evening.'

'Very good, sir,' Walsh said. 'Sissons will be here, too.'

'If they try to make a break for it before then—'

'I know what to do.'

'I need six men from the night patrol,' Harper said to Tollman as he walked into Millgarth. The sense of anticipation was rising. A few more hours and this would finally be over. He'd have the Smiths and wring them for every drop of information before he handed them over to the courts. As soon as the word spread that they were in the cells, it would be Councillor May's turn to feel terrified.

'I'm sure we can arrange that, sir. It'll stretch us thin, though.'

'Can't be helped. Give me the biggest ones you have. But with brains.'

The sergeant grinned. 'You have to make it difficult for me, don't you, sir? I might be able to scrape enough together who meet those qualifications.'

'Here at eight tonight.'

'Very good, sir.'

The sun seemed especially bright today. A clear diamond sky. Reed had to squint in order to see properly as he walked around Whitby. He'd covered West Cliff, going all the way to the bridge, shimmering splinters of light rising from the Esk as it flowed out towards the sea.

The streets were crowded. Elizabeth's tea shop would be doing a brisk trade in lemonade and cakes. Everyone looked happy, heartened by the weather, one of the best days he'd known since he moved here. Close to perfect.

Except for the arsonist. He was still on the loose. A check behind the buildings on Grape Lane, then along Church Street, working his way up the estuary. Reed strode through the arch into the courtyard of the Merchant's Seamen's Hospital.

And suddenly there was something. A hint of smoke in the air. Not coal; a different smell, paper and wood. Reed sniffed again, wanting to be certain. Very cautiously, he edged through a tiny stone passage to the back of the building, where the hillside rose sharply.

The fire had only just started to catch. Tiny yellow flames licked up and shimmered in the air as a figure vanished round the far corner at a run. Chase or stay? The years of being a fireman took over. He stamped out the blaze before it had any chance of taking hold, grinding down the embers until he was sure they were out. A few seconds earlier and he'd have caught the firestarter with matches in hand.

Nothing left but the burnt paper and charred wood. No damage done. Reed gave a satisfied smile. The arsonist was long gone, but that didn't matter. He'd caught enough of a glimpse to know who it was. He'd take care of that later. Billy Reed took out his pocket watch: time to eat dinner. Maybe he'd stop at Custom House and see if Harry Pepper the excise officer was around. Suddenly he felt ready to enjoy the weather.

'I thought I'd walk you home,' Reed said. He'd waited in the market square until Elizabeth came out, Catherine Bush beside her.

'That's lovely of you, Billy.' She stood on tiptoe and pecked his cheek. 'You don't mind Catherine coming with us, do you?'

'Of course not. How are you liking the work?' he asked the girl.

'I enjoy it, sir.' She had a meek voice, staring ahead as she walked quickly to keep up with them, not looking at him. 'And Mrs Reed lets me keep the tips people leave for me.'

'It feels good to be earning, doesn't it?'

'Yes, sir.' This time there was some warmth in her voice.

'She's such a hard grafter, too, Billy,' Elizabeth said. 'She does everything I need, doesn't matter whether it's clearing the tables or peeling potatoes.'

'Are you starting to feel settled here, Catherine?'

The girl's face lit up with a smile. 'Very much, sir. I still can't believe there's so much sea and sand. And it always smells so clean, doesn't it?'

'Yes.' He had to laugh. 'Better than Leeds?'

'Oh yes, sir. I'd like to live here for the rest of my life.'

They started up the twists of the hill at the bottom of Flowergate.

'What does your sister do with herself now you're working?'

'She plays, sir. Mostly by herself. But school will start again next month.' A pause. 'I think she misses having me around.'

'She used to get into trouble at the workhouse, didn't she?' He could feel Elizabeth's eyes on him, but he didn't turn towards her.

'Yes, sir, she did,' Catherine answered. 'She was only tiny when we went in there, you see. I'm all the family she has, and I don't think she's ever really understood what happened. Not when she sees other girls with their mothers and fathers.'

At the corner of Silver Street, Reed stopped and patted his pockets.

'There's something I've forgotten. I need to pop back to the police station for it. I'll see you at home.'

'All right, Billy love.' Elizabeth sounded doubtful.

He raised his hat. 'A pleasure to talk to you, Catherine.'

'How are you, Billy?' Annabelle's voice sounded faint on the other end of the line, as if he was an entire continent away.

'I'm fine,' he answered, 'and Elizabeth's well. Very busy, though, but that's good news.'

'If you're looking for Tom, he's not here. Have you tried Millgarth?'

'Actually . . .' He took a breath. 'I need to talk to you.'

The constables were waiting in the yard behind Millgarth. Tollman had done his job well; every one of the coppers was built like a battleship. They made him feel puny as he led them through the streets, the rhythmic tread of boots on paving stone behind him.

He left two of them with Walsh at the factory, taking Sissons and the rest of the coppers round to the Methodist chapel.

'Anything?' he asked Fowler.

'Curtains closed all day, sir. Impossible to tell.'

Harper gathered the men around, Ash, Fowler, and the bobbies. They must look like an odd group, he thought, coppers in a church, sitting on the pews while he stood in front of them like a vicar.

'I want you to listen very carefully.' His voice boomed off the high ceiling. 'This pair are dangerous. They beat one man to death, then cut him open. Another, they broke half his bones and tossed him into a quarry.' He paused to let the words sink home. 'They're brutal and they're killers. When you get them, you don't show any mercy until they're cuffed and helpless. Understood?'

Muttering. Disbelief. They'd learn quickly enough.

The Smiths were in there. He knew it as certain as breathing. They were waiting. But they'd have a plan. They weren't the type to simply wait around to be arrested.

'Four of you on the corner,' he ordered. 'As soon as you hear my whistle, take that front door down. Two of you cover that open area next to the house. Everything clear?'

This time there were nods and serious faces.

'And make sure you're careful,' he added. 'I don't want any of you hurt.'

The mill manager was right. Only a child could fit comfortably in the passageway. Harper had to move sideways, shuffling and praying to God he didn't end up stuck halfway. Rough brick brushed against his face and he felt a trickle of blood down his cheek. Then he was out into the waste ground, drawing in breath and knowing how stupid he'd been to try squeezing through.

The sky was growing darker, dusk coming on. But still enough light to see. Harper pulled the watch from his waistcoat. Twenty-nine minutes past eight. A little while longer to make sure everyone was in place.

The seconds ticked away. He had his whistle ready. On the stroke of half past he raised it to his lips and blew two long blasts.

The door to the mill burst open and his men came out, truncheons drawn, forming up in a line and advancing through the weeds. Up on the street they'd be running over the cobbles, big men putting their shoulders against the front door.

The passage was the ace. It had to be. Through there, out on to the street and away. But the Smiths would have a surprise if they tried.

The men moved forward at a steady pace, eyes fixed on the back of the house. Come on, he thought, get that door broken down.

And then he heard the dull boom of a shotgun.

TWENTY-EIGHT

C hrist. Without thinking, he took a pace forward, then stopped himself. Ash was there, he'd handle things. The Smiths wanted confusion, they wanted blood. Anything to give them time to escape.

The police kept marching steadily across the waste ground.

The brothers would have shot to kill.

Two men ran out from the back door of the house. Finally, after all this time imagining them, they were right there. They were real. But so ordinary, so nondescript. A pair he might pass on the street without a second glance. Yet these two were deadly. They both carried shotguns.

Together, without a word, they halted and raised their weapons.

'Down!' Harper called, just before they could pull the triggers. He saw tiny fragments of brick fly off the building and heard the splintering crack of a breaking window.

'Now,' he shouted. 'Go.'

The Smiths were running, raising their weapons again. Next to the house, coppers were running full tilt round the corner, the blood lust high in their eyes.

The brothers were cutting across the ground, sprinting towards the corner where he was waiting. A pause, firing off the remaining barrels as the police ducked, then running again. Straight for him. Just fifteen yards away. His men were rising, following.

Harper took the cosh from his pocket, feeling the weight in his hand. Two pairs of eyes stared at him with hatred, mouths set in bitter snarls. If he could stand his ground until the coppers were on them . . .

One of the Smiths lifted his shotgun like a club, putting all his strength behind the blow. Harper ducked, feeling it fly just over his head. But he couldn't move fast enough to block the other side, and the metal barrel hammered against his ribs, ripping the breath out of him.

Pain shot through his body, white hot. Another blow on his

shoulder and his arm went numb. The man was trying to push and kick him out of the way. He wanted to get to the passageway. Every nerve was screaming, he was on fire. But he knew he couldn't move. He dared not or the bastards would escape.

Suddenly there was space around him. Men were shouting. Someone screamed. It took more effort than he could believe to raise his head. The police had them. One of the Smiths was kicking, his yelling muffled under a scrum of bodies. The other had a knife in his hand.

Slowly, Harper sank to the ground. He tried to catch his breath, but it wouldn't come. He rested his back against the brick wall, hurting too much to speak. He clutched at his ribs. Drawing in air took all his strength.

He could only watch. One of the brothers was face down in the dirt, hands cuffed behind him, the biggest of the uniforms sitting on his back. The other was still dangerous. There was blood on his knife, one copper down in the dirt, moaning and clutching at his belly.

The man lashed out as a truncheon came down and caught him on the wrist. That was enough to stop him, all the bobbies needed to start raining down blows. Head, body, it didn't matter. Just pummel him into submission, Harper thought.

Moments later the second Smith brother lay unconscious, wrists bound.

A hand reached out and Harper forced himself to look up. Ash, of course. Hat gone, dust and earth on his suit. Dependable, always there.

'How bad is it?' His words came out like a wheeze, thin and reedy.

'The first blast came through the door. Caught McRae full on, sir. He's dead. And they knifed Pickford in the belly.' He lowered his voice. 'Doesn't look good. I've sent someone off for an ambulance.'

He extended his hand. Harper grasped the wrist and felt himself being slowly pulled upright. Christ, he hurt.

'We got them,' he said.

But was the prize worth the cost? He knew McRae. On the beat for fifteen years, a good, solid man, married with four children. Dead for doing his duty. Two of the others were kneeling by Pickford, trying to help him.

'I want Fowler and Sissons to go through that house. Top to bottom.' He had to pause after every word.

'Yes, sir.'

'You and Walsh down to Millgarth with the Smiths.'

'Don't you worry. We'll get everything from them.'

Harper nodded. 'Why don't you help me out of here? I don't think I can walk as far as the street.'

The coppers wanted revenge for their friends. He could see it on their faces. They deserved it. But they daren't take it when a senior officer was around.

It seemed to take forever, a trek that exhausted him. Three times he needed to halt. The effort was just too much. Finally he was sitting on someone's front step, watching as a constable guarded the body lying on the pavement outside number twelve. Someone had put a coat over the head. A crowd had gathered, keeping a safe distance.

'We'll have you off to the infirmary in no time, sir,' Ash told him.

'Pickford first,' Harper ordered.

'There'll be room enough for two.'

He tried to smile, but it wouldn't come. One man dead, another seriously wounded. The goods weren't worth the expense.

The nurse finished winding the bandage tight around his chest before pinning it in place. Harper winced; this must be what a corset felt like.

'You heard what the doctor said, Superintendent.' She stood with her arms folded, staring at him with a forbidding expression. 'Three broken ribs, and they'll take time to heal. You're lucky not to have a punctured lung.'

His chest had taken a battering, and he felt as if the stuffing had been knocked out of him. At least breathing was easier bound up this way. Not as painful.

'What about the man who came in with me?'

'The last I heard, he was still in surgery. You'd better look to yourself, though. You're going to have some very bad bruises for a few days. They'll be sore. And try not to cough or laugh.'

There was no danger of laughter. Not for a long time. Not after Cross Green. He needed to be out of here, to know what was happening.

'You can put your shirt on now,' the nurse told him. 'The doctor wants you back in a week. Any problems, come in immediately.'

'I will.'

He found Ash in the waiting room. No need for a question, just raising his eyebrows.

'Nothing yet, sir. But I do have some bad news.'

'Go on.' What else could have happened?

'One of the Smiths has died. The one with the knife. Blow to the head when we were subduing him. Sissons went through his pockets. Turns out it was Jack Smith.'

The man was breathing when Harper left; he was sure of that. But he wasn't going to say a word. Dead now or at the end of a noose, he'd be gone either way. This just saved the expense. Jack Smith was no loss to the world.

'What about the other one?'

'Cursing up a blue streak in the cells, the desk sergeant said.'

'Leave him there until morning.'

'You ought to go home, sir,' Ash said. 'I'll look after things here.'

There was so much to do. A report for the chief, checking on the other men who'd been there . . . Harper closed his eyes for a moment. His entire body ached.

'Sir?'

He blinked. 'What?'

'You dropped off for a moment.' Ash's eyes were kindly. 'Come on, let's find you a hackney.'

The man was right. He was in no fit state to do anything else tonight.

He glanced at the doors to the operating theatre. 'When you hear, you let me know immediately.'

'I will, sir. Get some rest before we talk to John Smith tomorrow.'

'Mrs Lyth?'

She was a soft-faced woman, barely five feet tall, fair hair gathered in an untidy bun. In her late thirties, Reed guessed, with the raw red hands of a woman who'd just finished scouring the supper pots.

'You live up the street,' she said. 'Your wife . . .'

'That's right.' He smiled. 'Catherine works for her.'

Worry crossed her face. 'You're a policeman.'

'I could do with a word, if you don't mind. It's important. It's about Charlotte, the little one who's with you. She's been trying to set fires around town.'

Harper slept until Annabelle came in and shook his shoulder. Already light, sun coming through the curtains, the air warm and comforting.

'You're—' She stopped as he pushed down the sheet and tried to sit up, clenching his teeth so he wouldn't yell. 'Tom. What in God's name happened?'

He told her, watching as her face grew darker. Very slowly, he forced himself out of bed, fighting the pain until he was upright.

'It looks worse than it is,' he assured her. 'But I think I'm going to need help with this shirt.'

Things seemed a little easier once he was moving around, although every jolt on the tram made him wince with pain. Walking into Millgarth, Harper held himself erect. He was in charge, he needed to put on a good front for the men. In the detectives' room he exhaled slowly.

'How's Pickford?'

'Out of danger, sir,' Fowler said as he looked up from a stack of papers. 'But it's going to be six months before he'll be back on the job.'

Heartening news. He'd live. But one good copper was dead because of this pair. He'd need to go and see McRae's wife.

'Are those the papers from the house?'

'For whatever they're worth.'

'Any names mentioned?'

'Not really. Looks like they were asking for loans from people they'd done business with. Everyone was refusing them.'

'Where are Walsh and Sissons?'

'Back out at the scene, sir, so they can put together a report.'

'What about Ash?'

'He's been interviewing John Smith for the last . . .' his eyes flickered over to the clock, '. . . hour.'

'Carry on. If any names pop out at you, tell me.'

'Yes, sir.'

Reed picked up the receiver.

'Whitby Police, Inspector Reed.'

'We got them, Billy.'

Tom should have sounded jubilant, he thought. Instead, his voice was as old as the grave.

'Congratulations.'

'We have one man dead, another wounded and gone for half a year.'

Now he understood. 'I'm sorry.'

'Jack Smith died resisting arrest.'

He wasn't going to shed any tears over that. Not after what they'd done to his brother and Hester and all the others.

'What about the other one?'

'Ash is interrogating him now. I thought you'd want to know.'

'I appreciate it. Turns out I'm going to be in Leeds in a couple of days.'

'Then come by. Stay if you want.'

'I probably won't have the chance. It'll only be a very brief visit.' He didn't say any more than that. Tom's mind would be too full of things to ask. 'But I'll stop at Millgarth.'

'I'll try and keep John Smith here for you.'

'Thank you,' Reed answered. 'But no need.'

It wasn't going to bring back Charlie and his wife. Much too late for that. Maybe it would be better to let the dead find their peace.

Harper stood outside the interview room, one hand on the door knob. He needed to see this man up close, to hear his voice and his words.

Smith was slumped back in his chair, wrists weighed down with heavy manacles that were attached by a chain to his ankles. His face was a mass of cuts and bruises. As he smiled, he showed gaps where his teeth had been knocked out.

'I should have done for you last night.' A rough voice, full of bragging and threats. Small, dark eyes pinpointed with hate.

'Then you missed your chance,' Harper told him.

'Your lot murdered my brother after you'd gone.'

'You killed one of my men.'

'Shame it wasn't more.'

'You're going to hang for it. And all the other deaths.'

'Prove it was me.' He raised his head, defiance in his eyes.

'I don't need to. Last night was enough. The two of you killed one copper and tried to murder another. That's a death sentence.'

Smith's expression changed. Something lingered on his face that Harper couldn't read. 'Doesn't matter, anyway. I was born to hang. Known it for years.'

'At least you won't be disappointed.' He turned to Ash. 'Has he said much?'

'A whole lot of nothing, sir. Round and round in circles.'

'Who put up the money for you to buy all those properties?'

A sly smile. 'Maybe we already had it.'

'No, you didn't.'

'Then you'll never know, will you?' With effort, Smith raised his hand to his mouth and made a locking motion. 'Never.'

He could feel the anger welling up, the urge to lash out with his fist. From the corner of his eye, Harper saw Ash raise his fingertips off the desk. A warning: let it go. No point in giving Smith the satisfaction. He'd seen the man now, he'd heard him. He wasn't going to break. He'd be laughing as they put the noose around his neck. The strange thing was that Harper felt absolutely nothing. No anger, no sorrow. A void.

'I'll leave him to you, Inspector.'

'Very good, sir.'

He'd no sooner seated himself in the office, trying to make sense of it all, than the telephone rang.

'It's Dr Lumb, Superintendent. I thought you'd like to know the results of the post-mortems.' No warmth in his voice at all, severe and professional.

'Yes, yes, of course. Thank you.'

'Your man McRae first. The shotgun blast sent a splinter from the door through his left eye and into his brain. Death was instantaneous, if that makes things any better. If he'd been standing a few inches to the right he'd still be alive.'

'I see.' The accidents of fate. At least there'd been no time for it to hurt. But that would be little comfort to his wife and children.

Lumb's voice hardened. 'The other man is a different matter. He was held face down in the dirt until he suffocated.'

'He was resisting arrest,' Harper said.

'By the time that happened, Smith already had a skull fractured in two places and his right wrist shattered. He couldn't have done any more harm.'

'I was there, Doctor. He'd just knifed one of my constables who's lucky to be alive.'

'All I can report is what I've learned from the body.'

'And I can tell you what I saw. He was armed and ready to kill again. My officers did what they needed to do.'

'On your conscience be it, Superintendent.'

No, conscience didn't come into it. The world was a safer place without Jack Smith. He wouldn't be losing any sleep over that.

Another hour and Ash appeared.

'He's still not saying anything worthwhile, sir. Won't give up the source of the money.'

'What do you think? Worth another go later?'

The inspector shook his head. 'We'd just be wasting our breath. He looks like he wants to die.' He frowned. 'Looking forward to it, in a way. Said at least he'd be with his brother and his mother again.'

'Then let's get him up before the magistrate and remanded for the assizes.'

'Yes, sir. I talked to Fowler. He hasn't come up with anything worthwhile from the papers. No mention of our friends on the council.'

'I see.'

'Sissons and Walsh will be back later, but I wouldn't expect much from them, either.'

John Smith. Was it loyalty that kept his mouth shut? Or just to claim some small victory? It didn't matter either way. They didn't have the name they needed. And there was only one other way to try and get it.

'We're taking a walk to Park Square,' Harper said. 'I want to try Dryden the lawyer once more. See if he'll tell us who owns this damned company.'

He knew Dryden wasn't going to give an inch. But he had to try. It was the last, desperate roll of the dice.

Halfway along Commercial Street, he needed to rest for a moment. His ribs hurt, a sharp pain that stabbed inside. Harper took shallow breaths, leaning against the stonework of the Leeds Library building. Eventually he nodded, ready to move on.

'Maybe you need another day off, sir,' Ash suggested.

He shook his head. 'I'm fine now.'

The ribs would heal. He was going to see this through.

They were shown straight through to Dryden's office. Better that than sitting in the waiting room, making his clients nervous.

'I hadn't expected to see you again, Superintendent.' The man was on his feet, the large desk a gulf between them. 'I thought I'd made my position clear the last time.'

'John Smith is in custody, charged with murder. His brother is dead. That means the Harehills Development Company doesn't exist any more.'

Dryden cocked his head. 'Why would that alter things?'

'When we find out who owns the North Leeds Company—'

'There is no legal way you can discover that.' Dryden's voice overrode his, growing more confident with each word. 'You're going to have to accept that.'

'And you refuse to tell us?'

'I do. I'm completely within my rights, as I'm sure your police lawyer has already told you. Was there anything more?'

'This involves murder,' Harper told him. 'The Smiths shot one of my men last night.'

'The North Leeds Company doesn't condone any violence. I'm sorry for what happened, but the company was in no way responsible. I trust you'll understand that. John and Jack Smith acted off their own bat.'

Harper turned on his heel and strode out. Ash followed close behind.

'We tried, sir,' he said as they crossed the small park in the middle of the square.

'No. We lost.'

Later, alone in his office, he gently ran his fingertips over the break in his ribs, feeling the tenderness and the pain, desperate to itch where the bandage rubbed against his skin. May and Howe were going to walk away from this. He had absolutely nothing to connect them with the Smiths. But they were guilty. There was no shred of doubt in his heart.

TWENTY-NINE

'Thoughts worth a penny, Tom?'

Crossley stood in the doorway.

He started to rise, but the chief waved him back down. 'I heard about it. How are the ribs?'

'Painful,' he admitted.

'It's a tragic business about McRae. I'm on my way to visit his widow.'

'I'll join you, if you don't mind, sir. I was going, anyway.'

'Is it ever really worth the cost?' Crossley stared out of the window as the carriage moved into traffic.

'I wish I knew the answer to that, sir. We have to hope it is.'

'I see one of the Smiths died resisting arrest.'

'He was the one who knifed Pickford.'

Crossley nodded slowly. 'What about the other one? Have you found out much from him yet?'

'Ash worked on him, but he's not given us a thing. Says he's looking forward to being with his brother again.'

'So we're never going to find out who's at the top of the tree.'

'That's how it looks, sir.'

'The councillors haven't been to see me again. I don't expect they will, now.'

A sly change of topic, Harper thought. Crossley knew the truth as well as he did.

'That's some good news, at least.'

'And more men are volunteering to be specials. We're going to need them very soon. Be grateful for that, too, Tom.'

What could you say to a widow whose grief was still so raw? Mrs McRae's eyes were red and swollen from all the tears she'd cried. She was trying to understand that her husband would never come home again. The children had gathered round her, the youngest just four, the eldest a grave, sombre girl of fifteen.

The chief handled it well, Harper thought.

'You'll receive a pension,' he finished, 'and there's a fund for the families of officers who die on duty.'

She gave a dull nod. Then it was his turn.

'He always did his job bravely, I know that. I worked with him. As good a copper as I've ever seen. We'll miss him.'

'Do you have children?' Mrs McRae asked.

'A daughter.'

'How do you think she'd feel if she was told you were dead? What about your wife?'

Just like the question May had asked when he issued his threat. But this time it was like a soft scream.

'Like you,' he answered, and she nodded.

The visit to the infirmary was easier. The ward sister allowed them five minutes with Pickford.

'He's dead, in't he? The one who got me.'

'Yes,' Harper told him.

'Good bloody riddance. Beggin' your pardon, sir.'

'No need. The other one will hang.'

'Not like anyone will miss 'im, sir.' He started to cough. A nurse came and bustled them away.

Out in the air, Crossley began to walk back to the Town Hall. It was only a few hundred yards, but he took his time.

'No great rush, Tom.'

'Thank you, sir.' The bouncing ride in the carriage had left his ribs complaining. He was just beginning to realize how drained he felt.

'I hear you and your inspector have been asking questions.' A throwaway sentence, saved until now.

'We have, sir.' No point in denying it when the man already knew.

'A couple of clerks told me.' He gave a smile. 'Don't worry, they have no love for our friends. Have you found enough?'

Enough for what? There was nothing to say they owned the North Leeds Company. And the council wouldn't care about corruption. They were probably all at it.

'Not for what I need,' he answered.

'Pity,' Crossley said. 'I'm sure your file would make for interesting reading.' That was all. 'Look after yourself, Tom,' he said as they parted. 'Let your ribs heal.'

*   *   *

A slow stroll back to Millgarth. His body ached, a mix of guilt and frustration filled his soul. He'd never expected the brothers to be armed. His fault; he should have anticipated it. What could his men have done, though? They still needed to break down the door . . .

Two murderers taken off the street. That was the headline all the men selling newspapers were shouting as he passed. Harper bought a copy of the *Evening Post* and glanced through the story. Praise for the dead and wounded police heroes. The details of the Smiths' crimes hinted at by the writer.

He'd achieved something. He should have felt proud. For the last few weeks, this was what he'd wanted, to have the brothers gone. Instead, he was empty. He'd never have the real truth – who put up the money, who pulled the strings. John Smith would hang and keep his silence. Whoever hired him would walk away, thinking their hands were still clean.

He entered the station through the yard. The back door opened and a constable led Smith out. On his way to court, still wearing the manacles. As soon as he saw Harper, the prisoner charged the copper aside, stumbling forward in his chains, pure hatred on his face.

'You did Jack. I'm going to kill you.' He had his wrists held high, fists clenched.

Harper stood his ground. No running, no dodging. Waited until Smith was close enough to smell his breath, then he grabbed the man's arm, sending him off balance and crashing down to the ground.

Smith was panting hard, flecks of spittle round his mouth, the vacancy of madness in his eyes.

'You,' he said. 'You, you, you, you.'

'I'm sorry about that, sir.' The embarrassed constable grabbed Smith and hauled him to his feet.

'Don't let it happen again.'

'No, sir.'

He watched as Smith was dragged away. Wanting to kill, wanting to die; maybe they were two sides of the same coin.

In the detectives' room, the men sat quietly. The map with its pins had been taken down from the wall, the reports written and filed away.

'I don't suppose Smith said more?' Harper asked.

'No, sir,' Ash replied. 'Just became more incoherent with every question.'

'Let's make sure his lawyer doesn't try to plead madness.' He turned to Fowler. 'It's all done. You'll be on your way to the army soon.'

'Next Monday, sir. I talked to my friend this morning. A month at Aldershot then I'm shipping out to Cape Town.'

'It's not too late to change your mind.'

The sergeant smiled and shook his head. 'That's very kind of you, sir, but I'm going. No fuss, though. Walk out of here and that's it.'

'It's your decision. But you'll have a job with us when it's all over.'

'I don't think it will be as soon as most people imagine,' Fowler said.

'Maybe not,' Harper told him, 'but the offer will always be there.'

Reed walked home slowly from the meeting. It had been an uncomfortable affair, sitting down with Mrs Lyth and Miss Tebbit from the Catholic group that brought the Leeds Workhouse girls to live in Whitby. He'd explained about the fires, that he'd seen young Charlotte Bush running off from one she'd just set. They knew about her past, her troubles at the workhouse, the things she'd done.

Then, finally, the sisters had come in together, sitting primly and quietly on the hard wooden chairs.

'Did you set the fires, Charlotte?' Mrs Lyth asked. The girl nodded, looking down at the floor. 'But why?'

'She missed me.' It was Catherine who spoke. 'She felt left out. She had no one to play with. The other girls don't like her.'

As simple as that, or perhaps as complicated. He didn't know.

'I'm afraid you'll have to go back to Leeds,' Miss Tebbit told her. 'We can't keep anyone here who does things like that.'

A silence hung in the room.

'Please miss,' Catherine said finally, 'I'll go back with her. She's my sister. She needs someone to look after her.'

'But you're doing well here,' Mrs Lyth said.

The girl had already made up her mind. 'Charlotte needs me.'

Now he had to tell Elizabeth. She'd be upset. But nothing was going to change Catherine's decision. He sat and watched the sisters leave the room, hand in hand. The girl loved Whitby, but

she'd give that all up in a moment for Charlotte. More than he and
Charlie had ever managed for each other. Another weight of guilt
to sit like lead in his heart.

Everything was arranged. On Friday, Miss Tebbit would take
the girls back to Leeds Workhouse. He'd travel with them, escort
and guard.

A key in the lock and he was inside the small house on Silver
Street. Elizabeth bustled through from the kitchen.

'What happened, Billy love? What did they say?'

He folded her in his arms. Sometimes, simply doing his job
was the hardest thing in the world.

Harper unlocked his desk and took out the folder. Pain filled his
chest. Why? He'd hardly done a thing, he hadn't strained himself.
Just two easy moves to put John Smith on the floor. He sat for two
minutes until it became a dull ache, a background, then waved Ash
into his office.

The inspector closed the door and sat down.

'The chief knows what we've been doing.'

'I—'

'He has a couple of pet clerks in the Town Hall. He wanted me
to be aware, that's all.' Harper drummed his fingers on the file.
'We didn't manage to find the connection.'

'No,' Ash agreed, 'and barring a miracle, we're never going to
find it, sir. John Smith will still be silent when they put the noose
on him.'

'Is he mad, do you think?'

Ash shrugged. 'Probably. Cunning, yes. Definitely not right in
the head.'

'Tell me honestly: do you believe May and Howe were the ones
behind the Smiths?'

A long pause. Ash's moustache twitched. 'Yes, sir, I do. We've
looked and looked and there's no one else likely. If we could just
get past that lawyer, we'd know for certain.'

'You've seen it for yourself. That won't ever happen. They don't
even feel guilty.'

'It's them, sir, and they're laughing their socks off because we'll
never be able to prove it.'

Harper sighed. 'I just needed to hear someone else say it. Go home, spend some time with Nancy. She must have forgotten what you look like.'

'Only if she's lucky, sir. Shall I tell the others?'

'Yes. We all deserve an early night. You know, I was beginning to wonder if we'd ever catch them.'

'All done now, sir.'

No, he thought as he heard the men leave, it wasn't all done yet. He took a piece of paper, dipped his nib in the ink and began to write.

The clouds had been looming all afternoon, growing off to the west and moving slowly towards Leeds. As he stepped down from the tram in Sheepscar, thunder boomed across the sky. He hurried across the road, ducking through the door of the Victoria as the first rain-drops fell.

By the time he'd climbed the stairs it was tipping down, bouncing loudly off the roof and the windows. Annabelle had a mug of tea cupped in her hands as she stared out at the downpour. A jumble of papers lay on the table where she'd been writing. He came up behind her, putting his arms around her waist.

'I suppose we need the rain.' Her voice was dull. Today she'd had a meeting with the Temperance man from the Board of Guardians.

'How was it?' he asked, although he sensed what her answer would be. 'What did he have to say to your ideas?'

She didn't move, face staring at the heavy rivulets of water pouring down the glass. Another roll of thunder boomed and a crack of lightning tore the sky open.

'Nothing,' she answered. 'Told me straight off the bat that he wouldn't have anything to do with a woman whose money came from men drinking themselves poor.'

'I'm sorry.' What more could he say?

'Now it all depends on the meeting tomorrow. I've spent the afternoon trying to write my speech.' She was silent for a long moment. 'We're elected to help people. That's all I'm trying to do, to stop another Annie and Ada dying. And these men are all playing silly beggars, just because a woman suggests something. And tomorrow I have to try and convince the lot of them.'

'It's wrong.'

'Yes.' She nodded and rubbed her eyes with the back of her

hand. 'Do you know what that man called me today? Hysterical.
I came this close to lamping him one and proving him right. It's
like a weight pressing down. I'm sick of it.'

He held her close and put his lips against her ear.

'Don't give up,' he whispered.

'Don't you worry,' she said. 'I'll be coming out fighting tomorrow.'

The chop house on Boar Lane was busy, men dining with colleagues
or friends, lingering over luncheon with a glass of brandy. Harper
sat by the window, gazing down at the street. The storm had passed,
leaving Leeds washed clean. Even the pall of smoke had vanished
for a few hours, letting the sunlight pour through, leaving the air
clean and fresh for once.

He sat back, one elbow resting on the folder, extending a hand
as a man sat down across from him.

'I'm glad you could come, Mr Russell.'

'I'm never going to turn down an invitation from a police superintendent.' He was in his late twenties, with a cocky, appealing
grin, wild red hair and a thin moustache. For the last five years
he'd been a reporter on the *Leeds Mercury*, covering the police
beat. A Liverpool accent still rang through when he spoke. 'Especially after a big case.'

'I'm going to disappoint you, then. All this is off the record.'

Russell's face fell a little, then brightened. 'As long as you're
paying, Mr Harper.'

'One way or another, coppers always do.'

'It's awful news about McRae. But I'm told Pickford's going
to recover.'

'In time. Quite a few months.'

'What did you make of John Smith, Superintendent? I only saw
him in court.'

Harper gave him a soft smile. 'I'm not here to talk about that.'

'Oh?'

The waiter brought their plates.

'Eat. Enjoy it, knowing you don't have to put your hand in your
pocket for the meal.'

Russell laughed. 'You don't have to tell me twice.'

After the food, as they sat and sipped coffee, Russell lit a cigarette
and said: 'So why did you want to see me?'

'What do you think of our esteemed local councillors?'

'A professional opinion, or an honest one?'

'I'll leave that up to you.'

'Venal, corrupt, and they all think they're untouchable.' A quick smile. 'That's the professional speaking.'

'Which ones are the worst, would you say?'

'May and Howe.' He didn't hesitate. 'If you don't already know that, Superintendent, you shouldn't be doing your job.'

'What do you know about the case with the Smiths?'

'I thought we weren't going to discuss that.'

'Humour me,' Harper told him.

'What your lot have told us, and a bit of digging on my own. They owned plenty of properties through a company.'

'Which was owned by another company. We can't discover who has that. The attorney is standing on his legal rights and refusing to tell us.'

'Go on.'

Harper knew he had the reporter's full attention.

'Someone put up the capital for the Smiths to buy all those places. Several thousand pounds. Every one of them was close to where applications had gone in to build new houses. Each of those applications was approved.'

'And this is where I put two and two together and remember which two councillors happen to be on the planning committee.'

'That's completely up to you, Mr Russell.' He took out his pocket watch, signalled for the waiter and paid the bill. 'I need to go. I hope you've enjoyed the free meal.'

'Nothing's ever free, is it? Don't forget your file.'

'What file is that? I never had one. Good day to you.'

The following day Harper picked up the telephone as it rang, the bell loud and jangling.

'You might want to be outside the Town Hall at four.' The line went dead. It didn't matter. The Liverpool accent was unmistakable.

The journalist was waiting near the Town Hall steps. Harper stood twenty yards way, leaning against a lamp post. The haze had returned overnight; all the soot and stink made Leeds feel curiously normal again.

His thoughts drifted. They'd seen Fowler off the evening before,

a few quiet drinks at the Victoria. Millgarth would be different
without him. At least Sissons seemed like a fine replacement.

Harper straightened, a twinge of pain from his ribs, as the council
members came out from their meeting and down the steps and into
the crowd. May was chattering away to Howe, not even noticing
the red-haired reporter until he was in front of them.

He was too far away to hear, but that didn't matter. He didn't
need to know the words. He saw the fury on May's face as it grew
darker and darker, and the way Howe stared in horror was enough.
Russell had done his homework.

As the councillors tried to walk, the reporter dogged them. More
questions and no answers, until May lifted his stick and swatted at
Russell. The blow missed, and the men climbed into Howe's coach
and drove off.

Harper strolled over to the reporter. 'I hope you have a good
article ready.'

'In tomorrow morning's paper.' He was grinning with joy. 'It'll
be enough to make them resign and face an inquiry, I can guarantee
you that.'

'My heart bleeds for them.'

'One other thing that might interest you, Superintendent. Lawyers'
clerks like bribes. I discovered who's the real owner of those
properties.'

'Who?' Harper asked.

Russell laughed. 'You'll have to buy the *Mercury* in the morning
to find out.'

The train pulled into the station with a thick hiss of steam. Reed
pulled down the suitcase from the overhead rack. It felt too light
to hold the contents of two lives. Miss Tebbit shepherded Catherine and Charlotte Bush through the concourse and out to a
hackney.

They hadn't spoken on the journey. What could any of them have
said? He watched the streets pass, knowing every one of them by
name, still able to feel the flagstones under his boots. At the entrance
to the workhouse, Miss Tebbit smiled at him.

'Thank you for the escort, Inspector.'

The girls hadn't lifted their heads. As they began to walk away,
he said: 'Catherine, I have something for you.' She looked up,

curious as he took a small envelope from his jacket. 'Mrs Reed wants you to have it. Your wages. A full week.'

'Thank you, sir.' She gave a small curtsey and turned away.

Much good it would do her in a place like this.

He walked back towards town. He could go over to Armley, stand by the cell and look John Smith in the eye. He could try to understand the man responsible for Charlie and Hester's death. Then he could go and beg a bed at the Victoria with Tom and Annabelle.

But what was the point? None of it would change anything. Maybe it was time to let it pass. Every last link with Leeds had been severed with his brother's death. He was the only one still holding on. Perhaps it was time for a clean break, to let go of all the guilt and the sadness. There was a train going back to Whitby in an hour. He could be home tonight, in his own bed with Elizabeth beside him.

THIRTY

Tom Harper was sitting and reading the newspaper and smiling with satisfaction when he heard her footsteps on the stair. She'd had the board meeting today, putting her proposals to change everything. He stood as she came in.

Annabelle unpinned her hat and tossed it on to the table. Her face was like iron.

'No,' she said. 'I fought for all I was worth but I couldn't convince them. They voted down every idea.' She began to pace around the room, then stopped and stared at him. 'Every single one. Tom. It's as if the deaths of those two little girls had been for nothing at all.'

'You're not giving up, are you?' Harper asked. He knew that look on her face. She was determined not to cry, not to show the pain of defeat.

She took a breath. 'Don't be so daft. I lost this time. There'll be others I'll win. I'll make absolutely sure of it, Tom.'

She needed a change of scene, he knew that. She'd been subdued for a week, ever since the meeting. And Harper craved a day away from Leeds, somewhere that wasn't all sooty red brick. Somewhere he could breathe clean air.

A little after nine on Sunday morning, he helped her into the railway carriage, then waited as Mary jumped up the steps. A blast of the whistle and they were on their way.

'What's in Ilkley, Da?' Mary asked. 'I've never heard of it.'

'You'll have to wait and see, won't you?'

She kept her face close to the window, staring out at the fields as they passed along Wharfedale. Stops at Burley and Otley and other small stations, then the engine gathered steam for the run, juddering over the points.

'Ilkley!' the guard yelled. 'All out for Ilkley!'

Only a few of them left the train. Mary stared around, curious about everything. And outside the station, an old man waited on his farm cart, a sway-backed brown horse munching slowly from its nose bag.

'How much up to the rocks?' Harper asked.

The man looked, calculating his wealth from his clothes. 'Threepence'll take you both ways,' he said.

Better than walking, he decided when they climbed down. It was a long, steep slope up from the town.

'I'll be back here in three hours,' the carter promised and pointed towards a small wooden shack. 'Cafe in there if you're hungry.'

The heather was at its best, brilliant purple and shimmering green on the hillsides. Mary scampered ahead, running along the tracks that generations of feet had made. Annabelle kept tight hold of his arm, button boots slipping once or twice on the pebbles.

'How are your ribs today? Up to this?'

'Mending.' Each day the ache faded a little. It would still be a while before he was back to full fitness, but things were improving. He could walk more easily. Still careful, though. One slip and he'd be back where he started. Just like life.

At least he had his satisfaction. Russell hadn't let him down. The story had covered three pages in the *Mercury*, the follow-ups still running days later. A dramatic headline, and the story underneath giving everything, showing May and Howe's corruption in minute detail. By evening the councillors had resigned. Russell had even named them as the men who owned the North Leeds Company, the ones behind the Smiths, and he'd challenged them to disprove it.

So far, neither the councillors nor Dryden the lawyer had responded. But all the records of the North Leeds Company had been subpoenaed and charges were being prepared. The prison doors were already opening for them.

Justice. In the end, though, it gave him little satisfaction. He hadn't managed to do it himself. That would always rankle. But perhaps it was a lesson; sometimes you needed to rely on others to make things happen. May and Howe would pay. Time to let it go.

'What are all those big stones?' Mary took the thoughts from his head as she dashed back. 'Why are they like that?'

'They're called the Cow and Calf Rocks. You see them there, the large one and the little one?' Harper pointed them out to her. 'They say that long ago they used to be joined together, but a giant was running along here—'

'Giant?' Her eyes widened, and he was grateful she wasn't too grown-up for stories.

'Yes. Some people claim his wife was chasing him. When he stamped his foot down, he split the calf from the cow.'

'Can we go up there, Da? Up on the top?'

'As long as you're careful.'

She ran a few paces and stopped. 'Why was his wife chasing him?'

'He'd probably been cheeky.'

They followed the path as it wound through the heather. Harper stood, Annabelle beside him, looking down at the town in the valley. The sun was soft and pleasant on his skin, a few fluffy clouds in the sky, and the air smelled fresh. No smoke, no smuts.

'Like looking down on the world, isn't it?' Annabelle said.

'On a bit of it, at least.'

'Do you know what it makes me think? How small we are.'

'You already knew that, didn't you?'

'I'd forgotten. I've been so wrapped up in things and feeling sorry for myself.'

'You're allowed,' he told her with a smile.

'I know, but . . .' She shook her head. 'It doesn't do any good, does it? I've had some setbacks. It's not as if I can win every battle, is it?'

'No,' he agreed and took her hand.

'I still feel guilty, though. I let Ada and Annie down,' she said. 'In the end, their deaths were for nothing at all.'

'You did your best.' That was all she could do. 'You'll have other fights. And you'll win those.'

'Some of them, at least. Enough of them, maybe.' She squeezed his fingers. 'Thank you.'

'For what?'

'Bringing us all out here. Putting up with me the last few days.' For the first time in a week, the smile reached her eyes, as if a weight had been lifted. Before he could reply, Mary was shouting in the distance.

'Da! Da! Come and look at these.' She was standing by some low rocks, close to the edge.

Names carved in the sandstone. E.M. Lancaster, 24th Foot, 1882. Jas Marshall, Bramley. Johnson, 1835. Dozens of others. All the letters so clearly etched, as if they'd been done the day before. Was Lancaster still alive or had he been killed in action somewhere? And Marshall, Johnson, what about them?

'Who were they, Da?' Mary asked. 'What does it mean?'

'They're all people who've been here,' Annabelle explained.

'But why did they do it?'

'So people would know and remember them. And little girls would ask questions.'

'Can we put our names in the rock, Mam?'

'Maybe when we come another time,' Harper said. 'I tell you what. After we take the cart down, we'll see if we can find a bookshop with the story of the giant and his wife. How about that?'

He could feel Annabelle smiling at him.

AUTHOR'S NOTE

Hiding the real ownership of property behind an attorney was quite common at the time. It happened famously with the London slum known as the Old Nichol. There, the true owners of the buildings were only discovered when demolition began and compensation paid. Among the landlords with extensive holdings was the Church of England.

The case of the Redshaw girls is very closely based on what happened to Ada and Annie Mellor in Leeds in 1900. Their father was hanged in Armley Gaol on August 16, 1900.

Helping with an exhibition called The Vote Before The Vote, I was researching in West Yorkshire Archives, and discovered that some religious societies did sponsor children from Leeds Workhouse to be boarded elsewhere – and two sisters, Maggie and Mary, were placed with a family on Silver Street in Whitby. They remained in the records for a few years, then vanished. Catherine and Charlotte Bush are those sisters in my imagination.

Those carvings do exist up on the Cow and Calf Rocks above Ilkley, and the view is magnificent, well worth the trip.

Many thanks to Ian Downes for the guided tour of Pontefract Castle, and to my good friend Candace Robb for inviting me.

I'm constantly grateful to everyone at Severn House for their support, and particularly Kate Lyall Grant and Sara Porter. Also my wonderful agent, Tina Betts, and Lynne Patrick, whose editing skills are little short of miraculous. Penny Lomas keeps me and my writing honest. And there are others who've contributed indirectly to this book, even if they don't realize it. Thank you all.

Finally, to all who buy my books or borrow them from the library. Without you, it simply wouldn't happen. I owe you, I truly do.